P9-DOA-662

RULES FOR 50/50 CHANCES

RULES FOR 50/50 CHANCES

KATE McGOVERN

FARRAR STRAUS GIROUX

NEW YORK

Farrar Straus Giroux Books for Young Readers
175 Fifth Avenue, New York 10010

Copyright © 2015 by Kate McGovern
All rights reserved
Printed in the United States of America
Designed by Kristie Radwilowicz
First edition, 2015
1   3   5   7   9   10   8   6   4   2

fiercereads.com

Library of Congress Cataloging-in-Publication Data

McGovern, Kate.
    Rules for 50/50 chances / Kate McGovern.
        pages cm
    Summary: "Seventeen-year-old Rose Levenson must decide whether or not
she wants to take the test to find out if she has Huntington's disease, the
degenerative disease that is slowly killing her mother"—Provided by publisher.
    ISBN 978-0-374-30158-3 (hardback)
    ISBN 978-0-374-30160-6 (e-book)
    [1. Huntington's disease—Fiction.   2. Sick—Fiction.   3. Dating (Social
customs)—Fiction.   4. Family life—Massachusetts—Boston—Fiction.
5. Boston (Mass.)—Fiction.]   I. Title.   II. Title: Rules for fifty-fifty chances.

PZ7.7.M4385Rul 2015
[Fic]—dc23
                                                                    2015003573

Our books may be purchased in bulk for promotional, educational, or business
use. Please contact your local bookseller or the Macmillan Corporate and
Premium Sales Department at (800) 221-7945 ext. 5442 or by e-mail
at MacmillanSpecialMarkets@macmillan.com.

For my parents; and for Gram

RULES FOR 50/50 CHANCES

FALL

Rule #1: Don't make plans you can't keep.

One

If you had a crystal ball, like in a fairy tale—or a magic mirror or one wish or whatever—would you want to know how you were going to die? Would you want to watch it happen, in slow motion, every day?

My mother is my crystal ball.

On Sunday I wake up to glass hitting the kitchen floor.

It's the Sunday before Labor Day, the last Sunday of my last summer vacation of high school. I have no ballet today, and what I'd really like to do is sleep late, then nothing in particular. No such luck.

It's a juice glass. I can tell because the sound is more like a tinkling-shatter than a heavy crash. My mother drops things with some regularity these days, so I've become aware of the particular cadences of different materials hitting the floor. This is a thin glass.

When I get down to the kitchen, my mother is standing barefoot by the sink. Her hands are shaking. And there's a glass, formerly used for holding juice, in shards on the floor.

"I'm sssuch an *idiot*," she says. "Sssorry." Her words slur gently, not a stutter but like her mouth is full of slick ice cubes, like they have more and more regularly over the last six months.

"It was an accident," I say. "Careful. You'll cut yourself." I bend over and pile a few shards in my palm.

My father pounds down the stairs in his towel, dripping from the shower. "What happened?"

"Just this fffool," Mom says. "Throwing ggglasses."

"That's my wife you're talking about. Don't call her a fool." He leans over and kisses her. "I'll get a broom." As he crosses to the pantry, he calls over his shoulder to me. "Get a move on, kid! Places to go, people to see! It's a beautiful day to walk for genetic research!"

Indeed. We've been walking for genetic research every Labor Day weekend since my mother's diagnosis, when I was twelve, which makes this my sixth Walk for Rare Genes. The walk is sponsored by an organization that does advocacy for something like seven thousand genetic diseases, most of which are too rare for anyone to particularly care about on their own. Unless, of course, you find yourself in possession of one, like we do.

Ours is a mutated gene on chromosome 4. The gene's called huntingtin, and if yours is messed up like my mother's, you end up with Huntington's disease. Don't ask why the two huntingtons—the gene and the name—are spelled differently; I have no idea. What I do know is that if you've got that mistake on chromosome 4, like my mother does—the tiniest typo in a book with billions of words—then your huntingtin gene goes haywire and basically wreaks havoc in your brain. Things start deteriorating in your mind and your body, until you're not the person you once were, and then they keep deteriorating until you die. Slowly, painfully, and without any chance of reversal.

Oh, and as far as my genes are concerned—it doesn't matter that my father doesn't carry the mutation on chromosome 4. I only need to inherit the mutated gene from my mother to be royally screwed. Which means that after watching my mother fall apart, I have a fifty-fifty chance of falling apart, too.

I shower quickly, and dig out a navy blue tank top to wear with jeans. Blue is the color of the day, because, you know, the whole genes/jeans thing. Even the rare genes ribbon is made of denim. I've gotta hand it to them, this organization may be representing diseases that affect only tiny groups of people around the world, but their marketing people know what they're doing.

Just as I'm rubbing down my wet hair with a towel, Dad pokes his head into my bedroom, knocking once as he opens the door. He's dressed head to toe in blue, too—blue T-shirt, blue jeans; even his Nikes have blue trim, but I think that's an accident.

"All set?" he says.

"Bells on, I assure you," I say.

"Look, I know you're not that psyched about this." He taps his fist against the door frame a couple times. "But it's important to your mother."

"Is it?" I'm pretty sure that at this point, Mom doesn't even care that we do this every year. Maybe she'd prefer to just sit in the backyard all afternoon and enjoy the nice weather without the fuss. Every time there's a beautiful day now, I wonder when it'll be the last day that Mom registers as beautiful.

The look on Dad's face makes me regret saying anything, though. A few years ago, I thought this walk was fun—joining all the other families in a sea of blue shirts and balloons, eating caramel popcorn and cheering all the way along the ten-mile route. Your feet hurt at the end, and that meant you'd done something worthwhile. There was a feeling of solidarity with all those other people whose lives had also been turned upside down by their own invisible bad luck.

But now, the sight of all those kids in wheelchairs and their parents plastering smiles across their faces like *they're actually okay with this* makes me feel kind of nauseous. Plus, Mom can't walk the whole way by herself anymore, so she uses her own wheelchair, and walking alongside her makes me feel like I'm supposed to be one of those smile-plasterers, too. It's all, "Hey, world, I'm so strong!" I'm not.

Still, I don't feel like bumming Dad out. "I'll be right down," I say, trying to soften my tone. He winks at me and disappears down the stairs.

When I find my family in the living room a few minutes later, Dad is loading bottles of water into a backpack and my grandmother is putting sunscreen on every visible inch of my mother and herself.

"Rose," Mom says, smiling at me, her mood already having shifted from our juice glass morning. "Ready?"

For the walk, maybe, Mom. Not for anything else.

* * *

When we get to the Boston Common, the registration area is already buzzing with blue-clad families. The organizers, recognizable by their enormous, spongy foam hats shaped like blue DNA double helixes, are chanting into megaphones: "Care about rare! Care about rare!" Across the grass, the starting line is marked by a huge, double-helix archway formed from blue balloons. There's a steel drum band playing some cheery Caribbean tune, and circus performers (in blue, obviously) walking on stilts and carrying signage advertising a free performance by Blue Man Group at the end of the day.

Even the sky is appropriately clad for the walk—bright blue, of course, tempered only by an occasional wispy cloud. The whole Eastern Seaboard is supposed to get slammed with a hurricane tomorrow, but today is beautiful. The air is unusually crisp for so early in September—there's no humidity, and it smells of freshly cut grass plus something like pipe tobacco. (I'm not sure it's really the smell of pipe tobacco—I don't smoke a pipe, obviously—but my dad used to when I was little, just every now and then on a nice fall evening, so that's what fall smells like to me.) It's hard to maintain an oppositional stance to this outing when the weather is so unrelentingly gorgeous.

Dad registers us, while Gram, Mom, and I stand around, taking in the scene. Or Gram and I do, anyway. Mom sits in her chair, looking mildly irritated every time one of us tries to fuss with something on her—her floppy sun hat, the pillow behind her back, the settings on her chair. Dad emerges from the crowd and passes around our T-shirts—all extra large, of course. Why do they only seem to order XLs and XXLs for these things? When I pull the T-shirt on over my clothes, it reaches my mid-thighs. My best friend, Lena, could probably find a way to belt this and make it look trendy.

"Right, so, we're in the ten a.m. kickoff group, so we've got thirty minutes until we need to head to the starting line. Anyone need a port-a-potty?" Dad asks. Gram, who's helping Mom into her blue T-shirt, waves him off.

I shake my head. "I'm going to find some orange juice. Want anything?"

Dad checks his watch again. "No thanks. Meet us back here in fifteen?"

I flash him a grim thumbs-up and wander off, trying to find a way through the crowd. By the registration tables, my eyes land on a young couple with two kids, one on foot and the other in a wheelchair, carrying a placard with a third little girl's picture on it. Blond curls frame a cherubic little face that looks almost perfect except that her features are slightly distorted—her forehead bulges out too much, her eyes protrude, her cheeks are distended. I look away.

The registration tables form a long border along one side of the park, and beyond them, there's just empty green space, where a few normal people are out for a nice Sunday morning walk (no doubt wondering how they ended up in this mess). I make a beeline for the normality.

"Hey there!" A guy a little older than me touches my arm as I try to get past the registration area. "Care about rare?" He grins at me. He's wearing a collared shirt under his blue T-shirt and one of those double-helix hats. I force a smile.

"I see you're here for the walk. Starting line's that way." He points, helpfully, in case I hadn't noted the giant balloon arch and multiple signs pointing in the opposite direction from where I'm headed.

"Right, I'm just—I was just getting some air."

He tucks his clipboard under his arm and takes me in for a moment, concerned. "The crowd's a little overwhelming," he says with an earnest nod.

"I guess, yeah."

"It's great to have so many people come out for this, though. Did you know that taken together, rare genetic disorders are one of the leading causes of childhood deaths in the world?" I didn't know that. "I'm Levi, by the way." He reaches out and practically grabs my hand to shake it.

"Can I ask you a favor?" he says, not waiting for me to introduce myself in return. "I'm short on volunteers handing out the ribbons over there." He gestures toward one of the tables. "Mind giving us a hand?"

I squirm. "Oh, I . . . My family's waiting, you know? I'm supposed to be walking with them."

Levi nods. "Sure, sure, I understand. I just thought, you know, if you're not feeling the crowd . . . I could use some help. No worries. Enjoy the day! Care about rare!" He gives me a little salute, and then saunters off into the crowd.

I stare out across the sea of blue, and for a second, I let myself wonder about all those people, about how their lives are like mine or not, and how much their genes dictate their every moment. Maybe it wouldn't be so bad to try something different for this year's walk.

"Hey, Levi!" I call after him. "Where are those ribbons?"

Levi gives me a big smile like he knew I'd come around, and introduces me to the lead volunteer at the ribbon table—a woman named Margaret—who explains that I'll need to pin the ribbons directly onto most of the children because they won't be able to manage the safety pins. I briefly wonder if we couldn't speed things up by handing the ribbons to the parents and letting them deal with the safety pin issue, but I don't say anything. Instead, I watch Margaret for a minute, grinning and calling out, "Care about rare!" as she waves ribbons at passersby. Then I plaster a smile on my face and follow her lead.

"Special delivery! Where do you want these, *Marg-oh*?" booms a male voice, coming up behind us. I turn, assuming it's Levi, but it isn't. It's a guy, my age-ish, carrying what I assume is another box of ribbons for the masses.

"Just put 'em back here for now," Margaret says, nodding toward our table. "Try not to leave the boxes someplace I'll trip over them, please, Caleb!"

The guy tucks the box of ribbons under the table and dusts off his hands. "All set." He notices me standing there and offers me his hand. "I'm Caleb, by the way."

"So I hear. Rose." His handshake is so firm that it's almost painful.

For a split second, I register that I'm surprised to see a black guy here, and then scold myself for it. There are plenty of hereditary conditions that are common in black families, I know, but I guess most of the people I've encountered so far through the Rare Genes Project have been white. I'm not sure what that says about the organization itself, but the realization makes my stomach twist a little bit with embarrassment.

Caleb is probably a foot taller than me, with a wiry build, an almost-shaved head, and thick, black plastic glasses—cute, in a skinny, nerdy kind of way. And the way he keeps his eyes on me, like we're going to exchange more than just our names, is disarming.

A kid tugs at my arm. "Hey! Can I have a ribbon, lady?"

"Lady! Who you callin' 'lady,' kid?" I tease, as I lean down to pin the ribbon on the little boy's shirt. He's probably six years old, pudgy-cheeked, and lacking in any discernible neck between the orb that is his midsection and the orb that is his head.

"*You're* a lady!" says Chubs, sticking his tongue out at me.

"Well, you're not much of a gentleman, are you?" I say, sticking out my tongue in return. Chubs lumbers off. When I straighten back up, Caleb's watching me and chuckling.

"What?" I ask, squinting at him.

Caleb shrugs, in a kind of casual-cool-attractive way. "Nothing, nothing. You have little siblings?"

"Negative. I just like kids." When I was in middle school I did the Reading Buddies program with the kindergartners. All I had to do was read Arthur books to a little girl named Annabelle for an hour every week, and she more or less thought I was the coolest person in the world. That's why I like little kids: they're uncomplicated.

Caleb leans against the ribbon table, his arms crossed. "Well, you can have my little sisters if you want them."

I laugh. "Uh, no thanks. My family is unwieldy enough as it is."

"Fair enough," says Caleb, taking a pile of ribbons from the table and coming around to stand next to me. "Mind if I join you for the ribbon-handing-out?"

"Are you trying to impinge on my ribbon territory, here?" I say.

"Clearly." He rolls one of the ribbons over in his fingers and chuckles. "Blue jeans."

"Get it?"

"Got it, thanks," he says, grinning at me. "Not my first time at the rodeo, my friend."

Standing so close, I notice the gap between Caleb's front teeth. It's probably big enough to slot a quarter in, but in a charming kind of way. It gives his smile character. Over his left eyebrow, there's a small, wrinkled scar. Whatever his genetic oddity is, it isn't readily on show.

"Where'd you get that scar from?"

He puts a hand automatically to his forehead and rubs his eyebrow. "This one? Kicked in the face, school playground, age seven."

"Are there others?" I ask.

"Others?"

"You said, 'This one?' like there are others."

"Oh, right. A few. I guess I played rough as a kid. Damaged goods."

I start to try to say something clever, about how since he's volunteering at the rare genes walk I already assumed he was damaged goods, but I can't quite come up with the right words.

Levi reappears, carrying a megaphone in one hand and a walkie-talkie in the other. "Ribbon bearers, I beseech you to listen up!"

. "Did he just say 'beseech'?" Caleb whispers, leaning toward me so that his shoulder is almost touching mine. The sudden shift in proximity bumps my heart rate up a notch.

"I'm pretty sure he did."

"I need to ask you a favor," Levi continues. "I've been asked to send a couple volunteers over to get some fresh boxes of T-shirts and bring them back to registration. Can I send you two?" he says, pointing to me and Caleb.

"Excellente," Levi goes on, without waiting for a response. "T-shirt boxes are in the main supply tent, which is thataway." He points across the Common to a huge white tent that looks like it could be harboring a college graduation or a decadent outdoor wedding. "Just take whatever they give you."

I check my phone and see that I have a text from Dad, wondering where I am. It's already ten o'clock. I send him a quick reply. I suspect he'll be fine with me volunteering instead of walking—that must count as showing my commitment to the cause—and sure enough, I get a text back right away: "Great! Love, Dad." He still hasn't learned that he doesn't need to sign his text messages.

Caleb and I set off across the green, threading our way through the crowd. "So you're not new to this either, I take it?" Caleb asks after a moment.

"No. We've come every year since my mom's diagnosis. I tried to get out of it this year, actually."

Caleb laughs. "I guess I can't blame you. It's a lot of . . . rare genes. In one place." I can feel him looking at me, but I keep my eyes on the ground. "I like it, though. It's nice to feel like part of a big thing. The cancer people get a walk so we should too, right?"

"Seriously. The cancer people get like ten walks."

"At least."

The truth is, the rare genes walk is a nice idea in theory, but in practice, most of the people here are dealing with different diseases and competing interests. We all want our disease to get the attention, because attention means funding and funding means research and research could mean a cure. I keep that uncharitable thought to myself, obviously.

"So, what's your—you know . . ." He trails off. My disease, he means. I can tell.

"My mom has Huntington's."

I sense Caleb sort of tighten up next to me. That's the Huntington's effect. For people who know what it means, who can picture the total terribleness of what you're talking about, it's always a shocker.

"That sucks," he says. I'm not sure I've ever gotten such a blunt reaction before, but he's right. It does. His honesty makes me smile.

"Yeah. It sucks." After a momentary awkward pause, I ask, "What about you?"

"Sickle cell. My mom and sisters have it."

"That sucks," I say. (Although frankly, sickle cell is basically a walk in the park compared to Huntington's. It doesn't even kill you anymore.)

At the supply tent, a double-helixed guy with a clipboard points us to the boxes we've been tasked with transporting, each marked in black Sharpie with their sizes. Caleb piles one on top of the other in my outstretched arms, and then hoists up a stack of three himself.

"Why do you think they have no small or medium T-shirts?" I ask over the top of my boxes. "Look, your boxes are all larges and extra larges. Mine too, right?" Caleb surveys my boxes and nods. "What about us small people? That's what I'd like to know. This is discriminatory."

"You could take a kiddie size," Caleb says, laughing. "Look—there are the baby ones. Five-T might fit you, actually. You're miniature."

"It's called 'petite,'" I correct him. Five foot one, and it's already a sore point. I've been the shortest girl in ballet since I was three years old. "And I don't need a kiddie size, thank you very much."

"Whatever you say, HD girl."

I'm glad the boxes are masking most of my face so that Caleb can't see me blush. "Okay, Sickle Cell boy." Over his pile of boxes, Caleb flashes me a gap-toothed grin.

We make several more trips back and forth across the green with boxes of T-shirts. They're not light, and even though it felt like a cool, fall day earlier, after all the schlepping, I'm sweating and exhausted.

"Snack break?" Caleb asks, when we drop off our third round of boxes. I nod, scraping the hair off my sticky neck and into a ponytail. We make our way to the refreshments area and grab a bag of caramel popcorn and two cups of a juice drink in an alarming shade of red.

"You'd think this kind of beverage could actually *give* a person a genetic mutation," Caleb says.

"Agreed. Didn't they outlaw this shade of food coloring in Massachusetts already?"

We find an unoccupied patch of grass and slump down on it. The crowd around the registration area has started to thin as more people have headed off on the walk, and I stretch my legs out on the grass and point and flex my toes a few times in my sneakers.

"So is your family here?" I ask, taking a handful of popcorn from the bag.

"They're walking. I've been doing the volunteer thing for a couple of years, ever since Levi got to me. You know Levi?"

"I just met him today."

Caleb crunches on some popcorn. "He's a pretty cool dude. He's Mennonite, from Pennsylvania."

"Mennonite, like Amish?"

"They're close, but not the same. Levi's got like five brothers and sisters with something called maple syrup disease, and now he's in med school up here."

Maple syrup disease—there's one I've never heard of. I'll have to Google it when I get home.

"Anyway, I met him at a fund-raiser my parents dragged me to, and he roped me in. He's hard to say no to."

"I noticed that," I say.

"So, your mom has HD? Symptomatic?"

Caleb talks like me, like a person who knows something—maybe too much—about this stuff. I cast my eyes out over the Common for a moment, taking a sip of toxic red juice.

"Sick people are a pain in the ass, right?" he says.

I practically spit Kool-Aid all over myself. One of the unspoken rules of Having a Sick Loved One is that you don't talk smack about them. In other words, you don't ever say what you're really thinking, because people who don't Have a Sick Loved One will think you're being cruel. They don't get it.

"Yeah," I say. "Plus, then they die."

Caleb and I sit in silence for a moment, picking at the caramel popcorn, each in our own world. It's nice, in a weird way—knowing that the person in his own world next to me understands a little bit about what my world looks like.

"What about you? Have you been tested for it?"

I'm not surprised that Caleb knows that there is a predictive test for my mother's disease—that I'll be able to find out whether or not I'll get sick, before it happens. It's not something I'd normally discuss with a stranger, but there's something about Caleb that makes me feel like I can talk to him.

"No," I say, plucking at some grass at my feet. "It's really expensive, and insurance doesn't cover it. Like a couple thousand or something."

That's how Dad explained it to me, when they sat me down and told me I was at risk for Mom's disease, but that I had a lot of years left before I had to worry about it. It was a year after her diagnosis, and I guess they wanted to avoid my learning about the whole fifty-fifty chance thing via Google, which most definitely would have occurred. They thought if they told me the truth about my risk factor, they could keep me from worrying about it. But it turns out that it's not so easy to just *not worry* about something like a fifty percent likelihood of death by drowning in your own brain.

"It's that expensive? Really?" Caleb asks. "That surprises me. Sickle cell testing's like a couple hundred bucks a pop. Why would the HD test be so different? It's still just a blood test, right?"

I don't know why it's so expensive. That's just what they told me. I never questioned the cost of it.

"Sorry," Caleb says, practically interrupting himself. "I'll shut up now." He wipes his sticky hands over his jeans and stands up.

"No, it's okay. Really," I say, even though I'm feeling a bit queasy. I'm not sure whether it's the conversation or the red juice that's turned my stomach. Caleb offers me his hand and pulls me up to my feet. His hand grasping mine feels . . . warm. And strange.

The commotion at the registration area has thinned out significantly, and when we get back there, Levi comes bounding over like an enthusiastic puppy. "Sorry to break up this excellent team," he says, "but I need to recruit Caleb for some heavy lifting. If that's all right by you?" he asks Caleb, who shrugs.

"Whatever you need."

"Excellent. Do me a favor and head back to the supply tent, and tell Bill that I sent you. He'll fill you in."

Caleb turns to me, almost apologetically, I think. "Nice meeting you, HD girl. See you later?"

"Sure," I say, swallowing the lump in my throat. "Good luck with that heavy lifting." I don't think I'm imagining that Caleb lingers there for just a moment, before he heads off toward the supply tent.

I stick around the registration tables, handing out ribbons to the last of the new registrants and, if I'm totally honest, waiting to see if Caleb's going to come back. But after an hour or so, I'm antsy and ready to go. I can't get our conversation out of my head. The truth is, I haven't looked into the cost of the Huntington's test because I've never really considered it an option. From the beginning, my parents always said it would be a choice I could make when I was much older, like getting ready to have a kid. They said children weren't allowed to get tested, and I believed them. I *was* a child, at the time. But now? I'm seventeen, about to head off to college. I'm old enough now to know what's really going on.

Charging across the Common toward the port-a-potties, my whole body feels like it's vibrating with nervous energy.

"Hey, HD!" I turn 360 degrees before I spot Caleb, jogging over to me. "I was looking for you. Look what I found!" He takes his hand out from behind his back and unfurls a blue T-shirt. Adult small. He's beaming.

"No way!" I exclaim. "What'd you have to do to score this?"

"Nothing . . . just tackled a woman with a tracheostomy, that's all. NBD."

"Thanks, Sickle Cell."

"My pleasure, HD. I'll see you around." Caleb gives me a light shove on my bicep, I presume by way of saying goodbye, and then turns to go. "Oh, hey," he says, turning back. "Do you have a last name, HD girl?"

"Who wants to know?"

"I do."

"You planning to stalk me on the interwebs?"

He makes a face like he's considering it. "We'll see. I'd like to keep my options open."

"Levenson," I tell him. "What about yours, in case I want to do some stalking of my own?"

"Franklin," he says. And then with a wink, which he manages to make kind of cool and not that cheesy, Caleb Franklin disappears into the crowd.

Right away, I peel off my giant blue T-shirt and replace it with the smaller one. On top of the tank top I'm wearing underneath, the small fits perfectly. I text Dad to tell him I'm leaving and cross Boylston Street to the subway, without waiting for a response.

At home, I unlock the front door and step into the quiet of our empty house. A draft is sneaking in through cracks in the floorboards and window frames, and the foyer feels almost too chilly for the first time in months. As if on autopilot, I go upstairs and wake up my computer. I've been thinking about this all the way home, and I don't really have a choice anymore. Now that Caleb's put the idea of getting tested in my head, I have to find out how hard it would really be.

Standing over my laptop, my pulse is racing and my mouth feels cottony-weird. I pull up Google and type, "Testing for Huntington's disease." Six hundred seventy-five thousand results come up in 0.32 seconds. How is it possible, Rose Smart-Ass Levenson, that you have never typed those words into a search engine before?

The very first result is a guide to HD testing from an insurance company. Sure enough, it explains that coverage of such tests varies between plans, but that the cost tends to run about three hundred dollars. Three hundred dollars. Less than I have in my savings account from birthday checks over the years. Less than a month of my mother's drug cocktail, the cost of a handful of college applications.

Another result, from a foundation that does Huntington's research (I recognize the logo; my parents are on their mailing list) says that minors are only tested in rare circumstances. But I'll be eighteen in a few months, and as far as I can tell, there are no other age restrictions.

Two hours later, I hear a key in the lock downstairs.

"Child! We're home!" Dad calls as my family tromps in the front door. "Where'd you disappear to?" I hear him flick the television on immediately, turning it to the Red Sox game.

Taking a deep breath, I gather the various pages I've printed and pad down the stairs. My family is in the living room, collapsed on the couches. I drop the printouts on the coffee table in front of my parents, just as Dad's leaning over to untie both of their shoes.

"So, you lied to me, is basically what this is."

"Sorry, what?" It takes Dad a moment to register that I'm talking about something serious. I hear the crack of bat meeting ball and the swell of the crowd—and then Dad mutes the television and looks at me.

"What is this?" He flips through the pages, squinting to read them without his glasses. Mom takes them out of his hands to look herself. "What are you talking about, 'we lied'? Do you want to explain this to me like a rational human being or are you going to act like an adolescent?"

I know I'm being petulant, standing here with my arms crossed over my chest, waiting for them to get the picture without me having to spell it out for them, but I can't help it. Gram gets up and sneaks out of the room, giving me a sideways glance as she leaves. I can tell she wants no part of this conversation, and I don't blame her.

"First of all, you told me it cost thousands of dollars," I say. "It costs three hundred dollars."

"Thousands of—I don't think I said that, did I? I have no idea how much the test costs."

I stare at him, holding my ground. Could I really have made that up? Maybe he never said thousands. Maybe he just said expensive. Maybe I assumed. I can't remember, to be honest.

Dad goes on. "We talked about this ages ago—they don't do predictive testing on children, Rose. It's a decision for adults to make when they're ready."

A conversation pops into my head out of nowhere, hazy, like I dreamed it: Dad leaning against the kitchen counter, Mom at the table, me hovering in the hallway where they can't see me. Dad says something about health insurance. "Can you imagine the premiums they'd make her pay? Her whole life, she'd be marked." And then Mom's voice, agreeing. "There's no point, anyway. What good will it do her?"

"You told me I *couldn't* take this test," I say.

"I don't think we ever said 'couldn't.' I think we said 'shouldn't,' not for a long time. Don't be ridiculous." Dad sighs. "Rose, we just got home from a long day. Do we need to talk about this now?"

"I'm almost eighteen. This is not ridiculous!" My voice catches in my throat.

"Rose, ssstop," Mom interjects quietly. "Calm down."

I turn from Dad to Mom and back again. "I'm sorry, but, Dad, you just don't understand the position I'm in."

"Excuse me?" my father says. "I don't understand? We're all living with this disease, Rose." Dad puts his hand on Mom's trembling knee. She holds the papers close to her face, scrutinizing them, her subtle tremors a reminder that none of this is hypothetical.

"You are not living with the possibility of getting it." I force myself to breathe in and out three times before I go on. "You should've told me the truth about this test. Maybe you thought I was too young to understand, but I'm old enough now. Or maybe you're just in denial about the truth, which is that I could end up like Mom."

At that, Mom's head jerks up. The look on her face, honestly, scares the crap out of me. It's sadness mixed with fear mixed with shame or something, I don't know. I don't want to hurt Mom. Her illness, my risk—none of it is her fault. She didn't choose this, and neither did my father. But I force myself to say what I need to say anyway. "Now I have this information. And it's going to be my choice if and when I get tested. End of discussion."

I leave the room before they can respond. I know we'll have to talk this through eventually. But for right now, I want to be alone with this new information, and the strange new possibility of doing something about it.

Two

THEY USED TO CALL MY MOTHER'S DISEASE HUNTINGTON'S chorea. "Chorea" because of the involuntary movements of any muscle group in the body that characterize Huntington's. It comes from the Greek word for dance. Which is kind of cruel/ironic, as far as I'm concerned, first because dance is what I *do*, and giving the same name to the thing that defines your life and the thing that swoops in to wreck it seems a little heavy-handed on the part of the universe, doesn't it? And second, because to dance one generally has to have control over one's body.

But as your chorea gets worse, you're losing control. I've seen videos on YouTube of patients with advanced Huntington's, and they look like they have no control at all: tongues sprawl out across their cheeks, feet jump, hands jerk this way and that way.

Among the other charming symptoms of our family heirloom: loss of impulse control; loss of motor skills; loss of the ability to walk, talk, and swallow properly; loss of empathy. Loss. It stops sounding like a word if you say it enough times.

* * *

Overnight, as predicted, a hurricane called Christine crept up the coast from the gulf. By nine on Labor Day morning, rain is already pelting my windows and a branch scratches anxiously at the side of the house. Outside, the trees lean hard with the wind.

I love storms, like my mother. We're New Englanders through and through, and I think there's something about being raised on the teetering edge of the mean Atlantic that makes you easily seduced by a weather forecast for big snow or thunder or gale-force winds. My father, on the other hand, sees only the inconveniences of weather: the snow he'll have to shovel, or the likelihood of a tree branch falling on the house.

When I was little and a big storm was heading for Boston, Mom and I would make a requisite Star Market run for Entenmann's doughnuts, the really bad-for-you kind with yellow cake inside and shiny chocolate coating outside. (It was the shininess that made them bad for you, that's what Mom always said.) We'd huddle in front of the television and compare the weather outside to the images from other parts of the Eastern Seaboard, checking to see if we were getting the good stuff or missing out. That was before our own storm hit.

I take the throw from the foot of my bed and wrap it around my shoulders, cozying up to the soft fleece as I tread down the creaky, uncarpeted stairs.

The living room, with big and not particularly well-insulated windows on two sides, sounds like it's in the middle of a car wash. Gram and Mom are already watching the news. I slouch down on the couch next to my mother and wait for someone to say something—anything—about last night's conversation. My words—*I could end up like Mom*—give me a sickening, guilty ache in my stomach every time I think about them. I hope Mom has let it go.

"Morning," Gram says without looking up. There's no hint in her voice of anything resembling a reference to last night.

I rest my head against the couch cushion and close my eyes, listening to Gram suck air through her teeth, like she has something stuck in them, while she works on her crossword. These days my grandmother makes a constant stream of soft, irritating noises: half-humming as she walks around the house, clucking her tongue as she reads the paper, this air sucking. It drives me nuts enough to not even want to look at her while she's doing it. I'm afraid I'll snap and say something mean, which I don't want to do, because she really does mean well. Gram moved in with us last year to help her only son take care of his steadily falling-apart wife, so I can't really blame her for being a little humorless about the turn her life has taken. Just as her friends in London were starting their "third acts," going on cruises all over the world, or at least passing the days playing bridge and gossiping about the neighbors, she made a return to caretaking that is undoubtedly more demanding than raising her own three children was.

Gram glances up from her crossword book. "All right?" she says with an uptick at the end. She still has a thick English accent, even after spending half her life in the States. The way she says it, it almost sounds like one word—"aw-right?"

"Fine," I say.

"Rose, this is a good storm, right?" Mom reaches over and squeezes my knee.

"Yeah, looks pretty good out there," I say. I turn to Gram in an effort to be less irritable toward her. "What are they saying on the news?"

"Landfall in two hours or so. The brunt of the damage will be farther south but we could still see some flooding, evidently."

On CNN, a British reporter named Alastair Dunsworth (which sounds more like a character out of *Harry Potter* than a real human) is currently standing in the middle of the street in Atlantic City, his feet planted wide apart so he doesn't blow over and one hand holding the hood of his official CNN all-weather parka over his head.

"Can I change the channel for a bit?" I say.

No one responds one way or the other, so I switch over to HGTV, where there's a repeat episode of *House Hunters* on.

"Oh, we've seen this one," I tell Mom. "They pick the two-bedroom under budget. The brand-new cookie-cutter one."

"Bad choice," Mom says, her body whirring like a quiet refrigerator beside me—the motor inside her just humming and humming. Mom and I always agree that period features, crown molding, and subway tile trump most things. Who needs double sinks in the bathroom? You and your spouse can't take turns spitting out toothpaste?

"Yowza," Dad says, bursting through the front door with a sodden bag of groceries tucked under each arm. He's got the thick, reusable shopping bags, but I can tell our food is still going to be damp.

"So it's raining, I guess?" I say.

"You could say that. The supermarket was downright post-apocalyptic. I think I managed to score the last batteries in the city of Cambridge."

Dad extricates himself from his soaked rain jacket and boots and drips his way to the kitchen.

"At least the power's still on. For now," he calls from the other room.

"Want to make your old mum a cup of tea while you're in there, love?" Gram says. My grandmother would have tea fed to her intravenously if she could find a doctor who would do the procedure.

"Your wife wants tea too," Mom shouts. She likes to assert that she still remembers she's his wife. One of Huntington's only kind features is that it tends to spare its victims' recollections of close personal relationships. Of course, when you lose control of your impulses and start saying horrifically nasty things to the people you know you love, it doesn't really help that you can remember their names.

"Oh, sure. No problem," Dad says, poking his head back in the living room. "Don't anybody worry about me, I'm only a little bit damp down to my bones. I'll just fix the tea for the ladies. I suppose the child wants one too?"

"Yes please." I shift myself off the couch and slink into the kitchen, where Dad's puttering around putting groceries away.

"Chicken soup?" I ask, noting the celery, onions, and carrots on the counter next to the cutting board.

"May as well, right?"

I take a heavy blade from the knife block and start chopping the celery. Chicken soup is our family's answer to all things challenging. Bad cold? Chicken soup. Bad weather? Chicken soup. Bad news? Chicken soup. We've eaten a lot of chicken soup in the last several years.

The kettle whistles. Dad puts a steaming mug next to me on the counter, and then takes the tea bag out after just a few seconds—he knows I like my tea weak.

"Thanks, Dad."

"Not a problem, my child."

"Hey, Dad?" I rest the knife on the cutting board. "I'm sorry about last night. I was sort of a jerk."

He stops puttering for a moment, holding Mom's spill-proof travel mug in both hands. The steam floats off it and coats his stubbly chin in tiny beads of sweat.

"Okay," he says. "And I'm sorry you felt blindsided. We were doing our best to protect you, and I still think it was the right call. But I can see why you would want to know all your options now. Okay?"

I nod. "Okay," he repeats. Then he kisses the top of my head and returns to the living room with two teas. None of this is okay, in fact, but that's all we can say about it right now, so I go back to chopping the vegetables for the soup.

I finish the celery and then start to quarter the onion. As soon as I cut into it, my eyes start to sting. Pretty soon, hot tears blur my vision enough that I can't cut anymore without risking my fingertips. I retreat to the living room, squeezing a dish towel to my eyelids one at a time.

"This is bullshit," Mom says, eyes still on *House Hunters.*

"Mom, I told you, they pick the wrong one."

"I know you told me that. You don't have to repeat yourself."

I breathe and ignore her mood swing.

"Let's see what's happening with the storm," Gram interjects, trying to distract Mom. The strangest things set Mom off these days, with more and more frequency—just another mystery of her deteriorating brain. She can be happy, almost her normal self, and then suddenly it's like an invisible switch is flipped and we can't reach it to flip it back.

It didn't start like that. The lightning-quick changes in personality are a more recent development of the last six months or so. In the beginning it was more subtle.

The first sign that something was wrong was that she got into three fender benders in two months. The first time, she hesitated a moment too long at a left-hand turn and got clipped. Neither car had been going very fast and there wasn't much damage. The airbag didn't even deploy on the guy who bumped her. But he was still pissed—he said he'd looked right in Mom's eyes as he'd first approached and he was sure she was going to wait. And then out of nowhere, she changed her mind, hit the accelerator, and burst out into the intersection.

The second time, she'd taken a wing mirror off a parked car while she was making a right-hand turn.

And the third time, she'd stopped short at a yellow light, and the woman behind her couldn't stop fast enough. It was the other driver's fault, obviously—it always is; they teach you that much in driver's ed—but it was still weird behavior for Mom, not taking the yellow light. Mom had always taken yellow lights.

Dad made her go to the emergency room that time, even though she wasn't really hurt—she'd strained her neck a little bit, that was all. But he joked to the doctor about prescribing a drug to improve her driving, because this was her third accident in a row. Three months of tests later, they named the thing that was changing Mom. Looking back, once she had the diagnosis, we saw that what all three accidents had in common was that she'd been unable to make the kind of quick decisions everyone makes behind the wheel—when to turn, when to stop. Decisiveness is one of the first things to go with Huntington's.

And no, we didn't see it coming. My mother's father died in his early fifties of some kind of crazy thing that no one talked about much—Mom always said he drank too much and lost his mind. Her mother had already been dead for years by that point. So Mom went out into her life unaware of the ticking time bomb she was carrying in her gene pool.

Gram switches the channel back to CNN, where Alastair Dunsworth is now clinging to a pathetic little tree that's swaying back and forth.

"This poor chap again," Gram says. "You know I think he used to be on BBC One back in the day. He's too old to be doing this nonsense."

Outside, the wind howls, and a sudden gust splatters fat raindrops against the window, making me jump.

I go to the window and look out at our near-deserted street. Leaves are plastered to the wet pavement, and no one's out except for one crazy neighbor jogging in shorts and a T-shirt, completely soaked through to the skin. I can sort of understand the attraction of going out there in the thick of it, just you and the rain and the big gusting winds. It must be kind of a rush.

I resist whatever impulse I have to run outside and tear my clothes off, however, and instead go back to the kitchen to brave the onion again. Once it's chopped, I scrape the chunks off the cutting board and into a pot of cool water, to get them out of the vicinity of my stinging eyes, then add extra garlic—two whole cloves. It's the garlic that seems to differentiate Jewish chicken soup from Asian chicken soup, I've noticed. When you get soup at a Thai restaurant, it's always nice and garlicky, but for whatever reason, us Jews haven't caught on. I'm personally changing that, one pot at a time.

I leave out the carrots. Mom would make me put them in, just for the color, but I hate carrots once they get soggy, and I figure no one will miss them once the soup is finished. Gram might, I guess—having grown up in London until she moved here with my grandfather a million years ago, it's sort of a point of pride for her that she loves vegetables with all the life boiled out of them. On second thought, I put a tiny saucepan of water to boil next to the big pot, and toss the carrots in. Carrots optional.

I dump the raw chicken in the pot with the vegetables and bring the whole thing to a boil, stirring it and watching the pieces swirl together as tiny bubbles rise to the surface. The steam makes my cheeks clammy. When it's bubbling nicely, I set it to simmer.

Within an hour, the smell starts to creep into the living room. On CNN, they're looping through the same correspondents up and down the East Coast and saying the same things. Landfall's coming; power outages are expected throughout the region; if you haven't evacuated yet and you're in an evacuation zone, it's too late and you should've listened to your mayor or governor or whoever earlier. In Cambridge, we're far enough from the water that we never have to evacuate, but one time we were up in Maine during a hurricane, when I was about seven, and we had to spend a night in the local school, sleeping on the library floor. I worried because I'd left my favorite doll behind. In the end, she survived.

I put my feet up on the coffee table again. Gram's disappeared upstairs to take a nap, and Mom is reading the magazine section of Sunday's *Boston Globe* next to me, probably going over the same page three times. Huntington's makes it harder for things to stick in her brain. Just as I lean over Mom to grab the arts section, the lights flicker around us and then suddenly we're in darkness.

"Shhhit," Mom says. "There it goes."

Dad appears in the living room, holding a flashlight under his chin and making what he thinks are spooky ghost noises. "Oh, laaaaaadies . . . mwa-ha-ha-ha."

Mom tosses the magazine at him, missing by a wide margin, but he stretches an arm out and grabs it midair. "What? Did I scaaaaaare you?" he says in ghost-speak.

"Dad, Casper, whoever you are," I interrupt. "I'm hungry. Did you get anything good?" I'm hoping he came back from the grocery store with popcorn or M&M's or something other than the bare necessities.

"Do I hear doubt in your voice, child?" he asks, shining the flashlight right in my eyes. "You think your old man doesn't know how my women like to prepare for a good storm?" He goes into the kitchen.

"What about this!" he says triumphantly, emerging with a box of Entenmann's chocolate doughnuts, the yellow cake kind with the shiny coating. "When was the last time you saw these babies?"

I can't remember. It feels like another life.

Three

Since our Labor Day weekend was marred by the combination of the rare genes walk and Hurricane Christine, Lena and I wait until the following Saturday to do our back-to-school shopping. Or her back-to-school shopping, more accurately—like every year, I'm really just along for the ride. We head downtown on the subway to exhaust ourselves combing the aisles of awful chunky platform heels and faux-leather boots at Designer Shoe Warehouse, all of which will undoubtedly look great on her and laughable on me.

Lena talks loud, and as she expounds on her theory about white guys with Asian fetishes, I glance around the subway car, trying to ascertain if anyone is paying enough attention to be offended. I've heard this monologue before: Lena will date white boys, but not, on principle, white boys who habitually date Asian girls.

"It's when they say, 'I'm so interested in *the Asian* culture' . . . that's when you know they have a thing for Asians, and they don't know what they're talking about."

"Lena, has anyone actually ever said that to you?"

"Yes! That guy Chris, at camp last summer. What, did he think I was going to tiptoe around the house and bring him tea and be all submissive and whatever? I really think that's what he thought a Chinese girl would be like. Clearly he'd never met one."

Her face flushes. She pushes a strand of thick, wavy black hair behind her ear.

"Yeah, but Chris was a jackass," I offer.

"That's my point. You'll never have this problem because no dude ever says, 'Oh, I love dating white girls because they're so . . .' I don't know. 'Perky' or whatever."

"You're right," I say. "I'm pretty sure no one would ever call me perky."

Lena's current boyfriend is Anders, who is Norwegian and hence probably the whitest white guy I've ever met. She's fine with that. He adores her, and his last girlfriend was as blond as he is, so she's confident that he doesn't have a fetish. Personally, he's not my type, but then I've never even kissed a guy. I'm pretty sure that qualifies me as not having a type.

The subway emerges from underground and rumbles up over the bridge. As we pass over the Charles River, I catch a glimpse of the red triangular flag flying over the Community Boating docks below. The red signals a windy day; my dad taught me that when I was little and we'd walk across the river together and get ice cream in Beacon Hill.

Across the subway car, two City Year boys eye us (or more accurately, eye Lena). They're earnest looking with baby faces that don't really need to be shaved but are anyway, judging from the red pinpricks and the little piece of gauze on one of their chins, and they're wearing the telltale City Year uniform: red hoodies, baggy khaki pants, and construction boots. City

Year is one of those programs that get well-meaning young people to do a year of community work for next to no money. A couple kids who graduated from our high school last year decided to do it to beef up their college applications.

Lena nudges me, hard, but I ignore her. She persists, leaning in and whispering without taking her eyes off them. "The blond is kind of cute. He's checking you out. Smile at him."

I jab her in the ribs. The boys get the message and chuckle, turning away to study the subway map more closely than they need to.

Lena sighs melodramatically. "Those ballet girls are a bad influence on you." Lena loves to insist that the girls at ballet are inferior friends in every way, compared to her. It's true: I've danced with those girls since I was three years old, but I've never quite fit with them, not the way Lena and I fit together. Still, I'm pretty sure it isn't their influence that makes me ignore the City Year boys.

"How are you supposed to get a boyfriend if you won't even smile at a totally cute guy who's looking at you? And, hello, he's into public service! He's perfect."

Caleb flashes through my mind unexpectedly for a second, carrying a box of T-shirts at the rare genes walk, finding me in the crowd to give me a small. I brush him aside as quickly as he appeared. I keep telling Lena I'm not looking for a boyfriend. Actually the thought makes me feel a little ill. How do you explain to a seventeen-year-old guy, "Hey, I know your plan is to just chill and make out with me and watch DVDs and have sex after prom, but guess what, when you come over can you also help me take care of my increasingly crazy and uncontrollable mother and also deal with this nagging little issue I have about a possible bum gene of my own?"

That's very attractive to a teenage guy, I'm sure.

Of course, then there's a teenage guy like Caleb, who already knows about bad genes.

Next to me, Lena shakes her head. "You overthink everything. It's probably taking years off your life."

She's right, obviously. I'm pretty sure I come by anxiety genetically, from both sides. When I was eleven, my mother tried to make me write my worries on slips of paper and hide them away in a box. She said I'd forget about them that way. But I never did write them down, which I guess explains why I never stopped worrying.

The first thing I remember worrying about was cancer, after Lena's father died of it—colon cancer—when we were ten. He used to take us ice skating on the Boston Common and buy us hot chocolate in paper cups with extra marshmallows, and then he got a stomachache and then he was dead, or at least that's the way it looked from my ten-year-old vantage point. For the rest of that year I wanted to know everything about the color and texture of my parents' bowel movements. Yes, I realize how totally weird and gross that is, and they set me straight pretty quickly. (Dad: "Rose, under no circumstances am I going to discuss my stool with you." That's how I learned the word "stool.") But I thought if I imagined all the bad things—the cancers, the car crashes, the burst aneurisms—they wouldn't happen. Because you can't predict the future, right? So if you predict every bad thing that could possibly happen, it probably won't.

Faulty logic. Plus, it turned out I wasn't able to imagine *all* the bad things. You can't possibly conceive of all the bad things that could happen to you or the people you love in a lifetime.

You'd think watching your best friend lose a parent would make you realize that you could survive something like that, too, if it happened to you. But when Lena's dad died, it didn't have that effect on me. Instead, I thought two things: one, Lena is stronger than I am. That's always been a theme of our friendship: Lena would swing upside down on the monkey bars with no hands and I was afraid to let go; Lena would bound up to Trevor McMahon on the playground and shove him if he took the dodge ball we were playing with, where I would just let him have it. Lena didn't cry when we got our ears pierced; I almost ended up with a piercing on only one side because I could barely go through with the other one. When her dad died, it was just further proof that where she could survive, I would crumble.

The second thing I thought was that when two girls are best friends, it's highly unlikely that something terrible will befall both of their families within a short span of time. Lena and I have always been intertwined, since preschool, like sisters, so it seemed like the big bad thing that happened to her counted for me, too. Like I'd already done my time. Again, faulty logic.

In some ways, Lena and I are just the same. We laugh at the same lame jokes. We get annoyed by all the same things (the little tuft of chest hair that pokes out from the top of our physics teacher's shirt, for example, and people who pretend they don't know your name, even though you've been in multiple classes with them for the last four years). We love the combination of popcorn and M&M's. We both understand that huge, bad things can appear out of nowhere and change everything you know about your life.

But somehow she manages to just get on with things without worrying, and I'm saddled with the anxious gene. She claims she doesn't bother worrying because she knows it doesn't help. Life still happens the way it's going to happen, with its instantaneous, irrevocable shifts, and you can't stop them so there's no point even thinking about them. Unfortunately for me, that message hasn't sunk in very well.

We get off the Red Line at Downtown Crossing and make our way across Washington Street. It's muggy out, and the sky is choked with low, heavy clouds. I can feel my hair starting to frizz as soon as we come up onto the sidewalk. Downtown Boston is busy with the usual weekend shoppers, and we have to thread our way through a throng of slow tourists with their Macy's bags and soft pretzels. A blond, sunburned family daring to wear Yankees gear is stopped dead in the middle of the sidewalk, consulting a map. I'd stop to help them but they're obviously busy, pretending to be in New York.

The DSW really does feel like a warehouse of abandoned footwear, a shoe orphanage, aisles and aisles of sad discount items lining the racks, their boxes stacked up by size and color on the shelves below. We make our way up the escalator to the fancy shoe section, Lena's target.

Lena can wear heels. I cannot—which is ironic, really, because I can turn a triple *pirouette* en pointe like it's nothing, but I'm so clumsy that I can barely walk five feet in a pair of three-inch heels without tripping over myself. This is before potentially losing my motor control, mind you.

"Ooh, cute!" Lena exclaims, holding up a pair of chocolate brown snakeskin stiletto heels.

I nod. "Do you need those, though?"

Lena pulls a size eight box from the shelf. "BCBG stilettos for under fifty dollars are not about need."

"Okay. I'm going to look at the flats."

Lena grabs my wrist, dropping her shoebox suddenly on the knee-high bench in the middle of the aisle. "No. More. Flats. For you!"

She's so serious about it that I can't help but laugh in her face. Lena has been trying to wean me off flats and into heels for, I don't know, all of high school. With limited success.

"We are finding you a pair of heels today. They can be wedges, it's fine—I'll settle."

"Tell me again why I need a pair of shoes I probably won't wear?"

"You are going to wear them, stupid. This is our senior year. Seize the day, Rose Alexander Levenson!" She only uses my middle name when she really means it. Alexander is my mother's maiden name. It's an annoying middle name because it sounds like my parents just wanted a boy. For the record, they did not. They were both quite pleased about my double-X chromosome-ness.

"I fail to see how wearing heels equates to seizing the day," I tell her.

"Fun! Going out! Parties on the weekends! Dates!"

"College applications, AP exams, ballet, my mother's doctors' appointments."

Lena slumps her shoulders and drops her head to her chest in a great dramatic show of defeat. "You're killin' me, Levs. Seriously. You can do those things and still have fun. Give me an inch, here. Or two point five inches, at least." Obviously proud of her joke, she gives me a goofy smile that looks like it ends with a question mark.

"Fine. Sorry."

"Excellent! In that case . . ." Lena pauses as she wanders down an aisle of party shoes. "In that case . . . these." She drops her hands on a pair of yellow suede wedges with round toes. "These look like you. Look, no sparkles, no pointy toes, no patent leather, and you'll be able to walk in these, no problemo."

I have to admit they're kind of cute. They're a nice color, bright but not insane, and I can sort of reasonably imagine wearing them with either jeans or a skirt, which my mother would say (or would have said, when she still thought about such things) makes them versatile. I flip one over to check the price: $29.99, marked down from $99.99.

"Fine," I tell Lena. "I'll try them."

She practically explodes off the ground, clapping her hands. "Yes! We're going to have a great senior year, trust me."

I can't say I'm completely convinced that one pair of wedge heels is an airtight prognosticator of a great senior year to come, but I find a box marked size seven and slip my feet into the yellow suede. The foot beds are padded so they're actually halfway comfortable. I look at my feet in the low mirror. Honestly, they look good. When I pull my jeans up, the heels have a nice lengthening effect on my calves, which are already muscular from ballet.

"All right, fine," I tell Lena. "Sold."

When we finally emerge from the last store of the day, the sky has darkened considerably, a thunderstorm clearly en route.

"This weather's been crazy," Lena remarks, glancing up at the sky. "Last week was pristine, then the hurricane, and now whatever this is." An empty plastic bag drifts by, skipping along the cobblestoned street in a gust of wind.

We duck into a coffee shop as the first drops of rain start to fall, and sit in the window, sharing an M&M cookie the size of my face. "I'll guess we'll be here for a little while," Lena says. Outside, a woman holding a newspaper uselessly over her head runs by, then turns back and comes darting into the coffee shop.

"We can stay here forever as far as I'm concerned," I say into my scalding tea.

I can feel Lena's eyes on me, observing. "What's with you?" she says.

"What do you mean?"

"Don't play dumb. You're acting weird. Like something is going on. Was the walk okay?"

Lena and I know each other's families about as well as anyone can know anyone else they're not personally related to. Between her dad's illness, her mom's second marriage last year, and my mom's diagnosis, we've seen each other through a lot of highs and lows. Mostly lows, actually.

I chew on my bottom lip, debating mentioning Caleb to her. But she'll just get overexcited, and there's no point. "The walk was fine. I found out something noteworthy."

"Oh yeah?"

"Yeah."

"And that would be?"

I shift my focus to the dark street outside. The rain has already slowed to a light drizzle. Finally, I look back at her.

"I thought I couldn't take the HD test until I'm like thirty or something. That's not true. I can take it whenever I want, once I turn eighteen."

"What do you mean 'the test'? For the disease?"

"For the gene. It'll tell me if I'll get the disease eventually."

I watch Lena process this information, rolling it over in her mind as she chews a piece of cookie. She stares at me for a moment. "Do you want to know?"

As if I can answer *that* so easily. "Obviously, I don't know," I say.

I'm not sure I'll ever *really* know if I want to know. It sort of depends on the answer, doesn't it? I mean, obviously, if I don't carry the gene, it would be nice to know that now. But if I do . . . I don't know. In the interim, every time I drop a pencil, or mess up a turn in rehearsal, or trip over my own feet—which is more or less all the time—I wonder if it's Huntington's. This is ridiculous, I know, because even if I am carrying the mutation, it's super rare for symptoms to show up before your thirties or even later. But still. That's the thing about the uncertainty. It puts the possibility of this disease in everything.

Lena rests her chin in her hands. Even with her hair falling out of its ponytail, a few strands plastered to her face from the rain, she's beautiful. Sometimes I look at her and I actually feel pride that she's my best friend and no one else's. Not just because she's beautiful and so much better dressed than I am, obviously, but because of all her Lena-ness.

"Here's what I think," she says. "I think if you don't know if you want to know or not, the answer for right now is that you don't want to know. Once you know, you can't *not* know again."

"Um, correct."

"Correct."

"But here's the issue," I say. "If I don't find out one way or the other, the answer to every question in my life is maybe. Do I want to eventually get married? Maybe. Have kids? Maybe. Join the CIA? Maybe."

"Do you want to join the CIA?" Lena interrupts.

"Probably not. But you get my point."

"I mean, I think that would be awesome, but it seems unlikely. You're not that good at keeping secrets. Or math, and I think CIA people have to pass some kind of big math test."

"No, they don't."

"Okay, well, whatever. Look, I get your point, but I sort of feel like it's normal for someone our age to have a lot of maybes. Right? I certainly hope so, because I have a lot."

Hardly. Lena has the next decade of her life at least already planned out. NYU next year (assuming she gets in, which she will), a degree in fine arts with a concentration in graphic design, a few years of working for a New York design agency, or maybe doing graphics in-house for a fashion designer, then a master's degree. After that, she'll probably be married with a bunch of gorgeous kids and ready to launch her own hugely successful design house out of her inevitably übercool Brooklyn brownstone.

Anyway, maybe she's right that most seventeen-year-olds don't really know what's supposed to come next. But to me, this feels different. Because here's what Lena doesn't get: It's not that I'm waiting to make a decision, waiting to see where life takes me, waiting to find out what happens next. What I'm waiting on has already happened. It happened before I was born. If I knew the answer, if I knew I didn't have the mutation, then the answer to those questions could still be maybe, but at least the maybe would be in my control. And if I have it, if I'm positive like Mom, what's the point in imagining all the possibilities? Might as well be real about it and get back to the business of dying.

Then again, if I have it, I'll still have probably the next twenty years before my symptoms really start, maybe longer. Do I really want to get ready to die ahead of time?

"Listen, girl." Lena pauses, pulling her ponytail loose and then twisting her hair effortlessly up into a messy bun. Her silver bangles clack together. "There aren't any rules for this kind of thing, you know. You're making it up as you go along."

I don't like making things up as I go along. I like to know what I'm doing. That's why I dance ballet, not modern. I like precise choreography, nothing improvised.

"Maybe there should be some rules," I say.

Lena shrugs. "Would that help?"

The espresso machine interrupts us with a sudden hissing loud enough to jolt me back to the reality of the coffee shop. Lena's eyes flicker over toward the counter, then back to me. She waits for me to respond.

"Maybe," I say finally. "Maybe it would help."

Four

I KEEP THE PRINTOUTS ABOUT THE HD TEST FOLDED UP and stuffed inside my journal. All week, I pull the pages out on the bus, at boring moments in the middle of class, when I get home at night and close my bedroom door. I roll it over and over in my head. One blood test. A few weeks. An answer. But I don't bring it up again with my parents.

"So, what's on your schedule for this week?" Dad says at dinner on Sunday night, clearing his throat. He shovels rice and refried beans from Mexican takeout containers onto Mom's plate.

"Usual," I say.

"Exciting stuff," Dad says. He leans over and cuts a piece of steak fajita for Mom. After a moment too long of quiet, he clears his throat again. "So. What happened last week? You didn't even give us any gossip. Did senior year start off with a bang?"

"It was fine. Same as every other year with an extra dose of get off your asses and apply to college."

I'm not just editing for my family's sake, although if there had been any actual good gossip—if anyone had come back pregnant or anorexic or converted to a new religion or something—I probably wouldn't have told them. I would've told Mom all of that stuff, a couple years ago when her symptoms were just forgetfulness and the occasional low mood, but now she doesn't get things in the same way she used to. She understands the words, but it's like the texture's taken out of the meaning. She's not a good gossip anymore.

We eat mostly in silence. As I get up to clear the table, Dad grabs a takeout container from out of my hands. "I got this, Ro," he says.

"Why?" I always clear the dinner table.

Dad shrugs exaggeratedly. "Consider it a beginning-of-senior-year present."

I eye him suspiciously as he crushes the Styrofoam platters into the trash. There's probably a landfill somewhere in the greater Boston area with our family's name on it. "Herein lies the waste produced by the Alexander-Levenson family. They used their oven for storage."

"What, Dad?"

"What what?"

"You're acting weird."

Dad gives up on trying to stuff the trash bin closed and yanks the full bag out, the detritus of many nights of takeout dinners stretching at the white plastic. "I'm not acting weird. Am I acting weird?" He glances around at Mom and Gram for backup but they both ignore him. "Maybe it's just sinking in that my only daughter is a senior in high school. You're growing up. A father is allowed to feel sentimental without being accused of acting weird, is he not?"

I look across the table to Mom and cross my eyes. She can't really cross hers in response, but she smiles crookedly.

"Anyway," Dad goes on. "Go do your thing. Talk to Lena. Go on the Twitter."

"It's not 'the Twitter,' Dad. No article."

"You know what I meant."

I'm relieved that he's just being sentimental about my senior year. I thought he might try to bring up the HD test again. I go over to him and give him a pat on the back. "Okay, Dad. Love you. Don't be weird."

"Love you more!" he calls after me as I head upstairs. "Not being weird!"

I already have a paper to start researching for my history class, but I decide to ignore it for now. I click on a new post on this hilarious blog I follow called *Teens with Bad Genes*, in which a kid whose sister has Tay-Sachs regularly turns life with genetic disorders into material worthy of Comedy Central, while also sharing news items of interest to people like him—presumably, teens with bad genes.

This week the blogger kid has written about an experimental program at some Orthodox Jewish high schools, where they test kids for a whole battery of genetic conditions that are common among Ashkenazi Jews—Tay-Sachs, Niemann-Pick, Canavan—a lot of pretty bad stuff. (Jews have a lot of lousy genetic luck—something about being a small population that has traditionally intermarried. We keep passing around those killer genes. I'm only Jewish on my dad's side, and I honestly think he feels a little vindicated, on behalf of his people, that I got genetically shortchanged from the gentile side of the family.)

Anyway, according to his blog post, each kid gets a number that goes with his or her test results, and when they start dating someone else from the community, they call up a hotline with both ID numbers and the person on the phone basically tells them if they're genetically compatible or not. If they both carry the gene for the same condition, they'll get a big fat no, and then they're supposed to stop dating and go back to the drawing board before things get too serious. Pretty clever, if you ask me.

Of course, I'm not surprised to read that the program only tests for recessive conditions—things where you have to inherit the bad gene from both parents. The program doesn't even bother testing for dominant conditions, where only one parent needs to pass on the gene for their child to get the disease. (Case in point: Huntington's.) Apparently the program directors believe it's "unhelpful" to identify someone as carrying a mutation for a dominant condition because in the community, those people would be "marked as unmarriable." And, clearly, who would sign up for that? I think of Dad, and wonder what he would've done if someone had handed him a genetic test before he fell in love with Mom.

I'm halfway through the blog post when a red Facebook notification pops up on my screen. "Caleb Franklin has added you."

My stomach lurches. So he was serious about the Internet stalking. I accept him as a friend and click over to his profile to see what's on offer, when a chat message appears in the corner.

Caleb Franklin: Ah, HD girl. Is it really you?

Me: Indeed. You found me. Stalker.

Caleb Franklin: Yup. I warned you.

Me: Next you're going to lure me into the woods?

Caleb Franklin: Considering it. Just out of curiosity, which woods would you suggest in the greater Boston area?

Me: Fresh Pond?

Caleb Franklin: Too many dog walkers.

Me: Walden Pond?

Caleb Franklin: It would be a little crass to stash a body in Henry Thoreau's place of peace and solitude, wouldn't it?

Me: Fair enough.

Caleb Franklin: In that case, I suppose we could skip the woods-luring stage of our relationship. All right?

I'm so thrown by his casual use of the phrase "our relationship" that I don't respond immediately to his message. Fortunately, he changes the subject right away.

Caleb Franklin: So what's on your docket this evening?

Me: My "docket," huh?

Caleb Franklin: Mock away, HD girl. Mock away . . .

My cheeks flush. I glance over my shoulder at my open bedroom door, just to see if Dad or Gram is hovering. Not that I'm doing anything wrong, but somehow the conversation feels private.

Me: History paper.

Caleb Franklin: Anything interesting?

Me: I guess. It's a women's history elective, so it's not bad. I'm writing about the early history of reproductive choice advocacy. Margaret Sanger, birth control, you know. Etc.

I can't believe I just said "birth control" to Caleb Franklin.

Caleb Franklin: Cool. So the whole medical thing is a big interest for you?

Me: "The whole medical thing" is sort of broad . . .

Caleb Franklin: Genes, birth control, etc.

Me: Fair enough. Sort of comes with the genetic-disorder-in-the-family territory, don't you think?

Caleb Franklin: You're a nerd, basically.

Me: Hey!

Caleb Franklin: Hey, I'm a major nerd. I like nerds.

By which he means . . . he likes this nerd? At the very least, he's still talking to me. Suddenly I want to tell Lena every word that Caleb Franklin has said to me to date, and let her dissect them all with me. I never thought I'd be that person, but here I am.

Me: So I did some research. You were right. The HD test's not that expensive.

Caleb Franklin: Oh yeah?

Me: I can take it once I turn eighteen. This February.

Caleb Franklin: Wow. What are you thinking?

If only I knew what I was thinking, Caleb Franklin. If only I knew. I hesitate before settling on a response. I want Caleb to think I'm self-assured, clever, confident—like he is. But there's no way to sound clever and confident about something so completely uncertain.

Me: It's complicated.

Caleb Franklin: Indeed.

Me: My HD status is this piece of information that hangs over literally EVERYTHING I do. Every choice I make about my future, about how I want to live, about the things I want to experience. You know? I had been going along with the idea that I wouldn't know one way or another for a long time. You kind of threw a wrench in that.

Caleb Franklin: Sorry about that. ☺

Me: Don't be. It's just opened things up for me. Possibilities. A positive result might make me . . . do things differently.

Caleb Franklin (after a long-ish pause): So might a negative result, right?

Me (after another long-ish pause): Yeah. I guess it would.

Caleb Franklin: Do you have to decide now? Maybe you're overthinking this at this stage.

I let out a snort at the computer. Caleb already knows his genetic lot. Some of us don't have that luxury. He might understand what it's like to live with sick people, but he doesn't get what it's like to have your whole life held hostage by one fifty-fifty chance.

Me: Maybe, Caleb Franklin. Or maybe not. I'll let you know when I figure it out.

After Caleb and I say goodnight a few minutes later—"Hasta la vista," he says, which makes me feel weirdly hopeful that I will "see him later"—I pull my phone out. I text Lena the words I know will make her call immediately: "I think I met a noteworthy boy."

Sure enough, her face pops up on my phone screen within seconds.

"Yell-o," I say. "What's up?"

"What's up?" she says. "What is up with the text you just sent me?" I can barely hear her—it sounds like there are people yelling in the background.

"Where are you?"

"Supermarket with my mother. Hold on," she says. "I don't care, Ma, chicken is fine." She sounds muffled, like she's holding the phone away from her ear. "I have to talk to Rose. She met a boy!"

"Lena!" I yell into the phone. "Please do not tell your mother about this! It's so not a big deal!" Lena tells her mother everything. They've been like that ever since her dad died, even after her mother got remarried. I can see how the disappearance of one parent can forge a kind of superglued bond with the other, but I can't imagine telling my father all the stuff Lena tells her mom.

Lena comes back on the line, with less background noise. "Sorry. I just went out to the car. So, wait. What?"

I tell her about the walk—she squeals at the part when Caleb brings me the small T-shirt—and then about our online conversation just now. When I finish, there's a long pause.

"Are you still there?" I ask.

"Mmm-hmm," she says. "Rose. I think this is a thing."

I stretch my legs out in front of me on my bedroom floor and lean out over them, pressing my face to my knees. I inhale and exhale twice before I roll back up to respond.

"I don't know. Maybe."

After I hang up with Lena, I go down to the kitchen and find my mother trying to make a cup of tea. We still have the knobs on the stove, but it's one of the things Dr. Howard says we're going to need to "deal with" soon. We're going to have to Mom-proof the house so she doesn't hurt herself or light us all on fire, in other words.

I stand in the doorway, watching her fumble with the kettle. She tries to get her index finger to engage properly with the trigger for the spout, but misses. Tries again, another miss. She sets the kettle down and takes a slow, shallow breath. The third time, she gets the spout open, and pours the boiling water to the left of the mug she's set on the counter. It splashes off the counter and splatters her hand.

"Dammit!" The kettle clatters to the floor, and Mom shakes her burnt wrist.

"Let me," I say. If she were normal, she would hear the slight edge in my voice and tell me not to be so impatient.

"I can make a goddamn cup of tea."

"You burned yourself, Mom. Here, run it under cold water."

I turn the tap on and hold her jerking arm under the running water. "Hold it there for five minutes." That's what Dad said the last time she burned herself trying to make tea.

"Fffive minutes is a long fffucking time."

She never used to swear in front of me. I can't tell if it's her frustration or her declining inhibition that makes curses come so easily from her mouth these days.

"Just do it, Mom. It'll feel better."

I let go of her wrist and watch as she makes an effort to keep it steady under the water. I pick up the kettle and drop a dish towel over the puddle on the tiles.

Quietly, her voice clearer than before, she asks, "Rose, cccan you make me a cup of tea?"

Gram appears in the kitchen doorway and just hovers there, assessing the situation. She looks from me to Mom with a slight crinkle at the edges of her eyes.

"She spilled the water for tea. She's fine," I say.

"I'm fffine," says Mom, her words slurring again. It's hard for her to concentrate on two things at once: keeping her arm under the running water, articulating her words clearly.

"Let me see." Gram reaches for Mom's arm and looks at the red splash across her wrist. "We should put some butter on this."

"No one puts butter on burns anymore, Gram. That's a myth." My grandmother also still thinks you get a cold from not buttoning your coat up all the way.

"All right, Rose. Do it your way." She turns on her heel and disappears.

Even a year ago, Mom would've snapped at me for talking back to Gram (even though I'm right—butter on burns? Come on). Now I don't think she can bother making the effort to be annoyed with me, if she even notices my snippy tone at all.

I don't mean to be short with my grandmother. It just slips out. She's a good grandma, and I'm pretty sure she did not see her life turning out like this. She had her three kids—two girls and my dad—and then my grandfather split, leaving her to navigate a foreign country and childrearing on her own. She got a degree in library science and once all the kids were out of the house, she picked up and moved back to England. She ended up in Stanmore, a little Jewish neighborhood in northwest London where she could be close to the sisters and cousins she'd left behind when she married the apparently quite dashing (and unfaithful) American who was my grandfather and followed him across the pond.

And then her only son, my dad, calls her up from the States one day and says, Hey, Ma, so the woman I married—you know, the not-Jewish one you didn't want me to marry in the first place—she's got this wacko genetic disease, and she's just going to keep getting worse, so can you give up your days doing crosswords and watching mysteries on the BBC and move back across the ocean to the country you thought you were done with, to play nurse/babysitter for a while? Possibly until she dies? Thanks.

I miss her sometimes—the grandmother she was before she was this person, in my space all the time, trying to take care of Mom and take her place at the same time. She used to be kind of funny. She'd come visit from London with bags of British things—P.G. Tips tea and HobNobs and huge, crispy Lion Bars. She'd say "poor yooooou" whenever I'd complain about one dance injury or another, but she didn't mean it sarcastically, the way an American would. She meant it for real: poor you.

I told Dad we could deal on our own, take care of Mom; it's a slow-moving beast, Huntington's. But Dad didn't want me to be the nurse. I was twelve when she was diagnosed; he saw adolescence looming, full of text messages and first boyfriends and AP classes. (In reality, of course, I've got the AP classes and the text messages—from Lena, anyway. Not so much the boyfriends. Of course, Dad couldn't have known that I'd be too neurotic to ever go on a date.) Anyway, about a year after the guillotine fell on Mom's head—I imagined her diagnosis like that—Dad called Gram, and she came, because that's what mothers are supposed to do.

I put another kettle on and wait for it to boil, standing guard by it so Mom won't bother trying to fix it herself. Maybe it's time to take the knobs off the stove after all.

Mom sits at the kitchen table with a wet dishrag draped over her wrist. "How's dance?" she asks after a moment—again, focused, her words almost clear.

"Fine. Usual."

"Usual?"

I sigh. "Everyone's a little weird right now because of next year, I guess. There are a couple companies some of the girls in my year are auditioning for, with like one spot for every bijillion dancers or whatever. So maybe that's why they're all acting a little cagey."

I say this to the tea kettle, more or less, and when I look up at Mom, I realize that I'd almost forgotten who I was really talking to. Every now and then I talk to Mom like she's still the same person she used to be. It's nice when it happens; I should do it more, that's what Dr. Howard says—he's always reminding me that she *is* the same person. I should keep acting as normal as I can with her, when I can. But it's easier said than done.

Mom's working hard at listening to me and processing my words, ignoring the dishrag that has now slipped from her wrist to the kitchen floor. This is what she does now, focuses extra hard on the tasks she really wants to do right. I pick up the dishrag and rinse it with cold water, wringing out the excess before I place it back over her hand.

"How are your college applications?" she asks slowly, chewing each word carefully before spitting it out.

We visited colleges last spring. One of them—Cunningham, in upstate New York—was sort of appealing. Their dance program is well known, at least for a liberal arts school without a conservatory program. Other than that, all the colleges blurred together. The truth is, there's only one school I've ever really imagined myself at, even though I've never visited. But it seems pretty unrealistic at this point—if I could even get in.

"Nonexistent, so far," I confess.

"Rose—don't put this off."

"Well, I'm guessing Dad won't like the idea of me doing a dance program. And I don't know what else I want to do."

Mom contorts her face into a smile. She used to be a great dancer, too. She never danced professionally, but she probably could have if she'd wanted to. She took ballet for a long time growing up, and when I was ten, she started going back to class occasionally, just for fun. Of course, that didn't last long.

"Your dad has two left fffeet. He doesn't get it."

I do a little impression of Dad's dance moves, an offbeat collection of disconnected twists and kicks, and Mom snorts out a laugh. She's right—I don't think Dad understands having a real passion for something creative. He's just more practical. He thinks I should learn something marketable, something I can turn into a reliable career path, like, I don't know, *real estate.* My father is a realtor. I like watching *House Hunters* with Mom, but I can't really see myself selling houses for a living.

"Just make a chhhoice, Rose," Mom says, suddenly serious again. "For next year. It'll be okay."

Back upstairs, I return to my laptop and open a new web page. The address comes up automatically after I type just a few letters, evidence of how many times I've visited this site. The Pacific Coast College of the Arts. One of the few—and certainly the best—combined ballet BFA/apprenticeship programs in the country. Here in Boston, I can dance or I can go to college, but there's no school like PCCA, where I can get that level of professional ballet training and a college degree at the same time.

I've had my eye on PCCA since probably sixth grade. As usual, I go to their admissions page and review the information one more time—not that anything has changed. They need all the standard stuff—transcripts, SAT scores, recommendations, a personal statement—plus you have to send them an audition video, or schedule an in-person audition. I haven't done either. It costs almost $50,000 a year to go there, never mind the flights back and forth. And it's on the other side of the country—from everything.

Caleb Franklin might be right: I might be overthinking the Huntington's test. Maybe my status shouldn't matter so much, and I should just continue living my life the way I was before I knew the test was a real possibility. It's just that now, when I consider how I want to spend the next years of my life—going to college, dancing, becoming a legitimate grownup human being and whatever else that entails—I can't help but think: What if I knew?

Five

Caleb Franklin's Facebook message a week later says, "Can I lure you out for coffee? In a public place, of course." I can't seem to shake the jittery, flushed feeling I have whenever his name pops up on my screen. Every time I remember sitting next to him on the Common, eating caramel popcorn and talking like we'd known each other for years, I feel the same rush of warmth mixed with anxiety. It's almost sickening, but I can't help it. I want more.

So I agree to meet him "for coffee"—even though I don't really drink coffee—at the bookstore in Porter Square late the next Saturday afternoon. I'm rushing, of course, after a full day of dance classes, and my hair is still damp from the two-minute shower I jumped in and out of. Through the swirled purple and yellow lettering on the window advertising ginger lemonade, I spot a huge book called *Information and Ethics in the Age of Genetic Medicine* propped up, masking its reader's face. I have to laugh.

"A little light reading?" I ask, as soon as I walk through the door.

He looks up from the book and shrugs. "I like to keep up with the latest research. You know."

"Mmm-hmmm. Okay." I fold my arms across my chest.

"Or maybe I just find that oversize scientific textbooks with long titles impress the ladies."

I laugh. "Oh, I see. So that's what this is. Do you really think that has the effect you're going for? I suspect most girls don't find genetics textbooks particularly impressive."

He flips the giant textbook closed and pushes it aside. "Indeed, you make a valid point. But you're not most girls, are you, HD?"

Color and heat rush to my cheeks, and I don't know how to respond, so I just stand there, awkwardly. It's nice to see Caleb again in person, but I'm only now realizing that in spite of the fact that we've chatted about some pretty personal stuff, we barely know each other. I look him over more closely, reacquainting myself with his face. His eyes, behind his thick glasses, are pure dark brown, not flecked with gray like mine, indecisive brown.

"So, um, do you want to stay here?" he goes on. "I don't actually drink coffee."

"Me neither," I admit.

"Ice cream instead?" he asks, his eyes flickering hopefully. "It's not too cold for that yet, right?"

"It's never too cold for ice cream. That's one of my dad's rules."

"He sounds like my kind of guy, then."

We cross the parking lot of the shopping center, headed for the ice cream shop tucked in a tiny corner unit next to the drugstore. It's takeout only, so we get our orders—coffee frappe for me, mint chip in a waffle cone for him—and sit outside. The cars on Mass. Ave. rush by and the breeze serves as a chilly reminder that sitting-outside-weather won't last long.

"You go to Roosevelt?" he asks, and I nod. My school, the only public high school in the city, is sort of an institution. My mom and uncle Charlie went there, too.

"What about you?"

"Barrow?" he says, in that way that Harvard undergrads tell you where they go to school, with a little half question mark at the end as if you may not have heard of it. I wasn't expecting him to name a private school. I guess my face reveals my surprise.

"I know, I know," he says. "Private school asshole, that's what you're thinking."

"No, I mean—" I stammer. Barrow is known for being one of the snootier private schools around. It's hard to imagine him there. "How is it?"

"You know, it's not bad, honestly," he says. "The people aren't as obnoxious as you'd think. And the teachers have been cool with my sisters, with the sickle cell stuff. They take it seriously. My parents sent us there so they'd get that kind of attention, so if they were having a bad day they wouldn't just get lost in the crowd."

I'm pretty sure no one at my high school knows about my genetic situation, except my favorite teacher, Ms. Greenberg. In English, sophomore year, she assigned us an essay on a moment that "cleaved our lives in two"—I remember her using those words exactly. She wanted us to think about a time when a single event—meeting someone, making a choice, taking a risk— changed us fundamentally. I could've written about setting foot in the dance studio for the first time, or the moment I went up en pointe, but everything I tried to write felt false, so I gave in and wrote the truth.

"Of course, half my classmates assume my whole family's on scholarship," Caleb says. "Because hey, you know, how else would we be able to afford it?" He throws up his hands exaggeratedly, pretending to be utterly baffled.

I register that he's making a joke about race, but I don't know how to respond in a way that makes me sound smart/funny/race-conscious in a sophisticated way, so instead I over-focus on my frappe, trying not to slurp. Slurping is something I am particularly paranoid about. It's almost inevitable when drinking ice cream through a narrow straw, but it's also an early symptom of Huntington's. My mother slurps a lot these days.

"Hey, so I read this thing last week that you'd find interesting, I think," I say.

If he notices that I've changed the subject away from his clever social commentary, he doesn't indicate it. "Tell me." He gives me a quizzical look.

"Have you heard of the blog *Teens with Bad Genes*?"

Caleb laughs, hard. He has a big laugh, the kind that shakes his shoulders up and down. It's a good laugh. "I have not heard of that, but I've obviously been missing out. What is that?"

"It was started by some kid whose sister has Tay-Sachs. He's really funny. You wouldn't think Tay-Sachs could be funny, I know, but trust me. This kid makes it hilarious. I mean, not the disease. But like, living in his family and dealing with all this stuff. And he posts cool genetics news articles and stuff."

"Oh yeah?" He raises an eyebrow in interest.

As I launch into a detailed explanation of the testing program in the Jewish high schools and all the fascinating questions it raises about genetic testing, it occurs to me that I am seriously nerding out on Caleb.

"Sorry," I say, cutting myself off. "I'm kind of a dork about this stuff."

"I already knew that, HD."

"I'm just saying, you should read the blog because it's funny and informative."

"Funny *and* informative, is it? Well, that must make it worth reading, then." Caleb shoves me gently. I push him back.

"At first I suspected that the blogger kid was probably a pedo living in his mother's basement and just posing as a teenager, you know?" I say. "But then I Googled him and he's legit."

Caleb laughs again. "Why do you think everyone is secretly a criminal? First you accuse me of plotting to lure you into the woods, and now you think this blog guy is a pedophile? I'm pretty sure most people are not murderers posing as teenagers with genetic mutations, even on the Internet."

"Truth?" I ask, putting my frappe down.

"Truth."

"I watched too many murder mysteries as a child. I'm damaged. Blame my parents."

"Oh, so that's what this is? And you'll never get in a taxi because you watched that movie with Denzel and Angelina, right?"

"Exactly!" I say, cracking up. "*Never*, ever take taxis!"

When our laughter naturally trails off, we both force a few extra chuckles out, just to extend the moment a little longer. Finally, I look at him, looking at me.

"What?"

"Nothing, nothing. You're funny, HD girl."

"I do what I can," I say, shrugging. Because you know, this is no big deal. Just me, hanging out with an attractive male, having a not completely awkward conversation. Like normal girls do.

"Anyway," I say, "I'll send you the link. For the blog. You sort of have to read it to get what I'm talking about."

"I'm looking forward to that," he says.

Ice cream consumed and all possible topics of small talk exhausted, we get up to go. Of course I manage to trip over my own feet going *up* the steps, and Caleb catches me by the elbow just as I go down on one knee.

"You okay?" he asks, stifling a laugh.

"Fine, fine." (Mortified, but fine.)

"Now you're probably going to accuse me of putting a roofie in your ice cream or something, right?" he says.

I brush my hands off on my jeans. "Actually, I won't try to blame that one on you. I'm the clumsiest ballet dancer you'll ever meet."

"Ah, I see. So you're graceful only when dancing?"

"And otherwise can't walk a straight line without tripping. Precisely."

We hover in front of the entrance to the subway station for another minute or two, even though neither of us is getting on. He told me he'd parked his car at one of the meters on Mass. Ave. and never mentioned needing to feed it again, even though

I'm pretty sure we've been sitting here for more than an hour. I wonder how many quarters he put in, how much time he thought we'd spend together. Then I wonder what percentage of that time I spent babbling about something ridiculous.

Finally, he gives me a weird punch on the shoulder.

"Well, I'll see you again soon, HD girl?"

"Sounds good."

"Get home safe. Don't catch a genetic disease on the way home." The light changes on Mass. Ave. and the walk signal appears, counting down in white digits from thirty seconds.

"You don't 'catch' a genetic disease," I say. "That's the point." He shades his eyes from the sun with one hand, just surveying me, while the walk signal drops down to twenty seconds. Of course, he *knows* you don't catch a genetic disease. "I mean, obviously. Well, you were kidding. Okay, I'm shutting up now." Nice one, Rose.

But he just laughs again, the shoulders going, and somehow I feel sort of okay being the biggest dork on the planet. Like I don't have to pretend I'm anything but.

"Okay, HD. Well, in that case, please don't experience the effects of epigenetics and have a mechanism in your present environment effect changes to your genetic expression. Better?"

Now I'm grinning. "Better." He grins back, then turns to jog across the street before the light changes again.

Six

"SO? DETAILS, PLEASE. THE DATE. TELL ME EVERYTHING."
Lena leans across her desk to whisper in my face when we sit
down for AP Calculus first period Monday morning. She looks
like a proud mother who's about to ship her kid off to college.

"Also, what do you think happens if a guy with the gene for
sickle cell and a girl with the gene for Huntington's make babies?" Lena muses. "Do you think those gene mutations would
magically cancel each other out and you'd have perfectly healthy
children?"

I roll my eyes at her. "Okay, first of all, you're incorrigible.
Second of all, he doesn't have sickle cell, his sisters do, and anyway, that is a totally scientifically unsound theory. And third
of all, it wasn't a date. It was ice cream and conversation. Very
civilized. You should try it."

At the front of the room, Mr. Petrilli is writing out some
warm-up problems involving standard deviation on the white
board. I like Petrilli; we all do. He's been teaching here forever.
Bowling ball head, thick Boston accent, and he takes three days
off every April to go down to Red Sox spring training. That,
and he's known for using Mrs. Petrilli's baked goods in class

from time to time. I still don't understand how Rice Krispies treats are related to the derivative, but it doesn't really matter.

"Come on, give me a clue," Lena whispers, leaning a little closer as she opens to a clean page in her notebook.

I start jotting down Petrilli's warm-up problems. "He goes to Barrow."

Lena's face contorts instantly, like she's just bitten into a sour gummy. "Seriously? Ick!"

"No, he's cool. He made a joke about it. He's funny. And smart."

"Funny and smart," Lena says triumphantly, nodding. "Like you." She gives me one of her huge, toothy fake grins. Lena acts like a goof a lot of the time, and she can sometimes sound ditzy, but she's actually one of those effortlessly smart girls who gets A's on everything without even trying that hard. I'd probably hate her if she hadn't been my best friend since forever.

Petrilli clears his throat and launches into today's lesson: "Ah-right, let's talk about stand-ahd deviation." I relax a little at the excuse to stop thinking about Caleb and set my eyes on the board.

But then I have no choice but to think about him, because he disappears. No text messages, no IMs or Facebook chats. He doesn't even respond to the *Teens with Bad Genes* link I send over. By the middle of week two with no sign of him, I'm convinced that he's vanished because he's realized that he made a massive mistake by hanging out with me.

"Maybe he thinks I thought ice cream was a date-date? And now he feels awkward about it?" I ask Lena over the phone when I should be finishing my English reading.

"If that's true, he's super lame. Maybe he's just been busy."

"Should I text him?"

I can practically hear Lena's exasperation in the silence on the other end of the line. "Really, do I have to teach you everything? You do not text him. That's rule number one for dealing with boys! You're way too busy with all the cool, interesting things happening in your life. Right?"

"Such as . . . ?"

"Such as ballet, school, getting into college, hanging out with *moi*, obviously."

"I just hope he's okay."

"He's *fine*," Lena says. Her lack of the anxious gene allows her to soar through these situations without jumping to the worst-case scenario. "Trust me. You'll either hear from him, or he's not worth the trouble."

When we hang up, I consider Lena's rules for dealing with boys. She's definitely savvier than I am about this stuff, but the idea of waiting around for some guy I barely know to call or text me just seems annoying. Besides, it's the twenty-first century. I pull up Caleb's last text to me. It was from five minutes before we met at the bookstore, when I'd written to say I was running late and he'd texted back, "No worries. No shortage of reading material here."

I start tapping out a text. "Hey, how are you? Haven't heard from you in a while, hope everything is ok." Then I delete it.

Next I try, "What's up? Missed you on IM this week." *Missed you?* Get a grip, Rose. Delete. Finally I settle on, "Breaking news: the blogger IS a pedo after all."

I hit Send before I can overthink it, and let out a sigh as I put the phone down. If Lena asks, this never happened.

I sit on my bed, scrolling through Facebook on my phone and waiting, and waiting. No more texts come through. I toss the phone aside and mark through the combination we worked on today in ballet, going through all the movements but with about fifty percent energy since I have limited floor space in my room. I pause on the part I kept messing up earlier and go through it a few more times until I nail it twice in a row. But my phone's still silent.

By the time I get home from dance the next night, my head is more or less exploding. I've even tried turning my phone off and on a few times to make sure no text messages got randomly lodged in there, but—big surprise—there aren't any.

I'd prefer to skip out on dinner and go straight to my room to obsess some more, but Dad has actually cooked for a change—chicken, salad, and rice pilaf—so I'm stuck sitting down for a meal.

It almost feels like our old life: real food, cooked by a person in our family instead of someone at one of our local takeout joints, and it's just the three of us; Gram's at her book club. Even Mom seems like she's having a pretty good night. Her body jerks involuntarily, constant slight, uncoordinated movements, but she hasn't had any outbursts or said anything inappropriate . . .

at least not since I got home. She's a little glum, which is her baseline these days, but other than that she seems almost normal.

"Can you help me with the rice, Rose?" she asks. I take more pilaf from the ceramic dish Dad hands me and pile a small heap on her plate.

"Thanks," she says, giving me a lopsided half smile. She aims a small forkful of salad at her mouth and brings it slowly in for a landing, letting a few lettuce leaves scatter to her plate.

"Let's talk about your college a-a-applications," she says after she's carefully chewed the bits of lettuce.

"Oh please, Mother, do we have to?" I groan.

"Yes. Dad sssays you're behind."

I shoot Dad a dirty look. "I'm not behind, guys. It's barely October."

"Okay, but the time is going to fly," Dad says. "Is your list all set? Including a safety school?"

I take a bite of pilaf to avoid answering. It scalds my tongue.

"Too. Hot," I say, fanning my mouth.

"You've got to get on top of this stuff, babe," Dad says. "I was talking to a client about his daughter; she's at Emerson, and he said she loves it. She's an economics major. You could do that or—have you thought about architecture? Like Mom?"

"Dad," I interrupt, taking a gulp of water. "Can we stop, please? I'm not ready to commit to a *major* when I haven't even applied yet."

"Sorry, sorry, you're right. What about your essays? Want me to look at them?"

"Ms. Greenberg is going to read them, she promised. She's also doing one of my recommendations. Mr. Petrilli is doing the other. Okay?" I look from Dad to Mom and back again.

"Fine. You're on top of it. Noted," Dad says. "But I'm just saying—"

"*Dad.* Seriously."

"Okay, okay." He pauses just long enough to cut his chicken, but I can tell he's not done. "But what about Cunningham? Have you started that application, at least? I thought you were thinking about applying early there."

I guess I did say that, technically. But there's still this voice in the back of my head, whispering about PCCA, that I can't get rid of.

I take a deep breath and smile at Dad. I get that he wants to be helpful. But what he doesn't understand—and what I don't want to tell him—is that I know he can't handle everything. He can't take care of Mom, and deal with all her meds and appointments and therapy, *and* get his own work done, and help me figure out this college mess. I determined quite a while ago that I was going to have to figure out this stuff on my own, and that's fine. It really is. I'm on it.

So instead of explaining all that to him, I just smile. It's a little forced, but I don't want to turn this into a thing, especially when Mom's having a decent night.

"I haven't decided yet about Cunningham. But I have a meeting this week with Ms. Greenberg, and she's going to help me figure it out. Okay?"

That should satisfy him. Dad knows Ms. Greenberg is trustworthy. I haven't had her since sophomore year, when I wrote about Mom's diagnosis for her class, but I still think of her as my favorite.

It works. "Sounds good," Dad says. "Just let me know if you want to talk about it." He turns to Mom, who's focused on getting food into her mouth. She looks up at me, a little piece of pilaf stuck to her chin.

"Good, sweetie. Ssssounds good."

After dinner, I'm trying to focus on my calculus problem set when finally my phone rings. Caleb. I let it ring a few times, almost to voice mail, and then answer casually. "Hello?"

"So you don't know who's calling?" he asks, without even saying hi.

"It's been so long since I've heard from you, I deleted your number from my phone." I'm surprised by my own boldness.

"Uh-huh. Before or after you texted me?" Dammit. Busted. "Hey, look, sorry I went MIA." He clears his throat.

"What's up?"

There's a little pause. "Been a rough couple weeks I guess. Sorry I didn't shoot you a text. My sister Ella had a bad pain crisis, and then Mom did. It's been a string of ER visits and hospital stays."

I know enough about sickle cell to know that it affects the red blood cells, so you can have terrible pain—a "crisis"— literally anywhere your blood flows.

"Oh man, I'm sorry," I say. Of course, it had nothing to do with us. Because *we're* not anything, really.

"Thanks. They're both a lot better now. It's just hectic when it happens, you know."

"Yeah. I mean, I can imagine."

I wander from my desk to my bed and pick at the pilling on my flannel duvet cover, trying desperately to think of something else to talk about so we won't have to hang up.

"So, how are things with you, HD girl?"

It gives me a little rush of warmth in my stomach, the way he says it. I never thought I'd enjoy being identified by my family disease.

"Things are fine. The parents are on my case about college."

"I hear you. My parents met at Yale. I'm dressed in bulldog gear in three-quarters of my baby pictures. No pressure."

I laugh, picturing Caleb as a baby. "So is that your plan? Yalie-to-be?"

"Hell no," he says. "They ruined any chance of that by talking about it so damn much over the years. Anyway, I'm pretty sold on RISD."

"RISD?" I repeat it the way he says it—Riz-dee.

"Rhode Island School of Design, in Providence. It's the best for painting. I know it's not the most practical career plan, but you know . . . life's short, right?"

Indeed. And sometimes it starts sucking long before it's technically over.

"I totally hear that. I always thought that in my dream world I'd go to a ballet BFA program. There's one in San Francisco that's, like, ridiculous. It's attached to the Ballet of the Pacific Coast, which is one of the top companies, and it's—" I realize I'm rambling again and cut myself off.

"It's what?" The way Caleb asks, it sounds like he really wants to know. The BPC is one of the premier companies in the country, probably in the world. Mom took me to see them when they came to Boston on tour when I was eight. I'd already seen the Boston Ballet, plenty of times, but the BPC was something special, Mom said. She was right, of course. Even at that age, I understood that what I was seeing onstage was extraordinary.

"I don't know," I say. "It's the best. Most of the other major ballet companies don't have actual bachelor's degree programs attached to them—usually it's one or the other. Dance, or get your college degree. Anyway, that's what I always imagined I'd do."

"Why the past tense?"

Across the room, on the wall over my desk, there's a bulletin board covered in pictures, including many of my different ballet performances from over the years. My eyes land on the one of me at three, dressed like a tutu-ed bunny rabbit. Ballet has been the center of my universe since then. It's hard to imagine living without it.

"Well, if my parents are paying for college, they sort of get a say in where I go. And my dad thinks I should be studying business or something else practical."

"Well," Caleb says, then stops for a moment. "I think you deserve to do exactly what you want."

"I'm sure my dad will appreciate your support for my lousy career choices."

"Career-shmareer." He laughs. "That's what I say to that! We'll make our lousy career choices together and prove them all wrong."

Seven

I'M TEN MINUTES LATE TO DANCE THE NEXT AFTERNOON, which is pretty unheard of and definitely frowned upon. My first class starts at three thirty on Mondays, Wednesdays, and Thursdays, which gives me just enough time to leave school at two thirty and get to the studio in time to change. Today, though, I slip in at three forty-two. I take my place as inconspicuously as possible at a barre by Eloise, but Miss Julia still shoots me a disapproving look from the front of the room.

"What's up with you?" Eloise whispers when we lean over to stretch.

"Nothing. Subway delay." It's a lie. I was sitting in the hallway by my locker, considering my conversation with Caleb last night and debating whether or not I was even going to go to ballet. I hung up the phone with a weird, nagging feeling, like two kids with pretty bad illnesses in their families should be worrying about more important stuff than whether or not we're going to pursue our "creative passions" after high school. Like we were being petty, or something. Plus, I saw the bill from my studio on Dad's desk the other night and it reminded me how expensive this passion is. Even when my mom worked, my parents saved wherever they could to pay for my dance training.

Now there's one income in my house and huge medical expenses, which are only going to go up. How much longer can I really justify doing this?

Eventually, though, I went to class—because no matter what, ballet is still the thing that makes me feel calm when everything else is confusing. Now that I'm here, stretching by Eloise like we've been doing three to five times a week since we were three years old, it feels good. Normal, solid, predictable.

Miss Julia teaches us a new combination. Thursday afternoon classes are usually fun—more of a mix of ballet and jazz, so no pointe shoes today. Eloise and I mark through the combination at the side of the room while half the class runs it first. Georgia, taller and thinner and definitely blonder than any of the rest of us, is at the front, as always. Even on Thursdays, when the rest of us wear our hair in looser ponytails, she wears hers in a tight bun, hair-sprayed within an inch of its life. Never a single strand out of place for Georgia.

Finishing up the combination, Georgia slips past Eloise and me and takes a swig from her water bottle. She gives us a tight smile.

"Did you hear?" she asks.

"Hear what?" Eloise says. I try to avoid giving in to Georgia's bait, but Eloise can't help it.

"BPC master class next week. They're in town." Georgia purses her lips. "They might be scouting for the PCCA program for next year."

"Where'd you hear that?" Eloise asks, not even bothering to try to hide her enthusiasm from Georgia, who shrugs.

"Just around. Your group is up." As we rush to the middle of the floor, Eloise turns to me, her face flushed with excitement. So much for giving up dance. That'll definitely have to wait.

Caleb said we would "obviously" talk soon, but I'm still startled when I see his name on my phone, buzzing away practically the minute I transfer from the subway to the bus, headed home from dance.

"Obviously, huh?" I answer.

"What?"

"You said *obviously* we'd talk again soon. I just didn't realize how soon."

Caleb laughs, and I picture those shoulders going up and down. "I wanted to talk to you. Should I have waited two-point-five days or something like that?"

"Why two-point-five?"

"Isn't that the requisite number of days a guy is supposed to wait before calling a girl?"

"I think two-point-five is actually the average number of children in a stereotypical American nuclear family," I reply.

"Okay, smart-ass HD. How are you?"

Somehow, coming from Caleb, that question doesn't feel like a total throwaway.

"Since less than twenty-four hours ago? Good. Just got out of dance, and I'm on my way home now."

"Little late, isn't it?"

I glance at my phone screen, even though I know it's after eight o'clock.

"This is pretty normal," I say. "Mondays, Wednesdays, and Thursdays are my long days." I'm used to the schedule: three days a week from three thirty until eight, the other two from four to seven, plus Saturdays from nine to four. Sometimes I forget that normal teenagers have more free time. That might be nice.

"So, what do you do in these mysterious ballet classes, anyway?"

"You really want to know? Pretty much beat up our bodies until we're bleeding, bruised, and busted—"

"Alliteration, nice work."

"Thank you."

"Are you guys supercompetitive with each other like in the dance movies?"

"Big *Center Stage* fan, huh?" I tease. Of course, it's secretly one of my favorite movies of all time. That and *Dirty Dancing* (the original, obviously).

"Two ten-year-old sisters, remember. I know dance movies, trust me."

"Oh, right," I say. "Sorry, I forgot you were well-versed in all things little girl." I hunch down in my seat closer to the window, and cup my hand over my mouth. I hate being that person who talks loud on the bus. Normally I wouldn't even answer the phone.

"We're pretty competitive, I guess," I tell him. Competitive is one word for it. Cutthroat is another that comes to mind. I think of Georgia's pursed lips. "Of course, we're not exactly in the corps at the Boston Ballet, so we're probably not the cream of the crop anyway."

I tell myself that, but the truth is every year a few dancers from our studio join major companies. I'm sure it's Georgia's plan, even though she's keeping her cards close to her chest, and I know Eloise is auditioning for a few. Miss Julia has hinted to me that it could be my plan, too, if I wanted it to be.

Talking to Caleb feels so normal, so natural, that I almost miss my stop. As I hop off and walk the half block home, he tells me about a kid from Barrow whose mom danced with the Boston Ballet until she was like forty. Turns out she's pretty famous. It's no surprise, of course, that Caleb has famous people's kids in his class, but I'm still impressed. Dance celebrities don't tend to be a big deal to regular people, but for me they might as well be Angelina Jolie.

When I walk in the door, I smell pasta—the second largest food group in our house these days, after takeout. Dad's probably left me some on the stove, still warm. Mom sits at the dining room table, surrounded by about a thousand photographs printed off from the travel Web sites she's obsessed with. She's got her big, easy-grip scissors out and she's making jagged cuts to the photos, letting shreds of paper fall lightly to the floor like broken snowflakes.

"Hey, Caleb?" I say in a low voice so she won't hear me. "I just walked in the door and I think I should go see what my mom's up to . . ."

"That's cool," he cuts in. He gets it.

"So how about I call *you* tomorrow?" But even as I say it—trying to sound all nonchalant, like I call guys all the time—my gut is churning with something between excitement and abject horror.

"I would very much enjoy that. Later then."

I hang up and dump my slew of bags by the foot of the stairs. "Hey, Mom. What's up?" I sit across from her, careful not to disturb the spread of pictures.

"Hi, babe. Adding to my collection."

By her "collection," she means her scrapbook of photos from train routes all over the world that she's never traveled.

"Uh, yeah—I can see that. What are these?" I ask, picking up one that's sitting in front of me.

"These are from the Hiram Bingham Orient Express."

"The Orient Express?" Maybe she's confused. I'm pretty sure she already has the Orient Express in her scrapbook.

"No. *Hiram Bingham* Orient Express," she repeats slowly. "It's in Peru."

"Oh, cool."

"It climbs Machu Picchu. You can get altitude sssickness on the train."

A train that climbs a mountain does sound pretty cool. "Want me to put these in the book?" I ask her.

"I can do it, Rose. Don't treat me like a chhhild," she says, suddenly harsh. She clutches the papers to her chest in her quivering hands, like she has to protect them from me.

This is how she is now—warm one minute, cold the next. I look at the pictures scattered across the table, some of which have been cut almost in half because her fine motor control is so weak.

I take a breath to steady my voice before responding to her. "Okay. I have homework."

"Don't talk down to me! I'm still your mother. Don't ffforget that."

I get up and leave her to it, surrounded by scraps of paper and all those imagined exotic trips she's never going to take.

Mom got her train obsession from her father, along with the Huntington's. My grandfather, apparently, was a bit of a rail buff in his early days, before Huntington's and alcohol took him away. He gave Mom's brother, Uncle Charlie, a toy train set for Christmas when he was eight or something like that, the kind that speeds around a track in a circle, forward and backward, with a caboose and a coal car and a heavy engine. My mother said it was the only nice thing he ever gave either her or Uncle Charlie, and she coveted it.

So when I was seven, Dad gave Mom a train set of her own, the gift she'd always wanted. He still sets it up every holiday season, and over the years we've added miniature fir trees and snow-covered bridges and a little station with a platform. It's become a dorky family tradition.

Mom says trains are romantic. She used to tell me bedtime stories that were all train-themed, stories of little girls named Rose who rode the rails and had adventures involving mysterious strangers and thieves and romances and other plotlines that probably weren't completely appropriate for a little kid.

"You never know who's going to sit next to you on a train," she told me. "It's a people's-eye view of the world. A plane is a bird's-eye view, but a train gives you something different."

Then she showed me all the classic train movies, unveiling them one at a time over the years of my childhood: *Murder on the Orient Express, Strangers on a Train, The Lady Vanishes.*

When I was eight, Mom and I rode the train to New York to see City Ballet, just the two of us. She knew exactly where to sit for the best views—on the left side of the train going down, right side coming back. We bought gummy candy for the ride in South Station—peaches, sour strawberry straws, and twin cherries. And she didn't let me read my book for the whole trip, even though I was reading *Matilda* and I was really into it.

"Just watch, Rose. Trains aren't about getting from point A to point B. They're about what's in between."

That person and the person downstairs, snapping at me for nothing, can't be the same. It defies all sense.

When she was diagnosed, Mom decided that she needed to take all the greatest train rides in the world while she still could. She bought a big world map and started doing all this research, comparing which routes were supposed to be the most scenic and then marking them out on the map with a red Sharpie: the Rocky Mountaineer in Canada; the Darjeeling Himalayan in India; the Glacier Express through the Swiss Alps. And the Trans-Siberian, which stretches all the way across Russia. The best American routes were on there, too: the Coast Starlight from Los Angeles to Seattle, the Empire Builder, and, of course, the California Zephyr—Chicago to San Francisco, supposedly the most scenic train route in the country.

She didn't make the Zephyr or the Trans-Siberian. Actually, she didn't make any of them. I wanted Mom to go to Russia and see the flat, white expanse of Siberia stretching out into eternity. I wanted to go with her, pack her up and ride all those trains as far as they would take us. But first there was the expense—trains aren't cheap—and then there was her health. Her symptoms progressed slowly at first, but still too quickly to plan a decade or two of international travel. I guess at some point, she just resigned herself to the fantasy of it.

Hence the mess of papers currently burying the dining room table. She prints them out and sticks them in these scrapbooks, and keeps telling and retelling the same made-up stories about what all the journeys would be like. Frankly, these days I'm not sure if she's repeating them on purpose or if it's the disease playing tricks on her mind. I don't know what goes on in there.

As I head to my bedroom, I pass by Mom's office. I still think of it as her office, anyway, even though she certainly doesn't do any work anymore. My mother stopped being an architect when she lost the ability to hold a pencil steady. She used to draw the most intricate, precise plans at the slanted desk by the window in this room, and she'd hang her plans on the wall so she could step back and look at them from afar. Now on the wall where those plans used to be, Dad's taped the huge map that documents all of Mom's train routes. She's stuck pictures to the map like a psychopath plotting a murder and then an elaborate escape route. Glancing at the map, I notice that the Hiram Bingham Orient Express isn't marked out. There aren't any red lines across South America at all. It must be a new one for her list.

In my bedroom, I fire up my laptop and quickly Google it. "Hiram Bingham Orient Express" brings up a bunch of hits from rail Web sites and blogs. "This Pullman train follows

Eight

FOR THE BALLET OF THE PACIFIC COAST MASTER CLASS, I show up at the studio wearing the least faded of my black leotards and a new pair of pale pink tights I picked up yesterday, after I realized that all of my hundreds of pink tights had some kind of run or hole in them, or looked otherwise abused. I don't want the BPC people thinking I don't take this seriously. When I get into the room, I notice that the rest of the girls look similarly polished for this occasion. Eloise is wearing what looks like almost full show makeup.

"All right, girls, let's do this," says the lead BPC dancer, Felix. "Ready to show us what you're made of?"

Felix warms us up with *pliés* and *tendus*, but the class quickly accelerates into a mix of exercises that make our regular classes feel like relaxing in front of the television. The BPC is famous not only for their gorgeous productions of the classical ballets, but also for being one of the most demanding companies in the business. Felix's class is a crazy-rigorous workout, and it's using muscle groups I didn't even know I had. Midway through the class, my obliques are pulsating and my quads burn.

Felix and his partner, a dancer named Nell with long, blond hair twisted high on her head, take us through a couple of combinations. Finally they announce that they're going to teach us the opening movement to *Ampersand*, the BPC's signature original ballet.

I throw a quick look at Eloise, who grins at me. We watch the BPC perform more or less every year when they come to town. I can practically see the *Ampersand* choreography in my head, but I've never had the chance to dance it. Even though I'm pretty sure I can handle it, I get a swell of nerves in my stomach as Felix starts placing us in a cluster in the center of the room, and gives us our counts for the opening sequence.

I'm practically dying by the end of class. My muscles are quivering, and I'm 99 percent sure I won't be able to walk tomorrow. We give Felix and Nell a round of applause, and Miss Julia passes a clipboard around for us to sign up for seven-dollar tickets to their shows this weekend. I put a one in the quantity box next to my name and am about to pass it to Eloise, but then I hesitate. I cross out the one and replace it with a two. Lena will come with me, I'm sure—but I'm not sure she'll be the first person I offer the extra ticket to.

At home, I soak in a bath with Epsom salts, hoping it'll offset some of the muscular agony I'm going to be in tomorrow morning. I'm not really a bath person, honestly, but sometimes, like tonight, I leave class knowing that I'll be punished if I don't give myself a good soak.

I lean back against the edge of the tub and try to relax, stretching my legs as far as they'll go in the near-scalding water.

I'm flipping through the magazine I brought in with me—*The Atlantic*, not very exciting—when there's a knock at the bathroom door.

"What?"

"Rose, someone's ringing you." It's Gram. I forgot to bring my cell phone in with me.

"It's fine, Gram," I call through the door. "I'm in the tub. I'll call whoever it is back."

"Want me to pass the phone to you?" she calls back. "It's someone called Caleb."

I know she's just trying to be helpful, but really, I'd prefer it if she'd just leave my phone where it is when she hears it ringing. Does she really have to go into my room, pick it up off my bed, and look to see who it is?

I try not to sound irritated. "It's okay, Gram," I say. "Thanks!"

Ten minutes is all I can stand before I start feeling nauseated in the humidity of the bathroom, and I haul myself out of the tub and stretch. Everything cracks—my neck, back, wrists, ankles. Seriously, my whole body is going to be wrecked long before Huntington's gets to it, at this rate.

On my way back to my bedroom, Gram pokes her head into the hallway.

"Who's Caleb?"

"No one. He's just a guy I know." Caleb and I have been in some kind of contact almost every day since last week—text, IM, a phone call—but it still makes my heart race with nerves to think about it.

"An interesting guy?" she asks.

"He's just a friend," I say. Gram's trying to ask the questions Mom won't know to ask anymore, but I don't feel like engaging in a dish session.

In my room, with the door closed, I take a deep breath to steady my voice before hitting his number to call him back. If I ask him to come see the BPC with me, will he think it's a date? Will he think *I* think it's a date? As much contact as we've had, we haven't made another plan to hang out.

I shake my head, as if the physical act will somehow rid me of all the questions. It doesn't, but I call him anyway. And he answers.

"How do you feel about ballet?" I ask.

"Is that how you normally greet people when you call them?"

I laugh. "Yes. Just a quick interrogation."

"Okay," he says. "Well, I told you. My little sisters are dance freaks. You're a dance freak. So I guess I have a lot of dance freaks in my life."

My hands are actually sweating. I wipe them one at a time on the bedspread. "So, would you like to come see some ballet with me? I have an extra ticket." I listen to the words hang in the air. "It's not a big deal, or anything."

"Of course I'll come see some ballet with you, HD. Obviously."

There's that word again.

Our cheap seats are all the way up in the nosebleed section of the Citi Center, row XX or something ridiculous like that. It's the actual last row. I rest my head against the back wall and look down to the tiny half moon of a stage below us. The ceiling of the theater, which, at this height, I could almost reach out and touch, is painted with intricate cherubs and clouds and ornate gold molding. I can see dust in the air, hovering in the beams of light.

"So this is the famous Ballet of the Pacific Coast, is it?" Caleb asks, flipping through the Playbill before the curtain goes up.

"The one and only," I reply.

"Your future employer, right?"

I squirm in my seat, wishing I hadn't mentioned to Caleb that the BPC was my dream company. It had been such an offhand comment—I didn't imagine he'd even remember. Go figure.

"So how come I haven't heard of them if they're so good?" he asks.

I scoff. "Trust me, dude, you don't know from good until you've seen these guys. They're insane. They're just based on the West Coast, so they're not in town that often."

"Okay, *dude*," Caleb says, flashing a grin at me. He glances around the theater, then leans in conspiratorially. "Also, I'm pretty sure I'm the only black person in this very large room."

I can hear the mischievousness in his voice, but his comment makes me blush anyway. It's true that the theater is packed with a lot of white people. Mostly old white people, in fact—the typical ballet demographic. It's not that I haven't noticed this little truism about ballet, but I guess I haven't ever *noticed* noticed. I'm relieved when the house lights dim before I can respond and the moment is cut mercifully short.

* * *

The first act is called "Classic BPC," a series of three beautiful pieces from their classical repertoire, and then after the intermission, there's a new original ballet called *Depths*, choreographed by the BPC's artistic director. It looks like a love letter to the ocean, with a *pas de deux* midway through between a man and woman, both dressed in swirls of chiffon in different shades of blue. As they dance together, they look like they're floating, treading water, reaching for each other. Their bodies separate, then come together again, barely distinguishable from each other as their limbs intertwine. I lean forward in my seat, my heart pounding, goose bumps rising on my arms. It's stunning.

When the whole company is onstage for the final movement, I spot Felix—even from this distance, I recognize the way he holds himself, how every inch of him responds to movements that start in his core: When he lifts an arm, his fingertips are alive. There's never a piece of him that isn't dancing. Nell, in the corps with so many other women designed to look identical, is harder to spot. At one point I think I recognize her, but then they all turn and I'm not sure again. That's the thing about ballet that I love so much, but that also frustrates me: the unison and precision of it. There's not a lot of room to be yourself.

"Well," says Caleb, as we emerge onto Tremont Street after the show, "you were right. That was pretty good."

"Not bad, right?"

"I mean, it's not like I couldn't do most of the stuff those dudes were doing—those leaps and turns didn't look *that* hard."

I jab him in the ribs. The act of touching him, even momentarily, sends a jolt of electricity up my spine, not unlike the time I touched an electric fence at a farm when I was five and got a brief but potent shock.

Outside the theater, we're caught up in the throng of audience members swarming around the stage door, hoping to get an autograph as the dancers try to escape. Pressing through the crowd on our way to the Green Line, we pass an older white woman, her blond hair flecked with gray, her arm wrapped around the waist of a stout black man with a shaved head and a silvery beard. They're smiling broadly and exclaiming over the performance, just like we are. They look like they've been that way for years, going gray and laughing together.

See, I want to say to Caleb, there was at least *one* other black person in the theater. As they go by, the man nods at Caleb, who nods back in a silent greeting.

When we've passed out of earshot, I lean into Caleb. "Did you know that guy?"

He laughs. "I don't know him. Code of black men."

"The 'code of black men'?" I ask, incredulous. "Is that a thing?"

"Oh, trust me, it's a thing."

"You greet every black man you pass on the street like that? Seriously?" There is definitely no code of white women. Or if there is, no one has filled me in on it.

"Not *every* black man," Caleb explains, chuckling. "But yeah. You've gotta give the nod. Be cool. Give the nod."

Now I'm the one nodding—slowly. "Okay. Whatever you say. I've just never noticed black men nodding at each other all over the place before."

"Don't worry," he says, smiling. "You're not meant to."

It feels vaguely condescending, but I let it go. I'm not sure Caleb and I are really at the point in our relationship to be talking about race, and it's come up twice tonight. Not that we have a *relationship*, per se. But then he presses against my shoulder, giving me a little nudge, and I get another of those shocks to my spine.

We walk the rest of the way to the subway in silence, but then as we get on the Green Line, Caleb clears his throat.

"So, I have a kind of weird request."

"Um, okay?"

"Can I draw you at some point this week?"

At first, I'm not even sure what he means. As in, draw a picture of me?

"You want to draw me?" I ask, really not wanting to embarrass myself by misunderstanding the request.

"Yeah, I want to draw you. For my art class. We're doing portraits this month."

Hearing that it's for his art class is both disappointing—he doesn't just want to sketch me in some romantic-Leo-and-Kate-in-*Titanic*-like way; he actually has an assignment—and also reassuring. It's *not* romantic. Or not too romantic, anyway. I can handle that.

"You mean you're not creating images of me that you're going to tape to the walls of the room you have hidden behind a fake bookcase?"

"What!" Caleb exclaims. "Who told you about that? That's my victim room!"

"That's what I thought! See, I knew you were really an Internet stalker!" We both crack up. The Green Line pulls in and we squeeze on board amidst a million other theatergoers.

"Seriously, though," he says, quietly now that it feels like everyone on the train can hear our conversation. "Can you model?"

"Umm . . . I can sit still. Will that suffice?"

"That will suffice. I'll even pay you in food."

"Oh really? What kind of food?"

He grins. "The best kind. My mom's."

The bottom of my stomach drops as the train lurches to a start. The crowd presses me up against Caleb's chest, and he rests a hand on the small of my back. I flinch when he first touches me, but it feels good to be tucked in against his chest. For a moment I imagine what we must look like right now: like one of those normal, happy, teenage couples.

But normal, happy, teenage couples always think they'll be together forever—because what could go wrong? I know things aren't that simple. Pulling away from Caleb a few inches, I snake my arm through the crowd and grab one of the silver poles to steady myself.

Nine

Caleb picks me up the following Saturday night, driving a slightly battered Honda Civic that doesn't seem like it would belong to a family that can afford to send their three children to private school.

"These your wheels?" I ask as I slip into the front seat.

"Yup. Fancy, right?"

"Fancier than mine."

"Oh yeah, what do you drive?"

"The subway, unless I'm borrowing."

The whole truth is, I could drive all the time these days if I wanted to. My mother's car is still sitting in the driveway, even though Dad finally took her keys away earlier this year. (Considering that the fender benders were her earliest symptoms of Huntington's, she was probably a danger on the road long before she stopped driving, but she and Dad had so many vicious fights about it for the first three years post-diagnosis that he gave up until Dr. Howard basically mandated the no-driving policy.)

Anyway, I don't drive Mom's car unless it's a real emergency. It just makes me feel weird, getting a perk out of her falling to pieces.

"So, I want to warn you about what you're in for here," Caleb says.

"What's that mean?"

"My little sisters are going to be very interested in you. That's all."

So he doesn't bring girls home for dinner very often. Okay. "So what can I do to impress them? Any tips?"

"Know anything about tween pop stars? I'm pretty sure any knowledge of the latest Disney hotshot will make you an insta-friend as far as my sisters are concerned."

"Sorry, but did you just say 'tween'?"

"I'm ashamed to admit that I did," he says. "Anyway, they're twins, so be prepared. Ella and Nina."

"Ella and Nina, huh? Great jazz names."

He smiles. "Yup. Dad's obsessed."

"So who are you named after? I don't recall a Caleb among the jazz greats."

"No obsession for me. I was born early so they were unprepared. They just picked a name they liked."

Caleb's family lives in a western suburb of Boston, known to me only for its literary significance—Louisa May Alcott lived there, I think—and for its affluent reputation. We take Route 2 for about fifteen minutes before he pulls off, and soon we're winding along slightly hilly two-lane roads with thick trees on both sides. The foliage is full of warm oranges and reds.

"It's nice out here in the fall," he observes. "The colors are insane."

"New England falls, man. They're the best," I agree. They're too short, but they're pretty spectacular while they last. "Okay, so, what about your parents?" I ask. "What am I in for there?"

"You'll be fine. My folks are goofy, but they're pretty cool. My mom teaches. She's a professor of economics at Harvard."

"So, she's not that smart?"

"Not really. Neither's my dad."

"Oh, what's he do? Brain surgery?"

"No, he's actually not *that* smart. He's a neonatologist at Mass General."

I laugh. My mother would've called them a power couple, if she still thought of things like that to say. "That's like preemies?"

"Like preemies, indeed."

I steel myself to be completely intimidated as we pull up to a big old Victorian tucked down a long, densely forested driveway. The house is lavender with white and gray trim, and there aren't any other houses in view—just land out the back and woodlands to the front. I already know Caleb's family has money, obviously, but I can't even imagine what this property is worth.

He opens the door and ushers me into what I can only describe as barely controlled chaos. The house may be pristine and peaceful from the outside, but on the inside it's a whirlwind of toys, kids' artwork on the walls, and backpacks and sweatshirts strewn across furniture and over the banisters on the tall center staircase. I like it immediately.

"We're back!" he calls into the house. Two little girls in polka-dot leggings and purple tunic-length sweatshirts come sliding into the front hallway, practically squealing.

"Ca-aaa-le," they call, each grabbing one of their brother's arms and tugging up and down. "Introduce us to your *friend*," says one of them slyly, eyeing me.

"My friend is Rose. These terrors are Ella and Nina." He points at one and then the other.

"Are you *sure* I'm Ella?" says the one on the left, who, admittedly, looks quite a lot like the one on the right. Even their hair is styled the same, in two curly puffs on either side of their heads.

"Yeah, who told you I'm Nina?" asks the other.

"Careful," Caleb says to me, ignoring them both. "They're cute but they bite."

"We don't bite!" they exclaim simultaneously.

"I actually shouldn't get too close," I tell Caleb, very solemnly. "I have that allergy I was telling you about."

He plays along. "Oh, right, right. That's very serious. You really shouldn't get within breathing distance of them."

"What's her allergy?" asks the one I think is Ella.

"I'm allergic to twins," I say, deadpanning. Their already huge brown eyes get even wider, four side-by-side saucers.

"That's impossible," says Nina, suspicious but, I can tell, also not entirely convinced of her own certainty.

"Oh, it's true. It's a rare but very serious allergy." I back away from them, covering my mouth. "In fact, Caleb's right, I really shouldn't even breathe near you."

"What happens if you breathe near us?" Ella asks, quietly fascinated.

I look at Caleb. He looks back at me and clears his throat.

"Well . . ." I say slowly.

"Well . . . it's very, very dangerous," he tells them. "She develops a potentially deadly case of . . ." He pauses dramatically, leaving the finale to me.

"Polka dot–itis!" I shriek, storming at them like I'm going to grab them.

The girls burst out laughing. "That's not real!" Nina exclaims.

"You're teasing us!" Ella says. And then earnestly, to her brother: "Mom says you're not supposed to tease us."

"Mom says no such thing. I think what Mom actually says is you both need to buck up and work on your comebacks." He shoves Ella affectionately by the forehead, then does the same to Nina. "Now please, go do something useful with yourselves. Play with dolls, write the great American novel, whatever it is you people are doing these days."

He takes my hand, just for a split second, to lead me toward the kitchen. I used to think holding hands would make me uncomfortable—too boyfriend/girlfriend-y. I was wrong.

"Parentals, this is Rose." His mother is pulling a roast chicken out of the oven in a Pyrex baking dish, while his father hovers over the butcher block island, chopping garlic and chilies directly on the wood. Both look up with wide grins—Caleb gets the gap in his teeth from his dad—when we enter the room.

"Rose, so nice to meet you," says his mother, putting the Pyrex to rest on a dish towel and wiping her hands on her jeans before reaching out to give me a hug. "Sorry, I'm a hugger," she says, chuckling. "Hope you don't mind!"

I'm not really a hugger, but obviously I'm not going to say that.

"Rose, pleasure." Caleb's father offers me his hand, which is so big that I momentarily picture it squashing one of the two-pound babies he probably deals with on a daily basis. He has the same, almost painfully firm handshake as his son.

"Thanks for having me . . ." I trail off, suddenly realizing that I have no idea what to call Caleb's parents.

"Richard, and Valerie," Caleb rescues me.

"That's right," says his mom. "We're not fancy people around here."

You wouldn't know it from looking around the kitchen, which has obviously been remodeled with high-end appliances and granite countertops and one of those deep, white ceramic sinks. It couldn't be more different from our old kitchen, with its mismatched appliances and warped drawers that are impossible to close without putting your full body weight behind them. This is not a kitchen that sees a lot of takeout.

"You guys want a Coke or something? Seltzer, OJ?" asks Caleb's mother from the fridge.

"I'll have a Coke," says Caleb. "HD? What'll it be?"

"Seltzer's great. Thanks."

Valerie grabs two cans from the fridge and passes them to Caleb. Leaning toward the doorway, she hollers for the girls to come take their meds. No response.

"Ladies! Meds time!" she repeats. Nothing. I glance at Caleb, who rolls his eyes.

· "I'll get them," he says, sliding off the stool he's perched on. I follow him into the playroom, where one of the girls is on the floor, braiding a doll's hair, while the other is bowling on the Wii. Both appear to be willfully ignoring any interruption from the outside world.

"You heard Mom. Meds. Get a move on." The one on the floor looks up at her brother and me like we're utter fools. She crosses her arms and juts her little chin out at us.

"We're on strike."

"You're on strike?"

"We have rights, you know."

Caleb bursts out laughing. "You have *rights*? Oh really? Where'd you hear that?"

"Miss Robles," says the twin who's bowling, not even turning away from the game.

The one on the floor continues. "We're learning about the Pullman railroad strike of eighteen ninety-three. People have the right to strike if they don't like how they're being treated."

· I look to Caleb, sideways. Good luck to him with this one.

"True," Caleb says slowly, considering his next move. "But this is not that kind of situation. You're not being paid unfairly for your work or something like that. No one's taking away your health care. On the contrary, we're trying to provide you with the things you need to stay healthy. Therefore, it's in your own interest to do what I say, and take your meds."

I like the way he talks to them, like they're real people, not just kids. They're listening now, processing his argument. The one at the Wii has put the controller down and leans against the arm of the couch, cupping her chin in her hands and tapping her cheek with one wiry finger.

"But what if we just feel tired of taking them?" asks the one by the couch. I really have no idea who is who at this point.

Caleb shrugs. "Listen, I hear you. It's your lot in life. You gotta bite the bullet and do it, or you'll have a pain crisis and you don't like that very much either, remember. It would be more sensible to go on strike from your chores if you want to go on strike. But don't tell the parentals I told you that."

The one on the floor puts her doll down resolutely and nods. "Fine. We'll do it." Standing up, she leans toward Caleb with a stern look on her face and wags a finger at him. "But don't think you can always get us to do whatever you want with logic alone." Then she and her sister march off in tandem to the kitchen.

I turn to Caleb. "Did she just say, 'do whatever you want with *logic alone*'?"

He laughs. "Yeah, they bust out with that kind of stuff all the time. I don't know where they get it."

"Is it always like that? Getting them to take their meds?"

Caleb sighs, nodding. "More or less, yeah. I mean, they go through phases. Sometimes they're fine with it, other times they get sassy, other times they just kick and scream like babies." He shrugs. "It is what it is, right?"

That's true, obviously, but it doesn't seem fair to be so young and have to deal with so much, to be always on the cusp of pain. Not that "fair" even means anything, really. But still, Caleb's sisters are so hilarious and smart and silly, it seems like they should be allowed to just be their hilarious, smart selves for a while without having to deal with heavy stuff like keeping a chronic illness under control. At least for now.

"Food's up, youngbloods!" Caleb's dad calls from the dining room, and we troop in and find our places around the long farmhouse table.

"So, Rose," Valerie says, passing me a colorful salad, "Caleb tells us you're a dancer." She smiles at me warmly. The girls giggle.

"Caleb tells us a lot of things about you," says one of them through her laughter.

"Caleb's like, 'And *another* thing about Rose, and *another* thing about Rose,'" the other one adds. They fall all over each other, hysterical. Caleb glares at them.

Valerie chuckles. "We may have heard a few things. Only good ones, of course. So, you're a ballerina? Our girls love ballet, too."

"Yes, the *evil* twins take all kinds of dance," Caleb says through his teeth.

"Um, well, I wouldn't exactly call myself a 'ballerina,'" I say. I can't quite reconcile myself in the dance studio—sweating, decked out in my faded black leotard with my feet bleeding into the inside of my pointe shoes—with the frilly word "ballerina."

"Come on, you dance practically every hour you're not in school. If you're not a ballerina by now, you should probably consider throwing in the towel and pursuing something else. You'd make a good librarian." Caleb's got the sarcasm down to a science, but there's something in his tone like maybe he's still a little nervous around me, too.

"A librarian?" I say, raising an eyebrow at him.

"It suits you."

"So, where do you dance?" his mother asks, interrupting our little flirtation, or whatever it is. "I work in Cambridge, so I'm familiar with some of the schools around there."

"New England Youth Ballet. It's downtown, actually, near Boylston Street."

"That's wonderful. What are your plans for next year? Are you looking for a school with a strong dance program?"

Ugh, next year. The question every high school senior dreads, and me probably more than average.

"Ma, maybe you could lay off the college interrogation until the *second* time you meet Rose?" Caleb says. "You think?"

"No pressure, Rose! I'm just curious! It's the mom-slash-college-professor in me."

"No, I don't mind," I say, stammering. "I just—I'm not sure yet. We'll see."

"Mom, we're learning about the Pullman strike in school, and Caleb says we should go on strike from our chores to practice!" one of the twins interrupts. Caleb tosses a balled-up napkin at her, which she bats away with barely a glance.

"I told you to keep your mouth shut about that, narc," Caleb hisses.

Valerie rolls her eyes at her children and asks me to pass her the breadbasket.

"Ladies, you know, strikes are usually about low wages or poor working conditions or things like that," Caleb's dad says.

"Yeah, and we work for free!" says the other twin.

"We don't pay you for your chores because you do them as a part of the family. We all contribute. And your working conditions are excellent, I might add," Richard says as he piles some chicken breast on his plate. "The Pullman workers did not have a Wii to return to when they finished working on the rails."

The buzz around the table continues all through dinner. There are three conversations taking place at any given moment, side chatter, giggling, platters being passed back and forth and forks crossing from one plate to another, grabbing the things one person likes and someone else hates—"Lemme get your avocado," "You can have my tomatoes." I sit in a sort of stunned silence for most of the time, smiling every time I catch one of them looking at me inquisitively. It really is nice, all the chaos. Dinners at my house are never like this. And you'd never know, really, that three of the five people in this family are—and will always be—sick.

After dinner, Caleb's sisters give me a grand tour of the house—which in this case actually merits the expression "grand tour." They show me the bedroom they share (apparently by choice, not for lack of space) and various bathrooms, the room where they practice the piano ("The parentals gave up on me. No rhythm," Caleb confesses when I ask him why he isn't required to play an instrument like his sisters), their parents' offices, and the finished attic space that holds a faded leather sectional and a huge flat-screen.

Finally, Caleb manages to free us from their admittedly very cute clutches, and takes me out to the back porch with his sketchbook and two thick pencils. I'd almost forgotten that I was originally brought here under the pretense of his art assignment. Outside, the air is brisk and smells like someone has their fireplace up and running nearby. I breathe it in deeply.

"Your family is cool," I tell him.

"By which you mean, these people are nuts and I'm never coming back here?"

"No, seriously. I've always wanted a sister. Someone to take the edge off with the parents."

Caleb laughs. "Yeah, they do serve that purpose, that's for sure. No time to overfocus on me."

On the back porch, we sit on a big, wooden bench with a faded canvas seat cushion. The porch light makes a low buzzing noise, and I watch bugs hover around the bulb. The air is cool now, and I'm glad I wore a scarf with my jean jacket, even though Gram commented that it was "too thin to be much use" before I left the house.

"You want me to just sit here?" I ask.

"Do whatever," says Caleb, picking up his sketchbook. "Just try to pick one thing and stick with it, if you don't mind."

I settle on a position that seems like it might be comfortable for a while, shifting my body toward Caleb, my back against the bench's armrest and my knees pulled up to my chest. I wrap my arms around my knees and rest my chin on them. Hopefully it looks reasonably non-awkward.

"I feel like the nice thing about siblings is that they're other people in the world who just get it, right?" I say after a minute. "They get where you come from, what your parents' issues are, that stuff."

He nods, shifting his gaze quickly between me and the sketchbook as he draws continuously. "That is true, indeed."

"Not that your parents seem like they have issues. They seem very . . . normal."

"Try living with them!" he snorts. " 'Normal' isn't exactly the word I would choose. They are truly bizarre individuals."

"I saw zero evidence of bizarreness," I say.

"They were on good behavior. Get to know them a little better. They've been known to sing show tunes while cooking."

"That's nothing."

"In pig latin."

"All right, so they're a little quirky. That's where you get it from, huh?" I flash him a smile.

"Yes, I won that particular genetic lottery."

"I'd say you won a few genetic lotteries, frankly," I say.

"True that," he says. "True that."

"So, your mom can work full-time, even with sickle cell?" I say, after a few minutes of silence except for the sound of his pencil scratching the paper.

He stops drawing. "Yeah. She's pretty hard-core. She hardly ever misses class, unless she's having a really bad crisis."

"How often is that?" I ask.

Even speaking of his mother's pain looks like it pains Caleb a little bit. "Often enough."

I wonder what it's like to have a mother whose illness you can't see. She could be suffering and covering it up, and he wouldn't know. At least my mother can't hide her pain.

Caleb frowns at his sketchbook, twisting his head first to the left and then the right, looking at the picture from different angles, I guess.

"What?" I nudge his leg with my foot.

"Nothing. I just can't get this line quite right."

He works at it for another minute or two, while I sit there in silence.

"So what's it like?" I ask finally, jump-starting the conversation. "Knowing you're never going to get what they've got?"

He taps his pencil against the notebook. "Don't know, really. I guess I'm used to it. I mean, they got me tested as a baby. I never didn't know, know what I mean?"

What would that be like, just being used to this big ugly thing in your family, having all the information about it right from the start. Never knowing anything different, or better.

"What about you? Do you want to know?" he asks.

"I want to know, and I don't want to know . . . you know? Sometimes I feel like I already know I'm going to get it."

"Yeah, but you don't. That's just you being pessimistic. You've got a fifty-fifty shot of being totally healthy."

"Yeah, and dying some normal way like cancer or a heart attack."

"Exactly. Or a car accident!"

"Death by polka dot–itis!"

We laugh for all of a split second and then return to silence.

"Let's face it," I say finally. "There are more ways to die in this world than to not die. There are exactly zero ways to do that."

"You are a very odd person, HD. One in a million, I'd say."

"So you're saying there are like seven thousand people on earth exactly like me?"

Caleb throws his head back and scoffs. "Oh, man. I cannot get one past you, can I, HD? Correction. You are one in *seven billion*, to be exact."

"Thank you. It's true, though. There are zero ways to avoid death."

"It is true," Caleb concedes. "You're going to kick the bucket at some point. So the question is, if you had a choice of knowing how you were going to die, or having it be a surprise, which would you choose?"

He phrases it like a rhetorical question, but it isn't rhetorical, not for me, not really. Sure, I could have the mutation for Huntington's and still get hit by a bus before I get sick. But assuming that one freakish stroke of bad luck is enough, I'll probably go the HD way: slowly and painfully, and as a huge burden on my loved ones. Everyone likes to say the people they love aren't burdens when they get sick, but that's bullshit.

"I don't know what I choose. Is ignorance really bliss?"

"Maybe if you have complete ignorance. But you don't. You have uncertainty. It's different."

"True that," I say, breathing in the smell of burning wood again and smiling at him. "True that." The sound of his pencil against the sketchbook gets louder in my ears for a minute, competing only with the buzzing of the porch light and the bugs around it.

"HD," Caleb says, "you're giving yourself a wrinkle between your eyes."

I relax my forehead, which had furrowed itself into a little knot. He's right, I'll have a permanent wrinkle by the time I'm twenty-five if I'm not careful.

"Let me see."

Caleb turns the sketchbook toward me. On the heavy paper, scrawled in strokes of pencil, is a girl with dark hair falling over her eyes, a scarf tucked around her chin and wrapped almost up to her ears. Her features are narrow, angled; her brow is tensed.

She doesn't look much like me, but she's beautiful.

WINTER

Rule #2: Falling in love
confuses everything
(so don't do it).

Ten

I THINK EVERY BALLET DANCER IN THE WORLD WOULD
tell you that they dread *The Nutcracker*. It's not *The Nutcracker*'s
fault, per se—it's a beautiful ballet. It's just that we all do *The
Nutcracker*, every year, just the same as the year before. I loved
it as a little kid. It's always the first real show you get to do, the
first time you get to dance on the big stage with the big kids, in
front of a real audience, and there's something magical about it.
There's the snow falling onstage, and the giant Christmas tree,
and of course there's the glamour of watching the senior girls
do their own makeup and break in their fresh pointe shoes in
the dressing room. But by the time you've done it for ten years
running, that stuff has more or less lost its luster. Now it's just
the annual holiday slog.

At least I'm not dancing the Arabian Coffee again this year—
I did that part three years in a row; it was my first part once I
graduated out of the ranks of Snowflake #6, Party Girl #3, Poli-
chinelle #10. I never did dance Clara; Georgia always managed
to snag that role. Now that we're the big girls, Georgia is dancing the Sugar Plum Fairy, of course, and I'm dancing Dewdrop.

My phone vibrates in my bag as I'm returning to the dressing
room after running my solo for the fifth time. I slump into a

chair by the mirror and put my feet up on the counter, stretching out over my legs for a few counts before I check the message.

"WHEN. CAN. I. SEE. YOU?"

No one's around, but it still makes me blush. I do feel a little guilty for having disappeared into *Nutcracker* craziness without adequately warning Caleb. It's been two weeks since I had dinner at his house, and we haven't hung out again—I've just been on autopilot from school to rehearsal to bed. If Lena weren't in half my classes, I'd never see her, either. This is why none of my ballet friends have boyfriends. Just when you think you're getting a little taste of normality, you remember that ballet comes first.

"The Land of Sweets," I write back. In response, he sends three question marks.

"Nutcracker. When in doubt about where I am between late November and January . . ."

"I see," he replies. "So when am I coming to see it?"

A lump catches in my throat. Somehow, dinner at Caleb's house—with his entire family—didn't seem like as big a deal as letting him watch me dance.

I write back: "Um, I don't know. Never?"

"Come on. Let me see what's taking up all your damn time."

So this teenage male actually wants to sit through the entire *Nutcracker*, for me? Seriously? I could try explaining that my Dewdrop solo is only about five minutes long, and the rest of the time I doubt he'll even be able to spot me in the crowd. But I don't.

Instead I say, "Well, if you insist."

"I insist. I also insist on hanging out with you at your next available time slot."

Eloise pops her head into the dressing room. "We're breaking for notes in five."

"Thanks," I say, tucking my phone quickly into my bag, but not quick enough to evade Eloise's eagle eye.

"Ooh," she says. "Are you keeping secrets?"

"Um, no."

She wrinkles her nose at me. "You're a bad liar, you know. And if you're lying about it, it must be someone interesting. Like a boy." Her freckled face lights up. "Am I right?"

"Trust me, it's no one interesting," I say, tossing a leg warmer at her. "Didn't you say we have notes now?" I throw my New England Youth Ballet sweatshirt over my leotard and head for the door.

My next available time slot is Monday afternoon, when we have no rehearsal, mercifully. My whole body aches, and even though all I really want to do on my day off is come home from school and sit in front of the television, alternating ice and heat on every muscle group in my body, I tell Caleb he can come over. Everyone's out of the house, at least for the next couple of hours, so I won't have to do any awkward introductions.

When he arrives, Caleb surveys our house closely, taking stock of the stair lift we had installed for Mom last year. He hovers by the mantel, too, picking up each framed photograph and staring at my childhood face. He holds up a picture of our old dog, Lionel (named for the toy train company, of course).

"This guy's not around anymore?" I shake my head. Lionel died when I was twelve, shortly after Mom's diagnosis. It was a bad year. "You didn't get another dog after him?" Caleb asks.

"Losing a dog is supposedly good practice for losing other things you love. My parents didn't think I needed more practice with that."

Caleb regards me quizzically, like I'm a puzzle he's trying to solve. Then (when he's probably determined that he's not going to figure me out) he turns his attention to the train set, which my father has dutifully set up in the living room in preparation for the holiday season.

"These yours?" He smirks at me.

"Hey, girls can play with trains, you know. Go ahead, give it a try. You know you want to." He kneels by the control switch and flicks it on. The train eases forward. Caleb toots the horn once and increases the speed, clearly enjoying himself. He watches the train shuffle around the track a few times. "Okay, this is pretty cool. I'm not gonna lie."

"It's my mom's. My dad gave it to her for Christmas years ago."

"That's awesome. Way cooler present than my dad has ever given my mom." He brings the train to a gradual halt when it comes back around to the mini-station platform.

"My mom loves trains. We're train people."

"Train people?"

"It's a thing, trust me." My mother always said there were two kinds of people in the world: plane people and train people. Plane people are focused on the destination and train people love the journey. When I was ten, she told me she was going to make me a train person if it was the last thing she did.

"I'll show you my mom's map of the world according to train people later. If you're nice. Snack?"

Predictably, it appears that neither of the able-bodied adults in my house has gone grocery shopping in ages, so the best I can offer Caleb is toast. I stuff two pieces of thick white bread into the toaster and turn the dial to medium. Gram leaves it on dark all the time—the woman loves to get in a few carcinogens with her breakfast.

"Your mom's?" he asks, nodding at the extensive collection of medications on the countertop, divvied up in a large pillbox organized by the days of the week.

The drugs cover anxiety, depression, motor control, the list goes on. They take the edge off the symptoms, but that's about it. "Just a little preview of my possible future."

"Why do you have to be like that?" Caleb leans against the kitchen counter like he lives here, his arms and ankles crossed. "Why are you so sure you're going to get it?"

"I'm not *sure*," I say, suddenly defensive. "It's just easier to plan for the worst."

"Is it?"

I don't answer. "No offense, but HD is way worse than sickle cell. Just FYI."

Caleb laughs again, throwing his head back and bellowing up toward the ceiling. He laughs with his whole body.

"Okay, so you're competitive," he says, pulling himself together. "Maybe I disagree. I say sickle cell is worse because you're sick your whole life. What do you say to that?"

"Oh, you want to do this?" I put my hands on my hips and get up in his face like I'm about to pick a fight. "To that I say, fine, but you don't die from it."

"You can, actually," he says, suddenly serious. "Not as much anymore, but it used to limit life expectancy quite a lot. It still can in some cases."

Now I feel like a jerk. "Sorry," I mutter. "I didn't realize that."

He gives me a gentle nudge with his elbow. "Anyway. Fine, I'll give you that sickle cell isn't as universally fatal as Huntington's, so from that perspective, you're right. Huntington's is worse. But that doesn't mean it's the *worst* of the worst. What about Tay-Sachs?"

He has a point. Tay-Sachs actually does give Huntington's a run for its money in the battle for the worst genetic luck. Watching your kid get sick and die—and potentially one kid after another—is probably worse than watching a parent get sick and die. At least, that's what parents always say. But Tay-Sachs is recessive. Genetically speaking, it's a less vicious mutation.

"Tay-Sachs is bad," I allow. "But consider the odds of actually getting it: only a twenty-five percent chance even if *both* your parents are carriers. I'd argue that a dominant mutation trumps a recessive one every time."

"Oh, so there's a hierarchy here? That's what you're saying?" Caleb takes a step closer to me. We're standing so close that he has to crane his neck down to look me in the eye.

I work hard to maintain a serious face. "That's exactly what I'm saying."

"You're very strict, you know," Caleb says. We're both cracking up by now. For a split second I think he might try to kiss me, but then the toaster pings. I duck away quickly and drop the slices on a polka-dotted dessert plate.

"I see you're still in ballet mode," he observes, and I realize that I'm moving between flat feet and tiptoes, stretching out my calves, while I search the refrigerator for butter. I do it so naturally that I don't even notice.

Caleb pulls up a stool at the kitchen island. If he thinks the toast is a lame snack—which, having seen his parents' kitchen, I'm quite certain he does—he doesn't let on. "So how are your infamous *Nutcracker* rehearsals going, anyway?"

I let out a big sigh. "They're fine. Exhausting. The music is beautiful, though. Tchaikovsky and all."

"Sure. My man Pyotr. He's all right," Caleb says. "Did you get my ticket yet?"

I search his face for signs that he's kidding. I don't want to take him at his word, get him a ticket, and then have him feel obligated to come.

"You really, really do not have to come see it. I am being totally serious. Really."

"Really, I am being serious when I say I want to. I want to see what you do. I'll bring my sisters—they'll be even more obsessed with you than they already are."

"Um, why are your sisters obsessed with me, again?"

"Because they think you're super cool and you're a dancer and you were actually nice to them when you came over. Just take it as a compliment."

The toast is still soft in the middle, not quite toasted enough, and it shreds as I butter it. I leave some ant-like crumbs stuck in the tub of allegedly spreadable butter. Then I hold a jar of raspberry Smucker's in the air and Caleb gives me a thumbs-up.

"Okay," I say, layering the toast with jam. "We open next Friday, so how about over the weekend?" I slide the plate across the island and he takes a slice of toast. "I'll leave tickets for you guys at the box office on Saturday. For the matinee."

"Excellent. We'll be looking forward to it," he says, grinning. "Thanks for the snack, by the way."

"Yeah, I'm sure a little soggy white toast is just what you were craving."

"Hey, whatever works. I just didn't realize ballet dancers were so big on the simple carbs."

I stick my tongue out at him. It's true that white bread soaked in high-fructose corn syrup isn't exactly my standard daily snack, but I don't eat like the stereotypical ballet dancer either. We burn a ton of calories dancing. I can't imagine *not* loading up on food.

"I pretty much eat whatever I want," I tell him. "I get quite the workout, so . . . you know."

"Yeah, for sure," he says. "Not trying to give you a complex! You look—I mean—you're . . . perfect."

The word hangs there for a moment, neither of us sure what to say next. "I mean, your body is . . . Never mind." He glances around, looking desperate to change the subject. "Where are your folks, anyway?"

"Doctor's appointment, doctor's appointment, work."

"Who's the second doctor's appointment in that equation?"

"That would be my grandmother. She's with my mom."

I can see him putting two and two together in his head, piecing together the finer details of my family tree and probably guessing at how our illness fits in. We're both quiet for a minute. I watch him, picking at the crumbs left scattered on his plate.

After a moment, he bites a crumb off his index finger and dusts his hands off. "Have I been nice enough to see that train map?"

In my mom's office, we stand in front of the map in silence. I can feel Caleb taking it in. Before this moment, Lena was the only person outside of our family who knew about my mother's train thing.

Finally, he says, "Wow."

"Yeah."

"You weren't kidding when you said you were train people."

He listens carefully while I explain the whole thing, running his eyes along the different train routes and moving closer to look at the pictures tacked next to the map.

"I wish I could take them all," I say.

"For real?"

"Yeah. I'd just like to be able to tell her what they're really like, you know? Since she can't see them for herself." I trace my fingers along one of the American routes out of Chicago, heading west—the Zephyr, to San Francisco. "This one's supposed to be the most beautiful ride in the country."

"You should do it," Caleb says. He reaches up and puts his hand against the map, his fingers brushing mine, tracing the same route.

Then, like the jackass that I am, I pull my hand away reflexively. "Should we watch a movie or something?" I ask, before anything else can happen.

An hour later, we're midway through one of my all-time favorites, *Evil Under the Sun*. Caleb teased me a little when I showed him my collection of old mystery movies, but he didn't refuse the Agatha Christie classic, either. I've seen this movie probably a hundred times—like all the Agatha Christies starring her famous Belgian detective, Hercule Poirot, but I'd forgotten—or never noticed—how the only people in the whole movie who aren't white are nameless, faceless, generally shoeless, and generally serving the white people. Sitting next to Caleb on the couch, it makes me cringe.

Car doors slam in the driveway, and my father's muffled voice floats up the front walk. He must've met up with Mom and Gram at the doctor's appointment. Dad likes to check in with Dr. Howard whenever he can, and his work schedule is pretty flexible. He didn't choose real estate because it was a decent business to be in while simultaneously caring for one's ailing wife, but it's worked out all right.

I silently curse myself for losing track of time. No choice but to make the introductions now. It occurs to me that my family might be surprised to find me at home, alone, with a guy. I've never done that before. In fact, I'm pretty sure the only person they've ever seen me sitting with on the couch is Lena. Caleb and I aren't touching, but I shift an inch or two farther away from him just as the door pushes open.

"Ro—" Dad starts to call, before seeing us there.

"Hi, guys," I say, sitting up and leaning over the back of the couch. "How was the doctor?"

"Fine," Dad and Gram say simultaneously—always their answer to that question.

Mom interjects, sounding agitated. "Bad, bad, bad. Dr. Howard is an asshole."

"El, give the guy a break. You like Dr. Howard. We all like Dr. Howard," says Dad in a matter-of-fact tone. I appreciate that he doesn't talk down to her, even when she's having a bad moment.

"Asshole. He's an asshole," Mom repeats. Dad sighs, and looks at Caleb expectantly.

"Oh, this is Caleb," I say, noticing a momentary look of recognition on Gram's face at the mention of his name. "He's my friend from the rare genes walk."

Caleb approaches my family, still clustered by the doorway, with his hand outstretched. Dad takes it.

"Caleb, nice to meet you."

"That's my dad, David, and my mom, Ellen, and my grandmother, Alice."

"Nice to meet all of you. Sorry to surprise you."

Dad's eyes flicker over at me for the briefest moment, then shift back to Caleb. "No, no problem at all. Always pleased to know that Rose has real, live friends. She doesn't always play well with others."

"Thanks, Dad."

"Listen, I'm going to get dinner started. Caleb, will you join us?"

I look from my father to Caleb and back again. Caleb gives me what I think is a little smirk. "I'd love to. Let me just call my folks and let them know."

When Dad said he was going to "get dinner started," he should really have said he was going to "heat up leftover Chinese food from last night."

"This isn't my father's finest culinary moment," I tell Caleb, thinking back to the multicourse homemade meal I ate at his house, as we sit down to slightly soggy scallion pancakes and pork lo mein.

"Hey, it works for me."

Caleb is sitting directly across from my mother, who looks at him intently, raising a piece of scallion pancake to her lips with a quivering hand.

"So, Caleb," Dad starts, a little awkwardly, "what, ah . . . so, you're involved in the Rare Genes Project?"

"Dad." I shoot him a dirty look. He may as well just bust out with "So, what's wrong with you and your relatives?"

"No, no, it's fine, Mr. Levenson," Caleb interjects.

"God, that makes me feel like an old man. Call me Dave, I beg you," Dad says. "This is Cambridge, anyway. Come on."

Caleb smiles. He has dimples in places I haven't noticed before. "Fair enough . . . Dave. Sickle cell runs in my family. I don't have the disease, but my mom and sisters do."

"I see. That's difficult. I'm sorry."

"It's all right. There are a lot better treatments now than there were when my mother was a kid, so that's good."

Dad nods, chewing on a spring roll. "Good, good. I thought they'd made quite a bit of progress with that."

"Caleb's dad works at Mass General. He's a neonatologist," I say, desperate to get off the subject of Caleb's sick family.

"That's something, isn't it? Ellen—Rose's mom, I mean—sees a specialist at Mass General."

"You didn't tell me that," Caleb says, turning to me. "What doctor does your mom see there?"

Mom pipes up across the table. "Talking about me like I'm not here is rude."

"Ellen—" Gram cuts in, sensing, like I am, that Mom's about to lose it.

"You're all talking about me like I'm not here."

"No one's talking about you like you're not here, El," says Dad. "We all know you're here."

"Who's the black kid?" Mom asks, staring at Caleb. "You're black."

"Mom," I interject, "don't be . . ."

"He's black."

Dad stammers something that sounds like an attempt at an apology to Caleb, but it comes out like he has a wad of Kleenex shoved in his mouth.

"It's okay," Caleb says. "It's just an observation." Then he looks right at Mom and smiles like he's having a casual conversation with a normal person. "You are correct. I am black."

"Black!" Mom goes on. "Black, black, black. Rose's boyfriend is black. Rose has jungle fever!"

"Mom!" I stand up, throwing my napkin down on the table. "Stop it! Stop!"

She laughs, this eerie, empty laugh that comes out sometimes now when she's worked up. It doesn't even sound like her. I'm frankly surprised she can conjure the phrase "jungle fever" at all these days. I wonder where that one was locked away. I glance over at Caleb, who's twirling his fork in a strand of lo mein.

"Rose, it's all right," Gram says quietly, looking to my father as if he's somehow going to rein in the situation.

"It's not all right. She sounds like a lunatic!" I stare at Mom, who's still laughing, in her own world. "You're humiliating me."

Mom stops laughing suddenly and looks right back at me. "Ungrateful bitch," she spits out.

It's the disease talking. She's not my mother when she's in this kind of place. I know that. She's having a bad day, a bad afternoon. But it still hits me in my gut. Grabbing Caleb's arm, I turn from the table and drag him with me out of the room so I won't say something horrible. I storm up the stairs two at a time.

Caleb shuts the door behind us. "Hey."

I don't even feel like crying. I sit down on the bed, frozen, staring into space. He sits next to me.

"It's okay, you know. I mean, she didn't offend me."

"Well, she offended *me*," I say.

"It's the disease—"

"I know. I know that."

He reaches out and tucks a stray piece of hair behind my ear.

"She's getting worse," I say. He doesn't say anything, just looks at me, like he's actually hearing me. "Sometimes it's like, she's more or less fine, or you don't notice it, anyway. And then suddenly, she's this totally different person." I shrug. "I guess that's what they mean by degenerative, huh?" I give him a fake smile, but he doesn't smile back.

"I'm sorry."

"It's okay."

"Okay. But it's not, really," he says.

I look away from him and toward the window. It's dark already, the days suddenly shorter as October turned into November. We stare outside for what feels like it might be five or ten minutes, although I know in reality it's probably more like two, before Caleb breaks the silence.

"On the bright side," he says, breaking into a sly grin, "I like that she called me your boyfriend."

"Oh really?"

"Yeah. Really."

I know what's going to happen next, of course. I've seen enough movies. He leans toward me until our faces are so close that I can almost feel a tiny breeze every time he blinks. And then I lean in a little closer, and then we meet in the middle.

His lips are softer than I'd expect for a guy's. We part for a minute, leaning back to look at each other. I feel shy, all of a sudden, like I don't want to make eye contact, and then we kiss again, longer this time.

I've seen a lot of movies, but I've never seen our movie: sickle cell kid meets HD kid and they fall in love. If that's what's about to happen.

Suddenly, the thought of it makes me feel sick to my stomach. Falling in love seems like one risk too many in a life that already has the odds stacked against it—or at least precariously balanced.

"It's late," I say, waking up my phone to see the time.

"You kicking me out?" he asks, smiling.

"I guess, yeah." I smile back, but I'm ready for him to leave.

Caleb looks a little skeptical as he gently traces my jawline with the back of his hand. "Are you sure you're okay?"

I'm okay and I'm not okay—that seems to be my constant state of being these days. For an instant I feel kind of annoyed by the question. So, we kiss and it's supposed to make everything better? Caleb of all people should know that's not how this works.

"I'll let myself out." He kisses me on the cheek quickly, then slips out the door. I hear him saying a muffled thank you and goodbye to my family downstairs, and I wonder if Mom has already switched back to a decent mood. Then the front door closes. From the window, I catch sight of him as he crosses the street and unlocks his car. Before he gets in, he looks up at my window and grins. I can't see the gap between his teeth from here, but I know it's there.

When his taillights are completely out of view, I flop down on my bed again and send Lena a quick text. "Mom's losing it. C and I kissed." Within seconds, my phone's buzzing. I barely even need to say anything when I answer.

"Mmm-hmm," I sigh into the phone.

"Do we need to divide and conquer here? I don't know what to ask about first."

"Caleb had dinner here and my mom lost it over leftover Chinese."

"Define 'lost it,' " Lena says.

"Oh, yelled at all of us, fixated on Caleb, made inappropriate racial comments, and called me an ungrateful bitch. You know."

"And then you kissed? So it ended well."

"I don't know. We kissed. It was—nice, I guess. But what am I doing?"

Lena doesn't answer for a minute.

"Hello?" I prompt her. "You're supposed to tell me what I'm doing."

"Rose," she says, "you're not required to sacrifice every kind of fun because you have a sick parent."

She's right, I know. But something tells me that this uneasiness isn't just guilt that I'm busy kissing a boy while my mother is getting worse. It's that whatever I'm feeling for Caleb—this thing that's like a tumor of good stuff, growing bigger every time I see him—is too scary, too risky. Maybe I need to just cut it out.

"Yeah. Whatever. We'll see." Suddenly I get an overwhelming desire to stop talking about this. "I'll talk to you tomorrow, okay?"

"Um, okay. Fine. Wait, though—how was the kissing? He didn't, like, lick all around your chin, did he? Because that can be a turnoff but it can be resolved with clear communication."

That makes me laugh. "Ew, no—there was no chin licking, thank you. It was . . . I don't know. It was nice?"

"You said that already. I need more information."

"I don't know—look, I told you, I'll see you tomorrow."

She growls a little. "Okay, fine. Later."

I hang up. I'm not sure I want to tell her how nice it was—that it was like the feeling of getting into a soft bed when your body is completely exhausted and all you want to do is relax. Because it's a slippery slope from kissing to boyfriend-ing to falling in love. And falling in love is like getting a dog: You're pretty much guaranteed to end up with a big loss.

Loss. It stops sounding like a word if you say it enough times.

Eleven

CALEB AND I DON'T TALK THE DAY AFTER WE KISS, OR THE day after that. It feels like something has shifted, like we've entered a period that can never be the same as before. I'm not sure if it's the kissing that makes it feel that way, or Mom's outburst, or Caleb's comment about being referred to as my boyfriend, but everything just feels different—in my head, at least. In reality, of course, I have no idea if anything has shifted at all because we haven't even exchanged so much as a text.

Eloise's mom gives me a ride after our *Nutcracker* dress rehearsal, and it's after ten by the time I get home. The house is quiet except for some scratching coming from the kitchen. It's Gram, who appears to be cleaning the floor harder than it probably needs to be cleaned. The sight of my seventy-something grandmother on her hands and knees, scrubbing at what I think is a long-standing stain in the hardwood, is a little alarming.

"What are you doing?"

She looks up, startled, then looks back down at the floor and at her raw, wrinkled hands, as though she's not actually sure what she's doing, as if I'd just woken her up from sleep-walking.

"I was just tidying the kitchen." She struggles to her feet. "Fancy a snack?"

I shake my head. "Not hungry, just exhausted." I drop my bag on the kitchen island and slump onto a stool.

"Where's Dad?"

"His study. Working away, I suppose. Earning his keep. Cuppa?" Gram asks. She means tea, and it sounds good, actually. I nod. She rinses out the sponge she was using on the floor, then fills the kettle and sets it to boil on the stovetop. We talk so little these days, my grandmother and I, I'm not even sure how to make conversation with her anymore. It wasn't always like this: We used to play cards—Oh Hell and War and Rummy, sitting opposite each other at the dining room table—and go to the aquarium and have tea parties whenever she'd come to visit. I used to look forward to those visits. But then at some point, after she moved here, everything shifted. Maybe it isn't her fault. Maybe it isn't anyone's fault, per se.

"All right?" she asks, setting a mug in front of me. She pulls a bunch of boxes of tea from the cabinet over the sink. "Mint Medley? Earl Grey? Peach something-or-other? So many bloody tins, a person can't even tell what's in here." "Bloody" is as close as she'll come to cursing, and it always makes me smile.

"Mint. Thanks." Gram drops the tea bag into my mug. The kettle goes, the whistle starting low and building to a high-pitched scream, but she just stands there, staring at me, as it gets louder and louder. After a moment too long, she turns the gas off and pours the boiling water into my mug. The steam rises off it and feels good on my face. I clasp my hands around the mug and wait as the heat sets into the ceramic, subtly at first and then so hot it burns.

"Sorry about the other night," she says, making herself a mug of decaf English Breakfast.

"It wasn't your fault." I take my tea bag out and get up to dump it in the sink. Gram sits down opposite me, warming her hands on her mug just like I do.

"You know it's—"

"It's the disease talking. Yeah. I've heard."

Gram blows on her tea, not taking her eyes off of me. "That's not what I was going to say, actually, although that is also true. You want to interrupt me again or can I finish?"

"Sorry." I burn my tongue on my first sip and curse quietly. Gram ignores me.

"I was going to say, it's okay to fancy somebody. It's okay for you to date."

Ugh. Do I really have to be having this conversation with my *grandmother*? She's not my mother—not that I'm sure I'd want to talk to Mom about this, either.

"You're allowed to enjoy yourself. I, for one, liked Caleb very much. He seems like a nice boy. He fancies you, clearly."

"Oh my god. Okay, Gram. Thank you." Slinging my bag over one shoulder, I take my tea and stand up, ready to go. But then I hesitate, for whatever reason. She's still my grandmother. She's annoying sometimes, but she's trying.

"He's just my friend. We're not dating."

Gram shrugs. "Well, what do I know? I'm just an old bat who hasn't been with a man in a very long time. You don't have to listen to anything I say on the matter."

The idea of Gram being "with a man," so to speak, makes me cringe a little, even though I know she means married, not "with" as in—*with*. And it has been a long time. Gram was younger than my parents are now when my grandfather split. As far as I know, she never really dated anyone after that. It's weird to think about old people dating, but it's also sort of weird to think about someone younger than my parents—like, a lot younger—deciding to throw in the towel on love just because she got burned once.

Of course, Gram might just have been being smart about things. Maybe my grandfather proved to her that love isn't worth the risk.

"I want you to see something." She gets up and marches past me, then stops short in the door frame and looks at me expectantly. "Well, stop faffing. Get a move on."

I follow Gram upstairs and into her bedroom, where she pulls a felt box out of the top shelf of her closet. It's full of old pictures, scuffed one-pound coins, and envelopes of who knows what. She digs through it for a minute, muttering something to herself.

"I have homework," I say, turning to leave.

"Hold your horses," she shoots back, not looking up. "Found it. I knew I'd put this in here." She holds up a DVD case, the kind you can buy in multipacks for burning your own stuff. "Sit."

I follow orders. Gram turns on her TV and pops in the DVD. There's no music, but a picture fills the screen: my parents, circa twenty years ago, on their wedding day. I've seen their wedding pictures before, of course. Dad's in a dark gray suit with a turquoise tie, and Mom's dress is a halter with a long tie down the back and a low V-neck. It's fitted through the hips and then billows out. Her hair is loose around her shoulders.

"Their wedding film," Gram says, clicking Play. "You haven't seen it, have you?"

I shake my head. I didn't even know it existed.

"I didn't think so," says Gram. "Years ago your mum told me she was waiting until you were old enough to enjoy it. I imagine she's forgotten by now."

It's surreal, watching my parents on video, practically in the flesh, when they're so much younger. I've seen footage of myself as a baby and a little kid, obviously, but usually my parents aren't in those videos. And even when they are, the focus is on me—someone's holding me up, or calling to me to walk toward them, or clapping for me when I've just finished performing one of my endless "recitals" in the living room.

In this video, Mom and Dad are just themselves. They get married outside, in the backyard of an old hotel in Maine, where we used to go every summer. Uncle Charlie walks Mom down the aisle, which is really just a narrow walkway of grass between uneven rows of folding chairs. Dad stands up at the front, under the chuppah, and cries (no surprise there). The wind howls and there are seagulls squawking loudly, which makes it a little hard to hear the vows—this video was clearly taken by a friend, not a pro—but I can more or less make out that they're not the standard religious ones.

"Ellen," Dad says, taking Mom's hands, "having you in my life is like wearing rose-colored glasses every day. You make every day a little better, a little brighter, a little closer to perfect."

Cheesy, Dad, but I have to hand it to him—it tugs at my throat.

"That's where you get your name from, you know," Gram says.

"What? I thought your mother's name was Rose."

Gram laughs. "Well, it was. She was your official namesake. Your mum didn't like the idea of naming you after a dead person, but she agreed on Rose because she said it wasn't all about the dead great-grandmother. You made everything better for both of them."

After their special vows, there are the regular ones: for better or for worse, in sickness and in health. They look at each other, and repeat those words, and they have no idea. They have no idea. Gram reaches out and rests her hand on mine. Just for a moment, I let her.

"Right, we can skip this part," Gram says then, all business again, fast-forwarding through a series of toasts. "Here we go, this is the good part." She hits Play again for their first dance.

Dad makes a joke over the microphone about how he's marrying up, and how everyone already knows that but in case there's any doubt in the room, this dance is about to prove it. Gram, of course, wouldn't have agreed with that proposition at the time—Mom always said that Gram didn't think anyone was good enough for her baby—but I guess both my mother and my grandmother have let that go, given the nature of their current relationship. After his string of self-deprecation, Dad takes Mom in his arms and they swirl around the dance floor, her dress spilling behind her when she spins.

My mother had a natural talent for dance, great rhythm, a body that generally did what she wanted it to. Dad just lets her show off—he spins her this way and that way, dips her, but mostly I can tell that she's leading and just making it look like he is. It's hard to believe that the person in this video and the person we have now, shaking and jerking continuously, are the same.

The DVD ends, and Gram and I sit there in silence for a minute. Finally, Gram pops it out of the player and puts it back in the jewel case.

"They were twenty-eight years old. More than ten years older than you are now."

"Yeah. I know."

"So?" Gram says.

"So?"

"A lot can happen in a decade or two, that's all I'm saying." She puts the box back in her closet and leaves me there, perched on her bed.

She's right, obviously. My mother was dancing at her wedding when she was twenty-eight. She had real love. Then she had me. And she didn't get diagnosed with Huntington's for more than a decade after that.

I tiptoe down the hallway to my parents' bedroom. Cracking the door just slightly, I see that Mom is in bed with her earbuds in, eyes closed but clearly awake. I knock hard on the door frame, but it doesn't catch her attention, so I go closer. She only notices me when I sit next to her and she feels my weight on the bed.

"What are you listening to?"

Mom pulls out the earbuds. "Mmmystery," she says, slurring. "Not very well written." She wrinkles her nose. I wonder if it's not good because it's not good, or it's not good because she can't process the story. I don't ask; I know she won't be able to tell the difference.

"I wanted to tell you. About the other night. It's fine. Caleb wasn't upset or anything."

She squints at me. "I'm sssorry."

I lie down next to her, with my head on Dad's pillows. "He's just my friend."

"Is he your boyfriend?" she asks. I think of Lena and her mother, sharing secrets. But nothing I tell my mother will stick. Maybe that makes her the best kind of secret-keeper.

"Just a friend," I repeat. "But I'm worried that I might . . ." I trail off. I don't know what.

Mom raises a hand unsteadily to my cheek and rests it there. "You might love hhhim?"

"Not love, but . . . something."

Mom's audio book is still on. I can't hear the words but I can make out the muffled ups and downs of the narrator's voice. I find her phone caught in the folds of the comforter and press Pause on the recording.

"How did you know you loved Dad?" I ask, when it's quiet again.

She focuses hard on my face and blinks forcefully a few times. "Because I didn't have to be anyone but myself with him."

I know one of Huntington's only supposed mercies is that it spares the short-term memory—it isn't Alzheimer's or something. But in this moment, I can't help but wish that it took that, too. So my mother could remember what it felt like to fall in love with my father more than twenty years ago, but could forget throwing around the term "jungle fever" over dinner with Caleb just the other night. So she could live every day completely fresh, except for the things that really matter. Maybe that would be the real mercy.

Twelve

Backstage before the Saturday matinee, I'm more nervous about a *Nutcracker* performance than I've been since my first year dancing a solo. What has become so routine, almost mundane, is suddenly an actual thing that I have to mentally prepare for. A series of neurotic thoughts are rushing through my head on a loop but I seem to be powerless to stop them. *Caleb is going to see me dance. This is the first time he is going to see me dance. I have to dance my best, or he will think I am a jackass.*

So I put on a *Nutcracker* like I've never done it before. Every time I step onstage, I picture all my energy going directly out to the audience. I'm extra careful with all the little details that are easy enough to let slide during a regular matinee. Somehow, having him there, looking for just me in the crowd, reminds me of how much I love being onstage. It's easy to forget that during *Nutcracker* season. But I really do love the rush that comes with the lights fading up and the music bounding in, and seeing the other dancers sweat and push and work so hard to make it all look effortless for the audience. The truth is, I never feel quite as at home, quite as secure and content, as I do when I'm dancing.

At intermission, I peek out through the wings, the heavy black velvet curtains that sweep the sides of the stage and keep us hidden from the audience while we're running around like chickens (in tutus) with our heads cut off. From stage left, where I'm situated, I should be able to see the seats where I think Caleb and the girls are sitting, just right of house center. But they're not where I expect them to be, and I can't crane my neck far enough to see if they're farther over to the right. They're probably waiting in line for the bathroom. Little girls always have to go to the bathroom at intermission.

After the show, I take a few extra minutes to make sure I don't look like a sweaty mess when I leave the dressing room. Eloise notices me putting on lip gloss. She crosses her arms and stares me down.

"Going somewhere?" Normally on a Saturday, with another performance at eight o'clock, we mostly just hang out in our sweats and listen to music for the couple hours in between.

"Just running out to see a friend."

She eyes me suspiciously. "The same male friend you were spotted with at the BPC performance, perchance?"

And I thought I was being so careful, taking Caleb to the performance that Eloise wasn't going to. I should've known the other girls at the studio were too gossipy to let my unidentified male guest go unnoticed.

"Who are you, Harriet the Spy?"

She smiles. "Just keeping tabs. Be careful, you know."

"Of?"

"Distractions." She leans over and lifts one leg to crack her back. I cringe at the sound. "As soon as *Nutcracker*'s over, we've got to think about the spring showcase. And there's next year. Have you even figured out what companies you're auditioning for?"

"You sound like Georgia."

Eloise looks hurt. "I'm just trying to be helpful."

"Sorry. I know. Thank you for your sage wisdom," I say, zipping up my fleece and grabbing my bag. "I have to run, though."

Before she can say anything in response, I push past her and head toward the stage door.

But Caleb and the girls aren't outside. I head back inside and up to the lobby, but it's mostly emptied out by now, just a few ushers cleaning up programs and candy wrappers, and a handful of lingering audience members. One quick 360 tells me that the Franklins are not in attendance.

I check my phone—nothing. No messages, no text saying they loved it but had to run, nothing.

"Who you lookin' for, Rose?" asks Marlie, the box office manager.

"Oh, no one," I say, turning away from her so she won't see the tears starting to work their way out from wherever tears are made.

"You had some tickets here for someone, right?" She flips through the ticket box. "Yeah, Franklin, right? Here they are. Guess they couldn't make it." She hands the envelope to me, but I don't take it. Instead, I thank her and hustle out into the cold. I can't go back down to the dressing room and face Eloise again, not right now.

Outside, tears almost freezing against my cheeks, I type and delete several messages to Caleb, ranging from "Are you okay?" to "What the hell?" to "Thanks for the no-show." But I can't settle on the right approach, so I don't send anything. Finally, after twenty minutes of walking around the block, avoiding the girls and checking and rechecking my phone to see if he's called, I wipe my face, pretend I'm fine, and go back downstairs to get ready for another show.

"How were your shows?" Dad asks, as I tear through the front hall and up the stairs after the evening performance.

"Fine," I call out, forcing my voice to be even, normal.

"That good, huh?"

I shut the bedroom door behind me. Something must've happened to him. Or to one of his sisters, or his mom, I'm sure. I sit on the edge of my bed, my coat still on, staring at the wall, then look back to my (not ringing) phone, then back to the wall. Something has to be wrong—or else he's just a huge jerk. That, or I did something wrong. I page back through our recent text exchanges, trying to figure out what it could've been, but I can't tell.

I turn on my laptop. There's no possible way that Caleb is going to be reachable. In my mind, he's already disappeared into the abyss. Maybe he never existed in the first place. My stomach is tied in about a million tiny, tight knots, and even though I'm exhausted, my heart is racing. I can't tell if it's more worry, hurt, or humiliation that's making me feel so sick. I just didn't expect to care this much. I thought I had this under control.

And yet, there he is, online just like it's a normal night. Probably moseying along, doing his homework, surfing the Internet, minding his own business. At least I know he's alive.

Something like fury roils up inside me while I wait for an instant message that doesn't come for the better part of an hour. Then finally, just when I'm gearing up to force myself to shut down—so he won't be able to message me even if he wants to—my computer quacks.

Caleb Franklin: How are you, HD?

How am I? Seriously?

Me: Um, fine?

Caleb Franklin: Why the question mark?

The playing dumb thing pushes me over the edge. Now I'm really mad.

Me: You seriously don't know?

He doesn't respond for a minute, and the back of my throat is starting to ache the way it does when you're about to cry but really don't want to, when my phone vibrates against the desk.

I pick up, but don't say anything.

"Rose? Are you there?"

"Uh-huh," I say after a moment.

"Hey, what's going on? Are you okay?"

I can feel myself snap and know my voice will come out sharp, maybe too sharp, but I don't care. "Um, you were supposed to be at *The Nutcracker* this afternoon. With your sisters. I left you tickets. Remember?"

There's a pause, and then I hear him exhale long and hard. "Crap. Crap, crap, crap. I'm so, so sorry, Rose—I just . . ." He trails off.

"We did say you guys were going to come to the Saturday matinee, right? I told you I'd leave your tickets at the theater," I say. I'm pretty sure that's what we agreed to, but now I'm starting to question my own sanity.

"Yeah, but . . ." he stammers. "I didn't even know what theater. Or what time, or anything."

All the racing in my mind stops for a minute. He didn't *know*? Does he seriously think that's a legit excuse? "But you didn't *ask*."

"Well, yeah, I guess I . . ." He trails off. "We said I'd see it over the weekend. But then the whole thing happened with your parents, at dinner, and then—"

And then we kissed. So that is what this is about. We kissed, and then he didn't want to see me again. I thought I was supposed to be the freaker-outer, but it turns out he is.

"Did you . . . Is it because of what happened? The thing with my mom? And then the—" The thing after that, but I can't bring myself to say it. My voice catches in my throat.

"No, no," he says. "It absolutely wasn't because of what happened. I just—honestly? We never talked about it again—and I didn't—I just thought it wasn't happening. Or I didn't really—I didn't really think about it, to be honest. I'm so sorry."

I don't respond.

"Rose? I'm sorry. Seriously. Can I make it up to you? Can I come see the show *next* weekend?"

I let out a long breath. People forget things, I know. But it hurts that he wasn't thinking as much about me as I was thinking about him. If he had been, he would have remembered.

"Let's just call it a day with *The Nutcracker*, okay?"

"Can I make it up to you with ice cream? It's never too cold for ice cream, right?"

I want to say no, I really do—I know I should take this as a sign that I should let this go. It would just be safer, easier, not to care. But the fact that he remembers my dad's rule—the one I told him about the first time we hung out—tugs at my resolve.

"I don't really have a lot of free time until after *The Nutcracker*."

"When is that?"

"Next year."

He laughs hard at that, and it loosens me up. I wish I could hold on to my anger at him, but already I can feel it dissipating.

"The very beginning of next year?" he asks hopefully.

"Yeah. Like January second." I sigh. I guess there's not really anything wrong with having some ice cream.

Thirteen

CHANUKAH AND CHRISTMAS—CHRISMUKAH, WE USED TO
call them when I was little, which we celebrate in equally half-
assed ways in my house—pass by in their usual blur, marred as
always by my *Nutcracker* schedule and this year by something
more insidious, too. Mom is in a festive mood one minute and
pissed off the next. Even the train set doesn't make her happy
like it used to. I almost wish Dad had left it in its box in the
basement this year, gathering dust.

When Caleb pulls up in front of my house to pick me up for
ice cream on January second, I put on my best slightly skeptical, slightly mad face as I walk out to the car.

"Forgive me yet?"

I shrug. "Undecided. I'll let you know. You're just lucky I've
shown up for this event. I almost forgot." I slip into the front
seat next to him and finally let myself smile at him like I really
want to.

"Phew," he says. "I thought you were going to give me your
serious face all day. So, long time no see. Happy New Year.
What's new?"

It's been more than a month since the fateful dinner with
my parents. It seems like a lot has happened between the

moment Caleb and I kissed and now, even though we've barely spoken.

"Well, I survived another *Nutcracker* season without sustaining any injuries," I say. "And I rang in the new year watching a Hitchcock marathon with my parents, so that was super cool of me." The truth is, Lena tried to drag me to a party at Anders's house, but I prefer Hitchcock movies to high school parties.

"It's good to see you, HD."

"You too, Sickle Cell." And it is.

Caleb and I get our ice cream to go in Harvard Square, but even though I really do believe my father that it's never too cold for ice cream, as soon as we step outside into the tundra that is January in Boston, I realize we've made a mistake. I jump up and down a few times, while the cold of my frappe seeps through my mittens.

"Did you know that they do not have frappes in the rest of the country?" I say, trying to distract myself from the impending frostbite.

"Of course they do."

I shake my head. "Nope. In the rest of the country milk shakes have ice cream in them. They have no need for frappes."

"Milk shakes have ice cream in them here too," he says. "Milk shakes and frappes are the same thing."

"Incorrect. Proper New England milk shakes are just milk and syrup."

"Milk and syrup . . . shaken?" He grins at me.

"Precisely."

"Well," he says, snaking an arm behind my waist and drawing me in closer to him, "I've learned something new today. Thanks for that."

It's warmer tucked in against Caleb's chest. "Can we go inside now?"

He nods. "I know a good spot."

I know I've been to the Gunn before, maybe when I was five or six, dragged around the museum on a Sunday afternoon with my parents, or maybe when Gram was in town for a visit; I can't remember exactly. It's on a quiet side street right behind Harvard Yard, a few blocks from my school—I've walked past it probably a thousand times and not given it a second glance in years. I'm not a big museum person, but I don't mention this to Caleb as he leads me quickly across the Yard—the grass is frozen solid, dotted with patches of gray snow—and up the marble steps of the old red brick building.

"You can't bring that in here, guys," the security guard tells us as soon as we push through the heavy door and into the warmth of the museum. The ice cream, of course.

"We'll finish it here," Caleb tells the guard with a smile. I get the feeling Caleb always gets what he wants when he deploys that grin.

Ice cream quickly consumed, we show the guard our school IDs to confirm that we can get in for free, and head inside. It doesn't bring back any particular memories—I think it's been renovated since I was here the last time—but Caleb seems to know it well.

"Come on," he says, leading me down a hallway. "I want to show you something."

We climb up two flights to a gallery called Modern American Art, 1950 to the Present. As we step into the first room, Caleb nods at the security guard standing watch. "Hey, Randall." The guard greets him back with a nod and smile.

"You know him?" I ask as we pass into the next room.

"I come here semiregularly."

The gallery is a bright, high-ceilinged room with crisp white walls and glossy hardwood floors. The rooms have the kind of solemn, silent feeling that always makes me a little uncomfortable in museums: I'm more used to the bustle of theaters, the backstage white noise of pianos being tuned and pointe shoes clacking on concrete floors. In the gallery, I trail Caleb through rooms only sparsely populated with artwork and museumgoers. Huge abstract paintings take up whole walls.

"See, I don't get that," I whisper to Caleb, nodding toward one of them. "It's just a big black canvas. I could do that."

"But have you?" he whispers back. Point taken. Nonetheless, it doesn't look like much to the untrained eye. "It's about texture, HD. And tone, and the way the paint interacts with the canvas, and the light, and—"

"So what you're saying is," I interrupt, "it's not just a big black canvas. It's a *fancy* big black canvas."

"Here," he says as we step into a room with, finally, some paintings that look recognizable as actual art. Along one wall is a series of three long, wide panels, hung side by side and running almost from floor to ceiling. They're painted in rich colors: at first glance, all I see is a blur of bright reds, deep browns, and shimmering golds, swirling together in a busy, vibrant mix. Looking more closely, I register that the first panel captures a scene from the famous slave uprising on the *Amistad*. Black men and white men are entangled on the deck of a ship while blue-green water sparkles around them. The painting feels familiar, and I've stared at it for a full minute or two before I read the name plate next to it—"Giles Henry Franklin, *Still Rising*, 1989."

"Wait, I know this painting," I say, it suddenly dawning on me that Mr. Sullivan, my tenth-grade U.S. History teacher, showed us a slide of it during the unit on slavery and the Civil War. It's sort of famous.

"You do?" Caleb asks, sounding surprised.

"From U.S. History. Are you related to Giles Franklin?"

"He's my grandfather. My dad's dad. He gave me my first sketchbook. Cool, right?"

"That's not cool—that's kind of amazing."

"He was commissioned to do this series for the one hundred fiftieth anniversary of the *Amistad* uprising."

I haven't seen the other two paintings before. One depicts a sit-in at a Woolworth's lunch counter; the other shows a series of scenes, each one blending into the next and clearly crossing different time periods. In one scene, there's a black man and a white man in suits, conferring behind a table in a courtroom. In another, a cluster of African-American students are walking into a school, and in a third, a white man and a black woman are exchanging wedding vows.

Caleb notices me surveying the third painting. "Oh, that one's major Supreme Court decisions." He points to each scene in turn, naming them as he goes. "Um, Powell versus Alabama, Brown versus the Board of Education, Loving versus Virginia." He falters on that one. "That's, uh, legalizing interracial marriage. Can't remember the year."

I swallow, hard. "Wow. This is—I mean, I didn't know your grandfather was a famous painter. These are awesome. It's awesome that they're *here*. You can just come see them whenever you want."

"He's got some other stuff in the collection here, but these are my favorites. When I was like ten, this museum bought them, and Granddad brought me here. Even then, he explained them to me, not like I was a kid, you know? I still remember what he said. 'Grandson, these are my paintings. They're about freedom. Don't let anyone tell you the struggle is over.'"

I take a step back to get a wider view of all three canvases. "We've come a long way since the *Amistad*, though."

He chuckles toward the floor. "Sure. But not all the way."

It's so quiet in the gallery that I can hear him breathing next to me. "I didn't mean . . . I know there are a lot of problems, still," I say. "Never mind. Thanks for showing these to me. They're awesome."

He puts his hand on my waist, sending a now-familiar shock wave through my spine. "We're allowed to talk about this stuff, you know. Race, et cetera. Et al. So on and so forth."

"I know we're 'allowed.'" I roll my eyes. "But it's like—I don't know. I don't even think of you as black."

Caleb's laugh bounces off the high ceilings of the gallery, so loud that I'm sure people all over the museum can hear him.

"Why is that funny?" I say.

He pulls himself together and takes my face in his hands. "Sorry, sorry. I'm not laughing at you—really I'm not."

"Except you are, clearly." I pull away from him.

"No—HD—really. It's just, how *do* you see me, then?"

I look around the gallery to make sure we're still alone. "You're just—you. Caleb. Do you look at me all the time and think, 'Gee, there goes that half-Jewish white girl again'?"

The bemused look on his face is bugging me. Suddenly I feel like the most ignorant person on the planet.

"No, but—HD," he says. "If you don't see me as black, maybe you're not seeing me as me. Because I *am* black."

"I know that, obviously. I didn't mean . . . We shouldn't be having this conversation." I'm officially mortified. But I'm just being honest. I guess I don't think of Caleb as being so connected to those struggles in his grandfather's paintings. It's not the same as the old days, now. His family is way richer than mine—and practically everyone I know. And anyway, we live in a place where people just don't think like that anymore. But now I feel like a total jackass for saying anything.

He takes my hands. "It's okay, HD. I get what you're saying. What I'm saying is, we still don't live in a world where race doesn't matter. This"—he points to the skin on the back of one of his hands—"still affects the way people see me. It just does."

I force myself to look up into his face, in spite of my complete humiliation. "Sorry. I didn't mean to be . . . an idiot about it."

"You're not an idiot, HD. You're just white. Can't be helped."
Then he cracks up laughing all over again. I shove him.

"But listen, HD," he says, calming down. "Look. At the end
of the day, I wouldn't want to live in a world that doesn't see
race. I want to live in a world where people aren't *disadvantaged* on account of race, but that's different. I like being a black
dude, okay? And I'm proud of where I come from. That's why
I brought you to see my grandfather's paintings."

We stand there for another minute or two quietly. I wonder
if this feeling of mortification will ever dissipate from my chest.
Finally Caleb nudges my shoulder with his. "Hey."

"Hey," I say back.

Then he turns me around to face him and leans toward me
slowly, his eyes on my mouth. I close mine for a moment, waiting, and then feel his lips brush mine. As we kiss, he takes my
hand and rubs his thumb lightly over mine. My whole body
goes calm. I see stars behind my eyelids.

After a minute or ten—I can't tell the difference—we hear
the sound of a throat being cleared and pull apart quickly. It's
Randall. He gives us a sly smile as he passes by. I catch Caleb's
eye; I must be blushing, I can feel the heat in my ears.

"Shall we?" he whispers. As we head down the stairs, he
threads his hand through mine and grips it firmly—like he won't
let me run away, even if I want to.

Fourteen

On Tuesday night, Studio D is quiet, lights off, as I know it will be at this hour. My pointe class just finished upstairs and it's the last class of the evening. I managed to slip away before Eloise could nab me to walk to the train station with her.

I don't even bother turning on the overhead lamps. D is the smallest and dankest of the studios, down in the basement, but it doesn't matter. I let the light from the street lamps outside filter in through the narrow windows that run along the top of the walls. The barre is solid under my hand, as always, and it makes me feel steady. I press up onto my toes, watching myself in the slightly warped mirror. I'm warmed up already from class—there's really no need to stretch, but I do anyway. I put one leg up on the barre and stretch out over it. Then I switch sides and stretch the other leg. I do a few deep *pliés* with my supporting leg and drape my upper body across my lower body, as my hand comes to its resting place on my foot. Being able to fold myself in half is pretty much second nature to me at this point—that's what happens when you start ballet so young that your body never even has a chance to stiffen up.

I don't normally stick around after class like this. But sometimes I come here for the alone time in the studio. Sometimes I just need to be in the half-lit room, just me and the music and the hardwood floor and the ability to control everything, if only for a moment.

I put my earbuds in and do the combination we just learned in class, pausing at the triple *pirouette* / triple *fouetté* combination that gave me trouble in class today. Thirty-two *fouetté* turns performed consecutively is considered a movement in classical ballet. *Fouetté* means whipped. It's a showstopper, the turn audiences love—the dancer moving from a flat foot to pointe as the other leg extends at a ninety-degree angle and whips around, turning and turning.

I do six. Then another six. Then another six. My heart is pounding out of my chest. Ballet isn't something you think about as you're doing it, not for me, anyway, not anymore. When I was younger I used to visualize the movements as I was doing them, the way Miss Julia or the other instructors would tell us to. But as I got older, it just became normal, like my body performed the movements without any help from my brain.

Lately, though, I've been thinking about it again. I think one step ahead: I'm going to rise up on my toes, I'm going to extend one leg toward the ceiling. And then less than a split second later, I do. I always seem to be just a little outside myself.

"Rose?"

I jump. I didn't hear the door open. The lights flicker on; it's Miss Julia. "I'm sorry. I didn't mean to scare you. I figured you'd be in here."

"Sorry. Do you need the space?" I take my earbuds out and start gathering my bags and jacket from the corner.

"No, it's okay. I just wanted to catch you before you head home. Can I talk to you for a minute?"

I grab my stuff and follow her into her tiny, cluttered office down the hall. She flicks off the NPR interview that's blaring from the old desktop computer.

"So, how are things?"

I shrug. "Fine. Okay."

"College applications? They're going all right?" I nod. By which I mean, I've filled out my name in the online common application that's due at the end of the month.

"Good," Miss Julia says. "Good. Look, I wanted to . . . put something on your radar." She says it slow, like she doesn't want to scare me, and my palms feel clammy.

"You know, obviously, about the BFA program at The Pacific Coast College of the Arts?"

"Of course, yeah. It's the best."

She takes a sip of tea from a heavy purple mug. The mug looks homemade, like one of her kids made it in a ceramics workshop at camp or something. "Yes. Exactly. It's one of the few combined ballet BFA/apprenticeship programs in the country, and obviously it's connected to the Ballet of the Pacific Coast, which is a fantastic company. It's basically the Harvard of ballet."

I know all this information already. I've been over and over it, but I just can't see myself—or my family—making the sacrifices necessary to make it happen.

"Anyway, they have a scholarship program, a full ride, for very promising dancers," she goes on. "It's called the Grierson

Scholarship. Don't be mad at me—I know you've been looking at schools closer to home—but I spoke with their director of admissions about you, and they've asked to see a tape of you. They think you sound like a strong candidate."

Miss Julia forges ahead while I stammer to pull some coherent words together.

"I know what you're going to say—it's too far from home. I know. Look. I just want you to have all your options open. I think you should send a video. You can tape it here in the studio. I was thinking of your Dewdrop . . ."

My Dewdrop solo from *The Nutcracker*, the one Caleb never saw. It's a beautiful solo, and I know I'm capable of dancing it well . . . at least, I was when I thought Caleb was in the audience.

Several beats go by while I'm still stunned. Miss Julia smiles at me, her forehead crinkling between her eyes. "So? What do you think?"

"Thank you, really. I'm so—I don't really know what to say." That's the truth. It's a huge opportunity. So huge that I'm pretty sure I wish I didn't have it. "I think I just need . . . to think about it."

"But you'll let me know? They need to see a tape in the next few weeks. There are in-person auditions at the beginning of April, but they'll do invites to those based on the tapes."

"In person? In San Francisco?"

"Yup. I know it's far, but I can talk to your dad if you want." She leans in conspiratorially. "Rose, I'm not recommending any of the other girls for this scholarship."

"What about Eloise? Or Georgia?" I ask.

Miss Julia shakes her head. "They both have plenty of options for next year. I want this scholarship for you. You deserve it. Give it some thought."

"I will, promise. Thank you, again. This is amazing."

"The Grierson is a big deal," she says, looking mighty pleased with herself. "Don't take this lightly." She grins at me, perky as ever, and pats my knee. "All right, get out of here."

I rush out of the studio and toward the train. While my stomach does *fouettés* and *pirouettes* of its own, I keep replaying the conversation in my head. And there's really only one person I want to discuss this with.

I text him. "Alert: High-priority convo. Meet up tomorrow?" Caleb writes back right away, of course, with a string of question marks.

"Will explain. Meet me at Angelo's at lunch?" Barrow kids are allowed to go wherever they want for lunch as long as they're back in time for class, so I know he can come over to Broadway, to one of the handful of off-campus lunch spots Roosevelt kids are allowed to frequent during school hours.

"See you at noon," he writes back. I rest my head against the window of the subway car. A full ride to PCCA. An apprenticeship with the BPC. On the other side of the country.

Angelo's Pizza is the kind of hangout that doesn't appear to have changed at all since the '80s or maybe earlier, with scuffed green linoleum tiles and a dusty Pepsi machine. It's almost disappointing when your Pepsi doesn't come out with a vintage logo on the can.

I sit at a back table, to avoid the possibility that Lena will walk by the window and realize that I totally lied to her about where I was going when I rushed off after English. Of course I'll tell Lena about this, of course I want her opinion, but for some reason, I just don't want it yet. I think I can only handle talking to one person about this situation at the moment, and that person is Caleb.

Unfortunately, he's late. I pick at my slice of cheese while I wait for him to show up, but by twelve fifteen, I'm starting to get irritated. Finally he rushes in, full of apologies.

"Sorry, sorry, sorry," he exclaims, wending his way through the crowd of my classmates in line for slices and dumping his stuff on the grimy table. "Really, we had to meet *here* for this serious conversation?" He looks around, incredulous.

"Shut up, I love this place. You're late, no complaining."

"Sorry. What's up?" he says as he catches his breath. His nose and cheeks are a little chapped from the wind, and a cold breeze wafts off of him as he sits down.

Caleb listens intently while I go through my conversation with Miss Julia, leaning forward when I get to the part about the admissions director wanting to see a tape of me. He doesn't interrupt, but when I finally come to my conclusion—which is, hello, what should I do?—he breaks into a triumphant grin.

"HD, this is amazing! Do you even get that? See, I *knew* you were an incredible dancer, although as you have pointed out numerous times, I have not yet had the pleasure of watching you dance."

"Because you were a no-show at *The Nutcracker*," I interject—never missing an opportunity to make him feel guilty about that.

"Yes, yes, because I'm an asshole! But now I'm obviously going to see you perform with the Ballet of the Pacific Coast. You *have* to go to the audition."

This kind of over-the-top exuberance is what I expect of Lena, not Caleb. From Caleb, I want measured, balanced debate. I want him to see both sides. I reach across the table and grab his madly gesticulating hands.

"Listen, calm yourself. First of all, making a tape is not even getting an audition, and getting an audition is not the same as getting *in* to the program. So slow down."

"Fine, fine, fine—details! You're so in."

In a burst of frustration that I can't control, I grab my Pepsi can and slam it down once on the table.

"Hey," Caleb says. "What's your problem?"

It annoys me to even have to explain this to him. He should know. "My problem is that this program is on the other side of the freakin' country! It's so far away, and it's not exactly cheap to get there, and the scholarship's not going to cover travel, and what am I supposed to do? Ask my dad to either let me disappear for many months at a time and barely see my mom at all, or shell out thousands of bucks to fly me back and forth all the time?"

"Hey, hey." Caleb rubs my arm and then squeezes my hand. "Hey. Calm down."

Just hearing *him* calm down, like he's finally hearing me, makes my eyes prick with hot tears. "I'm just not sure I should even try for this. What if I get in?"

169

Caleb studies me for a minute. "What *if* you get in? You will be able to pursue the thing you love? Is that so heinous?"

I laugh a little, in spite of my efforts not to. "I guess it wouldn't be 'heinous,' no."

"I didn't think so."

"I got you a slice," I say, shoving the almost-cold pizza across the table. It doesn't look very appetizing, but he doesn't hesitate for a moment before taking a big bite. A little trail of grease descends down his wrist and onto the paper plate.

"Okay, so it's not heinous," I say finally. "But it is far away. Would you go that far from your mom and the girls?"

He takes what seems like an unnecessarily long time consuming his mouthful of pizza before responding. "I don't know."

"See?" I start methodically shredding a half-grease-stained paper napkin.

"Yeah, but, HD, I don't know because the opportunity isn't in front of me right now. Something that would change my life? An art program across the country and a chance to go for free and jump-start my career? I'm pretty sure my mom would kill me if I *didn't* go."

"Well, you're a lucky guy."

Caleb sighs heavily. "This is kind of silly."

"What's silly?" All of a sudden I resent his know-it-all tone.

"It's silly that we're having this conversation. Why is this some big, indecisive thing? There's no way this is really about going far away from your mother, is it? You always say how much she loves dance. She'd *want* you to do this. So what's your real problem?"

The greasy napkin scatters across the table, torn in approximately a thousand tiny specks of paper. I wipe them into a pile in front of me, then look up at him. There's a pizza crumb stuck to the corner of his lip, but I have no urge to lean over and kiss it off him.

He's right, it's not just the distance. My mother does love ballet—she'd probably be happier than my dad if I went to San Francisco, if I spent the next four years dancing, so unlike what she's able to do now. So it's not really that. It's the whole thing. I think when you're maybe on the precipice of a long, ugly, early death, the "What are you going to do with your life?" dilemma that annoys the average high school senior is a little, shall we say, heightened. Is that so hard to imagine? I don't want Caleb to tell me what to do. I just want him to say that he understands why I don't know what to do.

"I'm freaked out," I say.

"When are you not going to be freaked out?" he says. "Rose—it's just—why do you make things so difficult for yourself? This is easy. It's a great opportunity. A lot of people would kill for it."

Heat rises in my cheeks. Maybe it does seem easy, to him—most things seem to be. "Fine. So let one of those people have my place."

"Maybe you should if you're going to waste it," he says. "At this rate, you'll waste your whole life thinking about things instead of doing them. You're exhausting to listen to."

I get up from the table and slam my tray down on top of the trash bin. Grabbing my coat and nearly knocking over the chair, I head for the door. Caleb follows.

Outside on the sidewalk, Roosevelt kids rushing by on both sides, Caleb grabs my wrist and spins me around to face him.

"I'm sorry," he says. "I didn't mean—I shouldn't have said that. But you can't not take chances in your life now, just because you don't know what's going to happen to you twenty years from now. That's absurd. There's too much stuff in this life that we don't know about anyway."

Absurd. Exhausting. It's so cold my face hurts, and I can't tell if it's the wind or Caleb's words that make my eyes water.

"I have to go," I tell him. I leave him there by Angelo's and rush across the street.

Back in school, I duck my head inside my locker, pretending to look for a book, to pull myself together before going to physics. When my breath has steadied and my hands are defrosted enough to function, I take my phone out and search for the number of the one person I know who, unlike Caleb apparently, can help me make an objective decision.

Fifteen

DR. HOWARD IS A CELEBRITY IN THE WORLD OF
Huntington's—patients come from the far corners of the universe to see him. Fortunately, his office manager still thinks of
me as an awkward twelve-year-old whose mother had just been
handed her death sentence, so she squeezes me in for a quick
appointment four days later.

Caleb's called three times since our conversation at Angelo's,
but I haven't been ready to talk again, not yet. On my way to
Dr. Howard's after school, I turn his words over in my head for
the umpteenth time. I don't want to be exhausting. If I get some
answers—one answer, in particular—maybe then I can figure
out everything else.

Dr. Howard must've seen my name on his schedule, but he
still looks surprised when he pokes his head into the waiting
room and sees me sitting there. He motions me into his office.

"Long time no see, Rose. What can I do for you today?
Everything okay?"

I'm pretty sure it's best to cut to the chase here. I don't even
take my coat off.

"I need all the information you can give me about taking the
test."

"The *test*. The test to determine if you carry the mutation," Dr. Howard says slowly. It's not a question exactly, but I can feel him questioning me regardless.

"Yes."

Dr. Howard is the person who sat my parents down, almost six years ago, and explained why things were never going to be really good again. Then they translated his speech into something they thought was kid-friendly enough for me—meaning they lied in places, certainly by omission. We were in Maine when they told me. (Way to end a summer vacation.) We'd eaten lobster rolls for dinner, a whole lobster in each one. We'd had soft ice cream for dessert. And then instead of playing cards or working on the thousand-piece puzzle we had splayed across the coffee table in the rental cottage, they sat me down in their bedroom and said, well, here's what this is. Their bedspread had a navy and white ticking stripe cover—I didn't know what that kind of stripe was called at the time, *ticking stripe*. Ticking stripe makes me feel sick when I see it now. I stared over Dad's head to a painting of a seagull, one foot raised like he was practicing yoga. Or working on his balance, which I was now told my mother was going to lose progressively, among other things.

Dad cried. Mom and I didn't.

"Rose, it's very rare for a person as young as yourself to take the test. The guidelines strongly advise against testing minors—and certainly without parental consent . . ." Dr. Howard trails off.

"My eighteenth birthday is next month. I want to know about all my options."

He sighs. "All right. Well, the test requires counseling beforehand. You would see a genetic counselor here at the hospital, at the Genetic Medicine Clinic. He or she would help you weigh the pros and cons of acquiring this knowledge, to ensure that you're making the right decision for you."

"Okay." So I have to get permission from a genes shrink. Fine.

"And you'll have three possible outcomes," Dr. Howard continues. "If your test is negative, if it shows that you have between ten and thirty-five repetitions of the DNA bases CAG on the fourth chromosome of the huntingtin gene, you are in the normal range and will not develop HD. If you have more than thirty-nine repetitions, you will develop HD at some point in your life. And between thirty-five and thirty-nine—"

"I know," I interrupt. I've read all this online. "It's considered borderline. I may or may not develop the disease." Certain uncertainty. A lifetime of questioning every decision I can't make immediately, every time I slurp my soup.

"That's right. Rose, really, speaking as a physician with a huge amount of experience with HD patients and families, I'd advise you to wait on this. You're seventeen. Even if you had a positive test result, it will be years before you develop symptoms of HD. Put it off at least a few more years. Consider it then, when you start thinking about having a family."

It's strange to like someone who's only ever given you bad news, but I like Dr. Howard. He has four daughters, laughing and falling all over each other in a photograph on his desk that looks like one of those staged placeholder pictures they put in the frames. He very rarely wears an actual white coat, preferring zippered sweaters over his collared shirts. Even though he's feeding me more of the same lines my parents already gave me—that there's no point in getting tested so young—I appreciate that he's being honest with me about the options.

"The testing centers do have the right to refuse you the test if they think you're not of sound mind to make the decision," he adds, almost as an afterthought. "Even if you're eighteen."

"Not of sound mind?" I exclaim. "So they'd rather wait until the symptoms actually set in? I haven't lost my mind yet."

"It's not about losing your mind. You're under a huge amount of duress for anyone, let alone a person your age. Your mother's disease is progressing—"

"I'm aware of that." I don't mean to sound as snotty as I probably do.

"Has anyone ever told you not to make major life decisions in a rush of emotion?" Dr. Howard looks so deeply concerned for me that for a moment, I think he's forgotten he's talking to me and not one of his own daughters.

"This isn't exactly eloping to Vegas, Dr. H."

He chuckles, his intense focus broken for a moment. "That, I can't advise you on. But this is an emotional time for you. And you can't unknow your HD status once you know it."

"So when will this not be an emotional decision? That's what I don't get."

"It's always going to be fraught, yes. But if you wait a few years, wait a decade even—"

A decade. I get it. "So, wait until my mother's dead?"

"Frankly, Rose, yes. Wait until you're not living with this thing in your face every day. Ten years from now you won't even be thirty yet. You'll still have plenty of time to do—to do whatever you want to do, either way."

"I want to talk to the counselor," I tell him.

Dr. Howard sighs again, takes his glasses off, and rubs his whole face and forehead. He has a high forehead, and his hair is thinning and graying like Dad's.

"Rose, you need to talk to your parents about this first. I can't come between you and them on this—I really can't."

My eyes flood with tears, which catches me by surprise. "If it were one of your girls, in my situation—would you want her to know?"

He looks at me long and hard, like he's just plain sad about this whole thing, or feels somehow responsible for it, or something. "I don't know, Rose," he says finally. "I really don't. I would want them to talk to me about it, though. Not keep it a secret."

"I just want to meet with the counselor. Just to think about it. Please, Dr. H. I *will* talk to my parents about it, I promise."

"You're giving me your word that you will not do this on your own? You know the counselor will want to verify that you have the support of your family?"

I bite my lip and take a breath. Then I nod. "I'll talk to them."

"Okay," he says. "I'll set up the referral. *Just* for exploring the possibilities. You will talk to your parents about this before you make a decision." It's not a question this time.

"I will. Thank you."

Outside in the wintry air, a few leftover, crisp leaves scuttle along the sidewalk in the wind. While I wait for the train, I pull my phone out and text Caleb. "Saw my mom's dr about the test. Maybe I just need more intel to decide about the audition."

I've already hit send before I realize that I want to talk to him again. And that wanting Caleb—wanting to know him, wanting him to know me, wanting him in my life—has become an inevitability.

"Walk me through this one more time," Lena says in a stage whisper, leaning across the heavy oak table in the reading room of the library. We have a study hall, but we're obviously not studying. I've just finished telling her, also in a stage whisper, about my visit to Dr. Howard. "You're legitimately planning to take this test now, to find out if you're going to get your mother's disease approximately twenty years or more from now?"

I notice the reference librarian shooting us a dirty look, and I think Lena notices too, but we both ignore her. "If you could find out if you were going to get colon cancer, wouldn't you want to know?"

"My dad's cancer wasn't genetic, so, moot point," she says, tapping a neon green highlighter against her physics notebook.

"Not moot point. If it *had* been genetic, if you *could* take a test and know with one hundred percent certainty, I'm going to get it or not, wouldn't you want to know?"

Lena stares past my head, into the middle space of the reading room. She chews her lip for a moment, unconsciously, squinting. Maybe she's thinking about what it was like when her dad was sick or something, I don't know. There were five months between Lena's father's diagnosis and his funeral. We were young, but not young enough to forget that mad dash from normal life to something unrecognizable.

"If it meant I could do something about it, then yes, sure. But if there wasn't anything I could do, then no. No way."

"I just don't think that's true. I think if you were in the situation, you'd feel differently." I see her point, though. There's no treatment for Huntington's, nothing you can do except wait for the first hand tremor, the first fender-bender, and watch it progress. It spares no one.

She shrugs. "Whatever you say."

It's probably time to tell Lena the real reason I've been mulling this over so obsessively. That there's more than one big decision hanging in the balance, and I have to nail something down or I'm going to go crazy.

"Miss Julia wants me to audition for a scholarship. At PCCA."

Lena's eyes snap to attention. "Wait, *what*? A full ride?"

"Full ride."

"Hello! Oh my god! That's amazing!"

"I don't have the audition yet. I have to make a tape and send it to them if I want to be considered."

The librarian trots over to our table. "Come on, girls," she says. "You need to leave the reading room if you want to chat."

"Sorry," I say. Lena waits until the librarian's back is turned, and then does a silent scream, pumping her fists in the air wildly. She leans in again.

"I can record you. That's easy. PCCA is your dream school! Unless you found out just this second, I'm offended that you didn't tell me sooner!"

I do feel a little guilty about that. I've never kept a secret from Lena for much longer than it takes to write a text message, let alone a whole week.

"I know. Sorry. I needed to figure out how I felt about it first."

"Figure it out? How could you possibly feel other than, hello, amazing?"

"You sound like Caleb."

Lena pulls away from me and sits back in her chair. "You already told Caleb about this?"

Flustered, I grasp for a loophole. "I mean, he called—I had just talked to Miss Julia—it wasn't like . . ." I can tell from Lena's blank stare that she's not buying it. I give up. "You never tell Anders anything before me?"

Her cheeks flush. "Not majorly important, life-changing things, no. Obviously I'll tell you first if I get in to NYU."

"Well, I guess you don't have to, now. Then we'll be even."

"It's not a competition, Rose. I would want you to know first. You're presumably going to be in my life a lot longer than Anders."

It's the first time I've ever heard Lena indicate that one of the guys she's dating isn't necessarily "the one," and it takes me by surprise. I wonder if there's something going on with them that I haven't noticed.

"Are things okay with Anders?" I ask.

"They're fine. You know, it's just . . . We'll be in college next year. What are the chances these boys will last?"

She's probably right. Acknowledging that whatever I have going on with Caleb might just be temporary is comforting on the one hand, and feels like a punch to the gut on the other.

Our argument in front of Angelo's was just over a week ago, but it's already fuzzy in my mind. We've talked every day since I saw Dr. Howard. I cast a glance over at the librarian, but she's busy droning on at what looks like a freshman (the oversize backpack is a dead giveaway).

"I'm sorry I told Caleb first," I say.

"I mean, I get it. We've barely even hung out in the last month," she mumbles. I start to protest, but then I stop. She's kind of right. We've seen each other in class, obviously, but it hasn't been like normal Lena-and-Rose hanging out time.

"Blame *The Nutcracker*."

"You know it's not *The Nutcracker*'s fault," she says, looking me squarely in the eye. I don't say anything. Finally, Lena flicks a balled-up piece of paper at my head and sticks her tongue out. "It's fine. You can make it up to me by going out on a fancy double date for your birthday and wearing your yellow heels."

Lena's been trying to get me to go on a double date with her and Anders for ages. She's met Caleb a couple of times now, but I've been avoiding the double date like an infectious disease. It just seems so . . . coupley.

I groan. "Please, do we have to do a big birthday thing? You know I'm not a party person."

"I didn't say a big thing. I said a double date. You, me, Anders, Caleb, and dinner. That's all. Fine?"

I sigh. I can tell I'm not going to win this one, especially since I'm already disadvantaged by my stupid slipup. "Fine."

Lena claps twice, then quickly slips her hands under the table when she spots the librarian eyeing us again. "Good," she whispers. "This will be most excellent, I promise."

"Just please, no candles or singing. Promise me that, too."

"Whatever you say," she says, her mood significantly brightened by the prospect of planning an event. "But getting back to this audition situation. It's awesome. What's your hang-up?"

"Honestly?"

"No, dishonestly, please."

"Here's the thing. I'm not really sure I can make any decisions about the rest of my life . . . without knowing," I say.

"Hence seeing your mother's doctor." It's not a question; Lena already knows she's right. She looks thoughtfully into the air over my head. "Yeah, I mean, dance isn't the most lucrative career. Maybe you should get rich fast if you have the gene. So you can get a really fancy house with an elevator."

This is why I love Lena. Because who says stuff like that? I hadn't even thought of it that way. But now I remember playing in our living room when her dad was sick, and Lena whispering to me that her mother was going back to work. They celebrated Christmas with us that year, not that it was much of a celebration. My dad joked that it was perfect because of the whole Jews-eating-Chinese-food-on-Christmas thing, but I don't think anyone laughed. Lena and I got all the same presents that year. My parents must've bought them for us both.

Lena gnaws on the end of her highlighter. Then she gets a kind of quizzical, serious look on her face and puts the marker down. "You know I'd take care of you, right? If you need me to?"

A rock forms in my throat. Then the absurdity of having this conversation in the reading room of the school library hits me, and I start cracking up at the same time that my eyes flood.

"I'm serious!" she says. "What's funny?"

"I love you, friend. Thank you," I say through my laughter-meets-tears. "But, like . . ." I gesture around the room.

"What? What's wrong with the library for a heart-to-heart?" Except by now, she's laughing too. The librarian has mercifully disappeared.

"But seriously, let's think about this," Lena says, pulling herself together. She twists her hair into a huge, loose bun and secures it with a pencil. "Have you ever considered that if you test positive, you could just, like, do whatever you want? Live it up. Travel anywhere you want, see all seven wonders of the universe or whatever, wear ball gowns to the movies. You know, anything."

"If you could do anything, you would choose to wear ball gowns to the movies? Seriously?"

She flicks her hand in the air. "It was a hypothetical. You know what I mean. In your case, you'd what—ride all those crazy trains? You could do that, couldn't you?"

I slump back as much as possible in the straight-backed library chair. Lena has a point, actually. I haven't considered that side of the equation. "That's what my mom was going to do," I say.

She nods. "I know. All I'm saying is, no matter what the test says, you don't *have* to call everything to a halt. You don't automatically have to stop living, stop dancing, stop falling in love with Caleb . . ."

"I'm not falling in love with Caleb."

Lena studies me, a smirk spreading across her face. "Whatever you say. Anyway, you get my point."

"I get your point. And my point is, if I know my HD status, at least I'll be better equipped to make choices about all those things."

"Okay," Lena says. "So you're taking the test. It's your call. I mean, I don't know what's right for you. Only you do."

I check my phone for the time. Five minutes until next period. I pile my notebooks on top of each other and slide them into my bag in one stack. "Well, this was productive," I say.

Lena looks down at the open notebook in front of her. "I highlighted one sentence. I'm glad we solved your life, because otherwise it would've been a major waste of time."

We're about to part ways in the hallway—I'm going to English, she's going to psychology—when she grabs my arm. Her eyes are sparkling, mischievous. "So when are we making that tape?"

I book Studio A for first thing on Saturday morning, before the first class starts at nine, because Lena says we have to have natural light for the recording. The truth is, I still feel uneasy about the whole thing, but I try to shake off those misgivings as I warm up. Whatever doubt I'm feeling, it can't come out in my dancing.

Caleb insisted upon coming along "for moral support," which is in fact making me considerably more nervous than I would be if it were just Miss Julia and Lena in the room. But I'm hoping that if the nerves wear off, I'll dance this solo as well now as I did in December—the first time I thought I was dancing it for him.

"I can't tell you how pleased I am about this whole thing." Miss Julia buzzes around the studio, making sure there aren't any stray ballet slippers or towels strewn where the camera will catch them. "This is a once in a lifetime opportunity. What'd your parents say when you told them?"

I stretch at the barre in the corner while Lena attaches her tiny camera to a tripod. To say I was anxious about telling my family about this would be an understatement. Mostly I was worried that my mother, so unpredictable these days as she loses her ability to regulate herself, would say something horrible, tell me I'd never get in, or that I didn't deserve it. But she didn't. For that moment, she was her old self, who loves ballet as much as I do. Even Dad—who I predicted would grumble about how "dance isn't much of a career path"—had nothing to say but carpe diem, more or less. Maybe Mom's good day was wearing off on him. Or all the bad ones were.

Of course, I didn't tell them the entire story—which is that in addition to booking the studio to make a tape for PCCA, I also booked an appointment with the genetic counselor to talk about getting tested for the Huntington's mutation. That seemed like it might sour the mood.

"They're excited," I say as I press my face against my leg.

Caleb comes up behind me and massages my shoulders while I stretch. He's wearing this black Boston Rugby Club hooded sweatshirt and jeans. I don't know where the sweatshirt came from; he doesn't even play rugby, but it looks good on him. I know I'm supposed to think he looks best dressed up, like he was when we went to the BPC, but the truth is, I think he looks pretty cute when he's all casual. It's mildly distracting.

"Your mom must be super proud," he says softly in my ear.

For today, she is. Tomorrow, who knows.

"Okay, people, we're all set here," Lena announces. "Are you warmed up?"

"Hold on," I say. "Not quite." I move to the middle of the floor and do a few quick leaps and turns, shaking out my muscles in between.

"Sit over there," I tell Caleb, pointing at a folding chair in the corner, next to Miss Julia. "And don't say anything. And don't laugh. And don't, I don't know . . ."

"Should I also wear my invisibility cloak?" he asks.

"I wish. Okay, I'm ready. We might need to run this a few times." I let Lena direct me to the right spot on the floor.

"Three, two . . ." Lena mouths the one like a movie director and points to Miss Julia, who starts the music. I close my eyes and take myself back to the theater. I can almost hear the quiet shifting of the audience in their seats, their anonymous faces packed in the dark. And then there's just me and the floor, and Tchaikovsky's music, calling me home.

Lena said she'd edit the footage and send it over later, so I go home after my last class and try not to think about PCCA for the rest of the evening. While I wait, I lie in bed with my laptop propped up on a pillow, staring at my online application to Cunningham College for the umpteenth time.

Last spring, Cunningham was just one stop on an epic road trip of practically every college within seven hours of Boston. Most of my classmates came back from their own college tours complaining about how annoying their parents had been—asking questions about things like shuttle buses around campus after midnight—but our trip was pretty fun. Mom's symptoms weren't that noticeable yet, certainly not to the strangers we took the campus tours with, and we strayed from the groups after a while to hunt out the best local ice cream and bookstores. It felt like a normal, family-ish thing to do. But for the most part, the colleges all felt the same to me—nondescript collections of old buildings around lush lawns, invariably dotted with college-y types throwing Frisbees.

Cunningham had its own share of Frisbee throwers and old buildings. But when we were wandering around campus, Mom spotted a flyer stapled to a bulletin board. "Common Ground: DanceWorks Spring Show."

"There's a dance performance tonight," she said—with total clarity, I remember that. She was slurring less back then. "We should go."

"We have to get on the road, ladies," Dad said. "Otherwise we won't get as far as Ithaca tomorrow."

Mom pulled the flyer off the board and scrutinized it more closely. She shook her head. "I think we should go to this. Ithaca will still be there on Friday. Rose wants to, don't you, Rosie?"

I shrugged. "May as well. We're here."

That's how we ended up in this black box theater space at Cunningham College on a Thursday night. The house was packed with all these college students carrying bouquets of tulips and bright gerbera daisies. And the show—which was a mix of jazz, modern, some hip-hop, and some that refused to be boxed into a category at all—was crazy good. Like stuff you expect to pay a lot of money to see. I've never danced much beyond ballet—there's something about modern especially that feels too uncontrolled, too lawless to me—but I know enough about the other genres to recognize that these kids were good enough to be dancing professionally. And there was a *feeling* in the theater that night. It reminded me of the annual showcase at NEYB, the buzz and energy in the air, the anticipation—a complete and absolute shared love for dance. Even sitting in the audience, I could feel it. I liked it.

Plus, as I pointed out to my father, at Cunningham, I could dance *and* major in business, if I felt so inclined. He seemed to like that idea.

The application is due tomorrow by 11:59 p.m. Mine's finished, just waiting there, ready to go. I give my essays one more read, and hit Send. At least I'll have a backup plan. Because I probably won't get into PCCA anyway.

It's almost midnight when Lena finally sends a text: "Just sent over your video. It looks awesome!!" My whole body tenses up, as if it's preparing in advance to be mortified. I almost never watch my performances on film. It's too torturous. Video never seems to capture the whole moment, the intensity and magic of it. But then I think of Caleb's face when I finished dancing this morning. He'd looked at me like he'd never seen me before. Is that because he's Caleb, and he doesn't know anything about ballet? Or because he's biased about me? Or is it really because of my dancing?

I open Lena's e-mail and click Play. She was right about the natural light—the sun streaming in through the studio windows gives the whole room a kind of soft glow. But there's more to it than Lena's videography skills. I think I forget for a moment that I'm watching myself. It's like looking at Caleb's drawing of me. I don't recognize her, but the person in this video is good—maybe good enough to have a shot at this.

Sixteen

Roxanna, the genetic counselor Dr. Howard referred me to, looks like a typical Cambridge therapist—flowy linen pants, a kind of purple tunic top, and a heavy beaded necklace. She has one of those granny chains attached to her glasses so she won't lose them, although it doesn't seem to help much. In the first ten minutes of our first session, I watch her search high and low for those glasses while they're perched right on top of her head, nested in her spiky white hair.

She looks like a therapist, but the thing about genetic counselors is that they're *not* therapists exactly. Although they're supposed to be, more or less. I researched this. Officially, they're supposed to practice something called "patient-centered therapy," where they don't tell you what to do—they're supposed to help you make your own decision. That's how the field of genetic counseling started out, anyway, when the main recipients were pregnant women who were at risk of carrying babies with genetic conditions. Of course, that was before there were actually any tests for the stuff, so the counselors were just working off the knowledge that something or other bad ran in the woman's family. Back then there really *wasn't* a right answer:

all a counselor could tell the woman was her general risk, but they couldn't tell her anything for sure.

That's no longer the case, now that we have access to more information about our genes. I imagined that Roxanna would explain all my options—even though I already know what they are—and then tell me that whatever I end up doing is the right thing for me. Not the case.

In reality, Roxanna lays out all the possibilities—I take the test, I get a negative result (good); I take the test, I get a positive result (bad); I don't take the test—and then starts pretty obviously pushing her own agenda. Which is: Rose, don't be an idiot, don't take the test.

Unfortunately, I have to put up with whatever pressures Roxanna wants to apply, because more than my parents, she's the gatekeeper to my genetic information. If I want to take the test after I turn eighteen, I'll need to see Roxanna at least three more times. They make you stretch it out, presumably to give you plenty of opportunities to change your mind. And at the end of it all, I'll still need her sign-off. I have to pass her test before I can take my test.

"Rose, can I ask you something?" she says ever so earnestly, cocking her head to the left. She squints a little bit and makes one of those sort of solemn, close-lipped half smiles. I stare over her head. On the wall opposite there's a mass-produced painting of some sand dunes that I think I've seen on sale at Target. Soothing, supposedly.

"I want you to close your eyes and imagine, just for a moment, that you take the test, and you get a positive result."

It's weird, isn't it, that getting a positive result is bad news. Why do they do that in medicine? HIV-positive. Positive biopsy. It's condescending. We're not dumb. We know bad news when we hear it.

"What's the question?"

"I'm sorry?" Roxanna cocks her head the other way.

"You asked if you could ask me a question. You didn't ask me anything."

"I'm sorry. Imagine that you get the positive result . . ."

Like I don't do that every day.

". . . And tell me, what do you do first? What's the first thing that happens?"

"I'm not going to kill myself, if that's what you're asking."

"That's not what I'm asking."

I think about what Lena said. I could just walk out of the doctor's office, go home, and book a train ticket. I could start with the Zephyr, Chicago to San Francisco. Then, after that, I could take all of Mom's train rides, one at a time, until I can't, just like she planned to do.

I elect not to tell Roxanna that particular plan.

"I'll join a support group," I say instead, assuming that's the right thing to say. My mother went to a few support group meetings when she was first diagnosed. Then she quit. She decided she didn't like being around sick people.

"That's the very first thing you'll do?" Roxanna asks, incredulous.

"No, I guess not. The first thing I'll do is drive home."

"You won't be alone. Who's with you, your dad?"

Unlikely, considering that Dad doesn't even know we're having this conversation. Again, I figure that's probably not what Roxanna wants to hear.

"I guess," I say. "We'll go back to our house and I'll make tea."

"You'll make tea?"

"Dad will be really upset."

"How will you feel?"

She studies me, like I'm a specimen in a research project—which I might as well be. There's a lot of research on how much people really want to know about their health, and about their genetic health, specifically. I've Googled this, and the results mostly contradict themselves. One study I found says there are two kinds of people: people who want information and people who would rather bury their heads in the sand—which isn't a surprise, really. It depends on the kind of person? Thanks for the insight, Science.

"Rose?"

"Honestly?" I ask Roxanna. She nods a little too enthusiastically. "I think I'll feel in control."

"Okay," she says slowly. "And if the test is negative? How do you think you'll feel then?"

When I was little and I couldn't decide something—stupid things mostly, like whether I wanted the blue Converse sneakers or the purple ones, or a birthday party with pizza or Chinese food—my mom used to tell me to flip a coin, but then as soon as it lands, to register my natural, automatic response. "Quick!" she'd say. "Are you happy or disappointed?" She'd smile knowingly (because she usually knew what I really wanted before I did) and say, "See, Rose? *That's* how you know how you really feel."

The strange thing is, when Roxanna asks me how I'll feel if the test is negative, my natural, automatic response—only for a split second, but still, there it is—is disappointment. It only occurs to me now that maybe I've spent so much time imagining life with my mother's illness that I've never considered life without it.

As soon as I get home, I pound up the stairs and open my laptop. It's been two weeks since I sent the tape in to PCCA, and according to their Web site, I should be getting an answer about the audition today. Sure enough, there it is. My hands shake like Mom's as I go to open the e-mail.

From: Office of Admissions, The Pacific Coast College of the Arts

To: Rose Alexander Levenson

Dear Rose,

Thank you for submitting an audition tape to the Gerald Grierson Scholarship Committee at The Pacific Coast College of the Arts. The Admissions Committee would like to invite you to audition in person on April 4. For your convenience and ours, this session will serve as your audition for both admission to the BFA program and the scholarship itself. Further information is attached.

We look forward to seeing you in San Francisco!

All best,

The Admissions Committee

This time, the first person I call is Lena.

Seventeen

"THAT CONVERSATION WAS BINDING, LEVS," LENA SAYS, one hand on her hip as she surveys the insides of my closet, trying to choose an appropriately celebratory outfit for the birthday dinner she wouldn't let me out of. "Listen, you are eighteen now: you can vote, you can serve in the military, you can take ill-advised genetic tests to determine your medical future . . ." She pauses and shoots me a pointed look. "And you're the best dancer in the universe, and you're going for free to the best dance school in the country. We have to celebrate!" She practically sings as she prances around my bedroom, trying to get me in the going-out spirit.

"Okay, let's not get ahead of ourselves, shall we?" I say. "It's only an audition."

There's no chilling Lena out right now. This dinner—Caleb's and Anders's first time meeting each other—is basically Lena's dream come true: the two of us on a much-heralded double date. But I still don't think of Caleb and me as the same kind of couple as Lena and Anders—one of those coupley-couples. Despite Lena's assertion that I'm falling in love with him, Caleb and I are just . . . people who sometimes kiss. And want to talk to each other all the time. And seem to be starting to care about each other.

"You're wearing the yellow wedges, obviously," Lena says as she begins laying clothing items out on my bed. Lena herself is already perfectly attired, looking like she always does—somehow like she didn't think about it at all, and happened to randomly throw on this just-right outfit. Tonight she's wearing tight black pants in some kind of stretchy material, a loose striped sweater that seems to always be sliding off one shoulder or the other, and high-heeled gray boots.

"Dress, or jeans?" she asks. I stare at her, already exhausted by what I know is about to turn into twenty minutes of trying things on and taking them off.

"Jeans." I sigh. "It's freezing out." I never understand girls who force themselves to wear tiny dresses and high-heeled shoes in the dead of winter. This is February in New England, people. It's freakin' cold out.

"We can do jeans. These," she says, pulling my only pair of decently dressy jeans out of my bottom dresser drawer. "And . . . wait for it." She wiggles her eyebrows up and down at me and goes over to the duffel bag—her stuff for spending the night—that she's tossed in the corner. Digging through it, she unearths a black V-neck shirt that looks too small for either of us. "Try," she orders, tossing it at me.

"This is not going to fit me in any way that is appropriate."

"Whatever. Do as your personal stylist says."

I really don't know how she does it, but she gets me every time. I peel off the T-shirt I'm currently wearing and finagle my arms into the shirt, which is made of some kind of thick, soft, stretchy cotton and is gathered around the sides.

"Yes," Lena says, like a proud parent, grinning at me. "Look."

I turn and examine myself in the mirror. She's right, actually— the shirt fits surprisingly well. It's low-cut, but not inappropriately so. Once I've wriggled into the nice jeans and the wedge heels, I have to admit I look pretty good. Like an almost-normal, decent-looking eighteen-year-old human.

Dinner is at a divey Mexican place with hockey on the televisions by the bar, and a guy with a guitar coming around to serenade the diners (automatically drowning out any conversation and requiring the entire table to smile awkwardly at him for two and a half minutes until he's finished).

Caleb busts out his best guy's-guy repartee with Anders. "You a Bruins fan?" he asks, nodding up at the hockey game. It's either a lucky guess, or Caleb is stereotyping about Scandinavians' love for hockey. Either way, he's right, and Anders launches into a monologue about injuries endured by the Bruins this season and why he thinks they're still on track for a Stanley Cup win.

Lena rolls her eyes at me across the table, and I smile and shrug. They can talk about hockey all night if they want—I'm happy to just sit and listen. The restaurant is warm, and Lena swore up and down that there would be no singing of "Feliz Cumpleaños" from the guy with the guitar, and the whole thing feels just about right.

I know Caleb noticed that I put a little extra effort into my ensemble tonight. When he first saw me take off my coat in the restaurant, he made an obvious "I'm impressed" face. Under the table, our knees are just barely grazing each other.

"Okay," Lena interrupts the hockey talk with a little clap. "Before dessert, presents!"

I groan. "Seriously, guys, you didn't have to get me anything. And you especially don't have to give it to me in public," I add, glaring at Lena. She just smiles, and pulls an envelope from her purse.

"Relax, it's nothing big to unwrap. This is from me and Caleb."

She and Caleb went in together for a present for me? That's weird. It's hard to imagine the two of them hanging out without me, or even talking on the phone. I give her a quizzical look, and then turn to Caleb, who just grins at me.

I take the envelope, slightly apprehensive now, and slide my finger under the flap to open it. Inside there's a pamphlet from Amtrak: "California Zephyr," it reads on the front. "Chicago— Denver—San Francisco." Folded inside is a gray-blue paper ticket.

For an instant, it's like the very last moment of a ballet, when the music and movement stop but hover, waiting for the audience to break the spell with their applause.

I look up at both of them. "What did you do?"

"It's the Zephyr, or whatever it's called. The most beautiful train ride in the country, right?" Lena looks at me like it's totally normal that the two of them would have just handed me a four-hundred-dollar birthday present.

"You guys bought me a cross-country train ticket?" I look from Lena to Caleb and back to Lena.

"Well, it's not technically cross-country. It leaves from Chicago, so you're on your own getting there," Lena says.

"Guys, this is nuts. This is way too expensive. I can't let you do this."

"We're not taking it back," Lena says, shaking her head. "Look, you keep saying how much you want to take this train, right? And you need to go to San Francisco. It's perfect."

I look at the departure date. This train will put me in San Francisco on April 3, the day before the PCCA audition. Of course.

"Anyway," Lena goes on. "Your dad already knows. And he helped us pay for it, so you don't need to worry that I've spent my entire college fund on your birthday. Okay?"

"Guys, this is just—this is too much. I don't even want my dad spending this much on a train ticket." I've looked online. I know what the tickets cost.

Lena's eyes flash from me to Caleb and back to me. She leans across the table and grabs my hands. "Listen. We know how much this means to you. Trains run in your family. You're doing this. We're not letting you *not* do this."

Hot tears spill down my cheeks. I try unsuccessfully to wipe the snot from my nose without making a disgusting mess of myself. Caleb slides a napkin toward me.

"I can't believe you're making me emote in public," I say through the napkin. "Thanks a lot."

Lena sits back in her seat, looking utterly thrilled with herself. "I knew this was a good birthday present. Didn't I?" She looks to Caleb, who concurs.

"I can't take credit for this," he says. "It was all Lena."

I blot at my eyes with the soggy napkin. "Here," Lena says, pulling a compact from her bag. Of course Lena would think to keep a small mirror on her person at all times. I take a quick look at myself in the unforgiving light of the restaurant. My nose is bright red and my eyes are puffy. The mascara Lena made me apply earlier is now running down my face in little streams of Maybelline brownish-black. I mop them up as much as I can.

"It's more than a good birthday present, guys. It's . . ." I stammer. "I don't know what to say. Thank you."

"I'm so good," Lena says, doing a little dance in her chair. "I'm so, so good."

"Let's get in your bed and watch *Dirty Dancing* like we used to," Lena says as I fumble for my house keys. "To celebrate your future life as a famous dancer."

"Please stop with the famous talk," I say, finally locating the keys in the bottom of my bag and shoving them in the top lock. "But yes to *Dirty Dancing*." I turn and wave to Caleb, who's waiting to see us get inside before pulling away.

We step into what I can only describe as a hurricane. But not the fun kind.

The first thing that happens is a ceramic vase is hurled across the dining room, missing my father's head by a matter of inches.

"Ellen! Calm down!" Dad lunges across the room to grab my mother, who has the china cabinet open and is smashing mug after bowl after plate to the floor. The pottery in the cabinet is the product of years of collecting, a piece here and a piece there, mostly from the shops we visit on the way up to Maine in the summers. Some of it goes back much longer than that—the tea cups and saucers with elaborate gold trim are from Gram's wedding. She always says the china was a much better investment than the marriage itself. Now I can see at least two of the set are shattered on the floor.

"I told you to leave me alone. I don't want you hhhere," my mother growls at Dad, throwing a green-and-pink-flowered creamer to the floor.

Behind me, I feel Lena's hand squeeze my arm. Then she steps instinctively backward, into the foyer.

I go toward my mother. "Mom, Mom," I say, putting a hand gently on her arm and taking a dessert plate from her hand. "It's okay. Stop. Stop doing this."

Dad exhales hard and crosses to the kitchen, letting me take over. We've gotten used to this choreography—one of us stepping in, wordlessly, while the other steps out to regain the patience required to not take Mom's words or actions personally.

Mom lets the plate go and looks at me, her eyes wide and sorrowful. "Rose," she says. "Rose." Her hands shake and she's out of breath, spent from the fury of the moments before. "I'm—I'm—I'm sssorry." She looks at the floor around her feet. It's covered in hundreds of shards of broken dishware. "I'm sorry I made this mess." she asks.

I take both her hands in mine and rub them until they almost stop shaking. Almost, but not quite. "It's okay," I say. "It was an accident."

* * *

Once Mom's in bed, I close my bedroom door behind me and stare at myself in the narrow full-length mirror. The warmth I felt at dinner—the nerves of being out as a foursome, like Caleb and I were really a couple; the excitement of them presenting me with the most ridiculously awesome birthday present ever—it all seems like it can't possibly have happened just hours ago.

My mother is disappearing, every day a little more than the day before. I get undressed and lift a leg up onto the ballet barre Dad screwed into the wall for me when I was eight. I stretch and *plié*, watching myself in the mirror, wearing nothing but my mismatched bra and underwear. With every inch that I push my stretch a little farther, I think of the look on Mom's face as she smashed those dishes to the ground. It wasn't even her. San Francisco seems even farther away now than it did three hours ago.

Twenty minutes after I've finally crawled into bed, there's a knock at the door.

"Where's Lena?" Dad says, poking his head in.

"Um, she left," I say. "A little too much excitement around here tonight."

"You okay?" he says, coming in. He's quiet for a moment. "I'm sorry about that. That I left you with that mess."

"It's fine."

Dad shoves a pile of T-shirts and leotards aside to make himself a spot to perch on my armchair. "It's getting a little crowded in here, isn't it?"

"It's fine, Dad," I say, waiting for him to say what he really wants to say. "What?"

"What what?"

"You want to talk to me about something specific, I can tell."

"You know, people always think dads are so predictable— what do you know, maybe I just came in to say one last happy birthday to my daughter whom I love and adore."

I glance at my phone. Eleven fifty. It's still my birthday for ten more minutes. Happy birthday to me. "Okay. But you also came in to say something else, I can tell."

Dad clears his throat. "All right, maybe I am that predictable. So they gave you the train ticket, I assume?"

"Yes, sorry. I forgot. Thank you. It's a great present."

It's a stupendous present, but after what I just witnessed in the dining room, the idea of leaving Mom—or more to the point, leaving Dad and Gram alone with Mom—seems almost impossible.

"Good. They were very excited about it, Lena especially. I personally don't understand what you and your mother think is so romantic about spending two days breathing canned air, but to each her own, I suppose."

"Will you be okay?" I say.

"What? When you're gone? Of course—we'll be fine! It's only a few days, anyway."

"No, Dad—I mean. If I went to school out there. Would you be okay?"

He gets up and spends a little too long looking at the pictures tacked to my bulletin board, as if he hasn't seen them all before: a selfie of me and Lena making stupid faces, and one of us as eight-year-olds, swinging in unison in our elementary school playground, grinning goofily with our hands joined across the gap between our swings. There's another of Mom and me after a ballet recital when I was eleven. It's one of the last pictures of our life before her genetic bomb exploded on us.

Dad takes that one off the wall. "Nice shot," he says, not looking up.

"Yeah."

"You look alike in this picture."

His sentimentality must be getting to him in his old age. Dad and I are pretty indisputable look-alikes—there's no resemblance between Mom and me, at least not phenotypically. Genotypically is a different story.

Finally, he tacks the picture back to the board and clucks his tongue, just like Gram does when she doesn't know what she wants to say. "Listen, you know *I* don't want you to go to college across the country. Personally I'd like you to go to college in this room."

"Okay, Dad," I say.

"Look, Ro. It's a great program out there. You can't get that anywhere else. We want you to do the right thing for you. Your mom and I both."

Tears prick at the back of my eyes and throat for the second time tonight. "I know that, Dad. But what am I supposed to say to her—what I want to do is leave you, now? Like this?"

He comes over and sits on the edge of the bed. I can't remember the last time he came in here and sat on the bed with me, like he was going to tuck me in and read me a story. "You're a good kid," he says, pulling my head into his shoulder and kissing the top of it. "The thing is, your mom and I can't . . . Parents just want to keep their kids safe from all the bad, messy stuff. And we can't. I mean, I don't know if anyone can, really. But we certainly can't. We *can* give you this. We don't want you to limit yourself."

Sometimes, around my parents, I have a feeling that's like love and appreciation, but it's so much bigger than that that I can't put a name on it. There's no word for it. This is one of those moments. "Okay," I say. "I won't. But, Dad?"

"But, child?"

"I need to tell you something."

His body stiffens up. "What's that?"

I can't hide it from him anymore. "I need to know my HD status. Before I go away to school. I saw Dr. Howard, to talk to him about the test."

"You what?" His voice is low and calm but laced with fear, I can tell.

"I can't make a decision about next year unless I know. If you want me not to limit myself, I have to know what kind of life I have to limit or not limit."

Dad rubs his hand firmly over his chin a few times. His forehead folds into more wrinkles than I can count.

"You didn't want to discuss this with me first?" He looks hurt, like I've gone behind his back about this. Which I guess I have.

"Well, I'm discussing it with you now."

"This isn't a discussion, it's an announcement."

I pull my knees up and squeeze them against my chest, hard. "Dad, I'm eighteen now. I'm allowed to make this decision."

"Just because you *can*, legally, doesn't mean you should—or shouldn't ask—or talk to us . . ." The words get caught in his mouth.

"Okay, so maybe I actually don't want your input," I say, as my heart rate picks up speed. "I'm sorry. No one else understands the situation I'm in, and I've made a decision."

He stands up and turns to face me, both hands resting on the top of his head. "So that's it, Rose? You're eighteen—your parents get no say?"

Heat rises in my chest. I knew Dad wouldn't be thrilled about this, but I assumed he would accept my decision once I'd made one. I don't want to fight over this. But it's my life. It's my call.

"I don't want to fight about this, Ro," Dad says, reading my mind. "Especially on your birthday." He lets out a long, heavy breath.

"You have to trust me on this," I say.

"Is it so hard to imagine why I wouldn't, though? I mean, Rose. Come on. This is huge. It's a huge decision." Dad's face is pink. I can see a vein pulsing on the side of his head. "I wouldn't know what to do if I were in your shoes. So how can you be so sure?"

I don't say anything.

"No. The answer is no," he says finally.

"*The answer is no?* I didn't ask you for an answer, Dad. I'm not asking your permission. I'm not even asking you for money. I have the money."

"You have the money?" Dad looks incredulous. The $375 fee is going to deplete most of my savings account, which is supposed to be for college, but technically, I have the money.

207

I nod. I'm afraid if I say anything else I'll start to cry again.

"No—*no*. You just—you cannot do this. We can talk about this again in a few years. Not now. I will not negotiate. No."

Then Dad does something he's never done before: He turns his back on me and leaves. He doesn't quite slam the door, but it shuts hard behind him anyway.

In eighteen years to the day, I have never seen my father like this. Rage pounds against my chest cavity, desperate to bust its way out, but I refuse to let it. My father can say no all he wants. I don't need his signature anymore.

I sit frozen on the bed, staring at the closed door, for who knows how long. Finally, exhausted, I flop back and stare at the ceiling. You can still see the outlines of the stars that formerly glowed in the dark against the white paint. Mom put them up there when I was six—I remember sitting on the bed and watching her on a step ladder, sticking them up there and trying to make the Big Dipper and Draco the Dragon and Orion. All my friends had glow-in-the-dark stars on their ceilings, but no one else had constellations. Mom used to do a lot of crafty things like that—stars on the ceiling, magazine covers wallpapering the downstairs bathroom, whole scrapbooks full of my baby pictures and locks of hair and swatches of fabric from my old onesies. Now she can barely dress herself, and her train scrapbook looks like it was made by a crazy person. Which it was.

I bet the stars are crazy bright when you're riding through the middle of Iowa or Nebraska on the California Zephyr.

Lying there, I try to imagine myself skipping the Huntington's test, running away to San Francisco to dance next fall, pretending there's no hurricane creeping up the coast of my life, ready to wreak havoc. But that version of me won't quite stick in my head; it's slippery, somehow. It feels like a lie.

SPRING

Rule #3: Knowledge is power.

Eighteen

THE MAN-NURSE, DEREK, IS SO SMOOTH WITH THE NEEDLE that I barely even feel it going in. It's taken a month, plus three more Roxanna appointments, before they finally let me schedule this test. My blood shoots through the clear tube into the first vial and he pops it off and pops another one on so quickly I almost miss it. When the two vials of blood are full and topped off with purple plastic stoppers, stickers with my identification info stuck to them, he spreads a Band-Aid gently over a piece of gauze on my arm.

"That's it," he says, smiling.

"Yeah, right," I say. "That's it."

I never mentioned the test to Dad again. We barely spoke for two days after our fight on my birthday. I stayed late at the studio rehearsing for the spring showcase and my audition, then slept at Lena's two nights in a row. I didn't want to give him the chance to raise it again. He'd made up his mind, but so had I. On the third day, he waited up for me to get back from rehearsal. I came home to find him sitting in the living room, reading. Sleep and the constant hum of our old refrigerator were the only sounds in the rest of the house.

"Long day?" Dad said, putting his book down.

"Tech. So, you know. Yeah." In the two weeks before the spring showcase, we're in the theater constantly, stopping and starting through our choreography while the lighting team focuses lights on us from every direction. It's more exhausting than dancing—standing around, waiting to dance.

Dad followed me into the kitchen and cleared his throat. I spread peanut butter on a rice cake and waited for him to say whatever he wanted to say.

"Parents, you know," he said finally. "The whole protection thing is our job. We've talked about this before."

"Yeah," I said. "And?"

"That's why I think you should not get this test right now. I hate to pull rank on you, but I have a lot more years of life wisdom here."

I took a bite of rice cake and watched the crumbs scatter across the counter. "You waited up to tell me the same thing you said the other night?"

"No. I waited up to tell you that I love you."

"I know that."

"Okay. Just checking."

I let him think he'd won. It just seemed easier.

Now I look over at the two vials of my blood, all my information stored in them, swimming around in microscopic sentences that tell my body what to do. Right there in those vials is all the information about the rest of my life and the end of my life. Just there for the taking.

I pull my sleeve down gingerly over the Band-Aid and layer on my sweatshirt.

"So, you know that you'll get a call when the results come back in—probably about three weeks."

"Tell me again why it takes so long?"

Derek smiles. "That I don't know. They like to keep you guessing?"

"Apparently."

"Do what you can to put it out of your mind, precious. That's what I tell everyone who comes through here."

"Sure," I say, zipping up my parka. It's still freezing out, even though it's already mid-March. "Think any of them actually manage that?"

"Doubt it," he says.

My phone vibrates in my pocket—Lena, waiting outside to pick me up.

I cross the street and tap the window of her mom's car. Lena pops the lock and I slip in next to her. I don't need to say anything. It's done. The information is out of my body, into the world, and in a few weeks, it'll be mine. For better or for worse.

Back in January, I told Caleb he could make up for *The Nutcracker* mishap when the annual showcase came around at the end of March. At the time, I'm not sure I really believed we'd still be hanging out by spring. A whole few months seemed like an unrealistically long time to keep up this thing between us.

But now the showcase is here and, of course, he hasn't forgotten this time. I get him a ticket for the final performance on Sunday evening—my last show with New England Youth Ballet.

In the back of my mind—or, let's be honest, the front of my mind—is the fact that the Sunday night show might not just be my last NEYB performance—it could be my last ballet performance, ever. Before I go to the dressing room to start my makeup regimen, I wander a big loop around the backstage area. Our theater is old and beautiful, with a high proscenium and ornate moldings, and lush, red velvet seats that haven't been reupholstered in decades. Backstage, it smells predictably of musty costumes, wet paint, and heat from lighting instruments. It's hard to imagine never coming back here again, never preparing for another performance by stretching on the cold concrete floors. Regardless of what happens with PCCA, I won't be dancing here anymore after this showcase.

In the dressing room, Eloise leans in toward the mirror and covers her pale, freckled face with even paler powder. On Eloise's other side, Georgia attaches her fake eyelashes with glue. We all wear them for performances. I used to think they felt incredibly strange, but now I'm pretty used to them.

"So," Eloise says without looking away from her own reflection, "is he here tonight? The distraction?"

I apply a thick layer of lip liner around my lips, exaggerating their natural shape, and fill the outline in with dark red lipstick. Blotting on a tissue, I roll my eyes at Eloise in the mirror. "I have no idea what you're talking about," I tell her.

"Oh, give me a break. You're still hanging out with him, right? I can tell. You seem—jittery."

She's right that I've been acting a little cagey around her lately, and I'm glad she's attributing it all to Caleb. She still doesn't know about my audition in San Francisco. I certainly don't need the ballet girls gossiping about me if—when, probably—I don't get in.

My face flushes under its heavy coat of makeup. "Wouldn't you like to know?" I say.

With that, I zip up the fleece I'm wearing over my leotard and shove my feet into my sheepskin slippers. There's still thirty minutes till curtain; no point in tucking and pinning myself into my costume just yet. I told Caleb to meet me at the stage door.

I rush down the chilly, concrete maze below the stage and shove the door open. Sure enough, there he is, just on time and carrying a single red rose tied with a white ribbon. He presents it proudly. "For the star of the evening," he says with a quick bow.

"Stop," I say with a laugh, although the sight of him, dressed up and holding a flower he's brought for me, gives me more butterflies than the thought of the performance ahead. "A rose, huh? Clever."

Caleb wraps a hand around my waist, grazing the sensitive spot on my lower back and sending a shiver up my spine. Pulling me in toward him, he kisses the top of my head lightly. "Break a leg."

"Thanks. I gotta go get ready. Here's your ticket." I pull the ticket from my fleece. "Great seat—third row center. Just don't wave at me or anything during the show. Oh, and you're sitting with my family. Good luck with that."

I kiss him one more time and scurry back toward the dressing room, feeling anxious and warm and lucky, all at once.

I'm dancing the *cygnets pas de quatre* choreography from *Swan Lake* with Eloise and two other girls—four little swans, holding hands. It's a tricky section with a rapid-fire series of intricate movements, *entrechat-quatre, passé, entrechat-quatre, passé, échappé, échappé, échappé,* all coupled with quick head and shoulder movements called *épaulement.* There's not a lot of room for mistakes—miss a beat and you'll ruin the whole thing.

The performance goes by in a blur. I'm aware of isolated moments, little snapshots that I seem to catch while the rest of it flies by. When we finally come to a fluttering, out-of-breath stop in the very last moments of the show, I close my eyes and try to hold on to the moment for an extra split second. The feeling of standing onstage, a performance freshly complete and an audience clapping, isn't something you can replicate any other way. It's only itself. I might never feel this again.

The lights fade up on all of us, standing in our rows for the curtain call, and I catch sight of Caleb and my family, standing up in the third row—the only people giving us a standing ovation. Even Mom is standing, leaning on Dad's arm. Caleb has a huge, toothy grin plastered across his face.

The curtain comes down after the final encore and we all relax immediately. Eloise rushes over to me, in tears, and squeezes me in a hug.

"Can you believe it?" she says. "Our last show together!"

I hug her back and force a smile, trying to look as moved as she and the rest of the seniors are by the moment. After almost fifteen years at this ballet school, thirteen years performing in this same spring showcase, having it just be *over* feels a little anticlimactic. It's not the big finish I was expecting. There's no rush of emotion of any kind. It's just over.

A tiny swan, probably seven years old, flutters past us, trying to run and remove her tutu simultaneously, undoubtedly overwhelmed by the performance and desperate to go find her mother. I used to be that swan.

I take a quick sip from my water bottle and blot my forehead with a tissue. "Congratulations," I say to Eloise, who's grinning through her tears.

"It's like, the end," she says, shaking her head. "Or the beginning. You know?"

I squeeze her hand. "I'm going to go find my family."

"And your boy?" she asks. I give her a swat on the hip and rush back to the dressing room to change.

I spot them as soon as I emerge from the stairwell. They're waiting together—Dad, Gram, Mom with her walker, and Caleb, looking dapper in a blazer and jeans. I pause for a moment in the doorway to watch them, just chatting together. I can't hear Caleb, but from the look on his face, I know he's talking about me.

"Damn," is all he says when I reach them. Then he kisses me, right in front of my family. Including my father.

"*Whoa*, there," Dad says. "That'll do, folks."

I pull away from Caleb, flushed. "So? What'd you think?"

"Superb," Gram announces. "Your best ever. Absolutely superb."

Mom reaches out with a wavering hand and pulls me into a hug. "Beautiful. Just perfect, my love."

"You're a talented kid," Dad says, giving me a one-armed hug. "What can I say? Your mother and I will accept full credit. You're welcome." He hands me a bouquet of yellow and orange tulips.

"You don't get all the credit, do you?" Gram says. "A grandmother has a significant influence on a young person, you know."

"Thanks, guys," I say. "So, I guess this is it. Last spring showcase."

Dad looks around the lobby. "It's been a great run here over the years." His eyes shine.

"Don't cry, Dad. Please."

"Who's crying? No one's crying. How about a celebratory dinner? What do you say?"

I catch Caleb's eye. "I'm starving," he says. "Dinner sounds great."

I hug Dad one more time. "I want to show Caleb around backstage. Can we meet you at home in a bit?"

Dad looks surprised. "Oh . . . I thought we'd do an actual restaurant. Something nice—a.k.a. not takeout."

"I know," I say. "But . . . I just want to spend some time in the theater. Take in the whole last performance thing, you know?"

"Sure, hey, of course." I can tell Dad's disappointed, but he'll get over it. He turns to Gram and Mom. "We'll just mosey home, and whenever you guys get there, we'll figure out some food. Don't wait too long, though . . . this guy looks like he needs a solid meal every few hours." He thwacks Caleb on the shoulder in that awkward man-hug kind of way.

As my family leaves, I glance around the emptying lobby. Eloise is probably lurking, staking out an opportunity to introduce herself.

"Come on," I say, grabbing Caleb's hand and pulling him toward the stairwell. I lead him around the hallway to the orchestra pit door. "Want to see something extra cool?"

"Always."

"You're not afraid of heights, are you?"

He laughs. "Have you noticed how tall I am?"

The theater has a catwalk snaking over the stage and the audience, a huge iron walkway in the shape of a capital I, where they hang the front lights for the shows. From up there, you can see everything, even the set pieces hiding up in the fly space over the stage, waiting to come floating down on cue. Aside from being onstage, the catwalk is my favorite place to be in the theater. You can see the whole magic of the thing.

Right outside the orchestra pit door, there's a set of stairs that leads up to the catwalk entrance. Because I'm friendly with the tech crew, I happen to know it's usually unlocked on show days. When we reach the top of the stairs, I pull down on the sticky door handle and motion inside.

"Duck," I warn him. Even I have to bend over to avoid smashing my head on the ceiling.

We make our way gingerly to the middle of the catwalk, where I sit down with my legs hanging over the edge, looking out across the now empty seats. Down below, a couple ushers check the aisles and between the seats for trash.

"Something tells me the dancers aren't technically supposed to be hanging out up here."

"Perks of being friends with the tech guys." I grin.

"Oh, tech guys?" He tucks a strand of flyaway hair behind my ear, and traces my jaw with the back of his hand. His skin is smooth against mine, and sends a little tickle up the base of my spine, like someone is brushing my lower back with a feather. He leans in and gives me a light kiss on my lips, then one on the tip of my nose, then one on my forehead.

"I don't think you need to worry about the tech guys. You do need to worry about falling, though," I tell him. "I will definitely get in trouble if I let an audience member fall to his death."

"So you're saying I'm a liability right now?"

"Um, yeah."

We kiss again, his hand pressing the soft spot where my head meets my neck. His glasses slip down and bump against my forehead. When we pull away, he grins goofily with his eyes crossed. I clamp a hand over my mouth.

"Don't make me laugh or someone's going to hear us," I whisper, still giggling. Caleb drops the silly face, then squeezes me closer to his chest. He breathes into my hair.

"You were amazing out there, HD. Seriously." He's looking at me like he feels genuinely proud.

"I messed up one part."

"HD. Accept the compliment."

"Fine. Thank you." I don't know what to say next, so I punch him in the bicep. "And thanks for actually showing up to this one."

"I'm never going to live that down, am I?"

"Meh," I say. "Eventually. Maybe. Thanks for hanging out with my family, too."

"You mean sitting with them? Your family's cool. I like them."

"My mom didn't say anything crazy to you this time?"

Caleb shakes his head. "Not a word. But it wouldn't bother me if she did."

"It bothers me, though." I press my head into the nook between his chest and his shoulder. "I just wish it would stop."

"That what would stop?" He's speaking so quietly now that I can barely hear him, even in the silence of the catwalk.

"The getting worse."

I crane my neck to look up into his face and kiss him again. If we could freeze this instant and stay here forever, in the dark theater, just hit Pause on life, that's what I'd do. There's a calmness in my chest, in my stomach, even in my head, that I can't remember ever feeling before, at least not in the last six years. For a split second, I feel what I'm pretty sure other people call certainty.

"Hey, HD?"

"Hey, Sickle Cell?"

"I could sit up here all night with you," he says.

He must have been reading my mind. "I thought you said you were starving."

"I am starving, that is true. But I'd never get bored. I could watch paint dry with you and I wouldn't get bored."

"You could watch paint dry with me? That sounds delightful," I say.

"I'm making a point here! Paint drying is about the most boring thing I can think of to watch, and I would enjoy doing it with you."

I want to say something nice back to him—I really do. I want to tell him how I feel. My heart thuds so fast I figure he must be able to feel it thwacking against my chest. I'm pretty sure that heartbeat is the only sound, the only movement in the whole theater right now. But I can't make my mouth form the words.

Finally Caleb puts an arm around me and kisses the top of my head. I know he wants to make me think it's totally fine that I can't seem to express my feelings in the same way he can, but I feel him sigh in the dark. I wonder how long he'll wait.

Nineteen

IN TWENTY-FOUR HOURS, I'LL BE WINDING MY WAY ACROSS
the western half of the country, toward California.

My flight to Chicago is tomorrow at nine a.m. I land by early
afternoon, and then I'll take the Blue Line to Clinton, and walk
about three blocks, take a right, walk one block, and then I'll
reach Union Station. Where I'll board the Zephyr.

I've laid out everything I might need across the bed—leotards,
ballet slippers and pointe shoes, warm-up clothes, snacks for the
fifty-two-plus-hour ride: trail mix, pistachios, almonds, peanuts.

("What are you, nuts?" Dad said with a little chuckle, when
he saw me pile all the snacks on the conveyor belt at Star Market over the weekend.)

Dad comes in with Mom's medium-size suitcase. My parents
have matching luggage sets, which were apparently once pretty
nice but are now frayed around the edges, patched in places,
and showing the wear and tear of the decade of traveling my
parents did together when they were young and had a life before me.

"Check out what I found in your mother's suitcase," Dad
says. He holds up a wrinkled postcard. "Prepare to be impressed
with your father's romancing skills."

The postcard is to Mom, from Dad, sent from Scotland, according to the postmark. I know Dad spent a semester at St. Andrews when he and Mom were undergraduates. He must've sent this then.

His handwriting hasn't changed much over the years, unlike Mom's, which has gone from tidy, almost clipped little letters to a sprawling, looping mess.

"Dear El," my undergrad dad wrote, "Greetings from the Land o' Scots, once again! Where the weather is dreary, the people are beasts, and the golf courses are plentiful. I still couldn't hit a golf ball if my life depended on it, and you're still the most beautiful woman I've ever seen. Don't abandon me for Steve Branahan. He's a jackass. I miss you, I love you. Yours."

He sounds like himself, already. Like a just slightly less grown-up version of himself. And it makes me smile, because "jackass" is my favorite insult. I didn't realize I got it from Dad.

"Who's Steve Branahan?"

"Your mother's other suitor. He tried to make a play for her while I was studying abroad, but he had nothin' on me."

I hear muffled voices and laughter coming up the stairs, and Caleb appears in the doorway. "I've come to say farewell before the epic journey."

"Well, on that note, I'll leave you kids alone," Dad says.

Caleb assesses my packing progress as Dad slips out the door. "So. Here's the thing. I don't trust that you're going to come back. I think you might just jump off in Utah and set up shop."

"Would I have to convert to Mormonism?" I ask.

"Nah," says Caleb. "You could just hang with them. I think Mormons and Jews get along."

"I'm only a half Jew."

"I'm sure Mormons and half Jews get along, too." He gestures at the postcard, which I'm still clutching. "What's that?"

I hand it to him and let him read it for himself. His eyes get wide and his mouth spreads into a sly smile.

"All right, Dave," he says, grinning enthusiastically. "Way to play it with the ladies."

"Really, that's uncalled for," I say, grabbing the postcard back.

"I didn't know your folks were college sweethearts."

"Well, they were. I mean, I knew they were together back then, but I didn't realize they were that serious. Jeez."

"Come on, it's cute," he says, smacking me lightly with a leotard.

"I guess," I say, shrugging. "Seems kinda young to be so in love."

I catch what might be a look of disappointment flash across Caleb's face, but he covers it quickly. "You're too young to be such a cynic, you know."

"I'm not a cynic! I prefer to think of myself as a realist."

I start layering the folded piles of clothes into Mom's suitcase. Caleb sits down on the bed, gingerly so as not to disturb my piles.

"So what's the realist's problem with young love, then? This optimist would like to know." He folds his arms and looks at me expectantly, like it's going to take a good dose of logic to convince him.

"I don't have a problem with it. I just don't know—I guess I think, you might *think* you're in love when you're twenty or whatever, but if you haven't been through something with the person that's really hard—life stuff—then I'm not sure you know what love is. Not for real."

He's quiet for a minute. "Sometimes you bust out with things that you have no business knowing about, HD."

I laugh. "What? I know about love. I know about my parents. My dad certainly didn't see *this* coming." I gesture around the room, as if Huntington's is in the air. "And he's stuck around. That's love."

"That's crazy love," Caleb agrees.

"I'm just saying that I think the love he has for my mom now is not the same as what he had when they were in college."

"Of course it's not the same. That doesn't mean what they had then wasn't for real," he says. "I think young love is kind of—I don't know—it's its own thing. It's special. Yeah, okay, maybe it's cheesy, but it's cool. It's lucky."

"Lucky?"

"Yeah. Why not?"

I shrug. "I guess I've never thought of falling in love as lucky. It seems like a big risk, to me."

"And that makes it a bad thing?" Caleb shakes his head at me. "You're a massive pain, you know that?"

"What? I am not!" I toss a pointe shoe at him.

"So what are we, then?" he asks, his tone suddenly serious. He leans back on the bed and props himself up on his elbows. I take the shoe back and press it down into the suitcase with its torn satin mate.

"We're just—us."

He gives me a sort of bemused look, like he knows this conversation isn't going where he wants it to go. "You need help with that thing?" He points at the overstuffed suitcase that I'm now trying unsuccessfully to zip.

"Yes, please."

"You're not a realist when it comes to packing, I see." He leans over the suitcase, pressing down hard with both hands. "Zip, come on."

I drag the zipper closed, almost all the way until it catches at a spot where the suitcase's two halves haven't come together evenly. Caleb shifts the top half of the case, then presses down again. This time it closes.

"Voilà," I say. "Now, I hope I don't need to add anything to that after you've left."

"Guess you're on your own from now on."

Bending over the stuffed suitcase, our faces are just inches apart. His breath smells like peppermint, even though he's not chewing any gum.

This time, when we kiss, it's not like any of the other times. For a moment it's tentative, but then suddenly it feels urgent, hungrier, like we can't kiss each other fast enough. At first he cups my face in his hands, and I grip his shoulders, but then our hands drift down, unbuttoning things and roving around each other's bodies. We crawl back onto the bed and he runs his fingers along the base of my spine and then up under my shirt. His hand grazing my skin makes me feel like every nerve ending in my body is at attention.

He kisses my neck, behind my hair, along the edge of my ear. For a split second he slips the tip of his tongue right into my ear and it's such a weird feeling that I pull away suddenly.

"What?" he whispers.

"Sorry," I say, giggling. "That's weird."

"Weird how?"

"Like tongue-in-ear weird. Sorry."

He laughs. "My bad. I got lost in the moment." He takes his glasses off, puts them on the bedside table, and pulls me into a hug. Then he starts kissing the base of my neck. "Neck okay?"

"Neck okay," I confirm. We stay there for a moment, not moving on the bed. The room's getting darker as the sun goes down.

"You have an early flight tomorrow?" he asks.

"Sort of."

"I should go. You probably want to hang out with your folks before the epic journey."

"Guess so, yeah." But we keep lying there, our hands tucked in secret places—mine in his back pockets and his resting right on the bare skin of my hip bones.

"What do I look like without your glasses on?" I ask after a moment.

He squints at me. "You look like an elderly black man. Like my grandfather."

I swat his arm. "Shut up."

"You look like you. Only blurrier." He kisses my nose, then pulls away.

"Okay," I say finally, getting up and buttoning my jeans. "I guess you should go now, for real."

I follow Caleb downstairs, and at the front door, he turns to me again. "Do come back from the epic journey, HD. Don't join a hippie commune in San Francisco."

I smile. "I don't think they have those anymore."

"Fine. Then don't become a Scientologist."

"Fair enough. I promise not to become a Scientologist."

A breeze sneaks through the cracked door and I shiver, even though I'm not really cold. Caleb pulls me to his chest. He's like a human heater.

I strain up on tiptoe to be closer to his height and kiss him again. He turns me around and pushes me up against the door-frame, not forcefully but not gently either. We're still making out when there's a rustling behind us. We pull away quickly, looking around, but there's no one there. Caleb slips his fingers through the belt loops of my jeans and pulls my hips toward his. We bump against each other and he smiles at me.

"It's more fun to be an optimist. Trust me."

My lips feel almost swollen and a little numb, so I can barely string together a response. I push the door closed after him and lock it. That's when I hear more shuffling in the next room. Turning, I see Mom, emerging from the shadows of the dark-ened dining room, shoving a walker in front of her like she does more and more around the house now.

"Mom, what are you doing?"

"Wanted a sssnack," she mumbles.

She shuffles toward the stairs, crumbs adorning the front of her robe. As she passes me, she pauses and leans in close to my face. "You're allowed," she whispers. Then she settles herself in her stair lift and takes off, leaving me standing there by the door.

*   *   *

It's drizzling the next morning when I drag my suitcase down the stairs, much too early. Mom is sitting in her wheelchair by the window. She's not up for me; she's always up at the crack of dawn now.

I leave my suitcase by the door and go to her, perching on the ottoman closest to the window. "I'm out, Ma." She ignores me for a minute. "Love you."

"Wwwhere are you going?" she asks, spinning her chair around to face me. "Where" sounds like it has twice as many syllables as it should, the way she slurs now. It still takes me by surprise, how everything keeps getting worse. I should be used to it by now, the progression—I know how it works—but still it never fails to surprise me that she wakes up a little bit harder to understand, a little bit less capable of caring for herself, than she was the day before. Even if the changes are almost imperceptible from day to day, they're constant.

"I'm going to San Francisco. For the audition. At The Pacific Coast College of the Arts. Remember?"

She nods slowly, which is more like an exaggerated version of what her head does on its own these days. "Obviously. I knew that."

"I'm taking the train. The Zephyr, from Chicago."

She blinks several times, hard, staring at me. "The Zzzephyr," she repeats, slowly.

"I told you I was going to take the train. It was my birthday present. You told me it's the most beautiful ride in the country."

"I didn't tell you to take the train."

So we're not going to have a pleasant, easy farewell this morning. "No," I say, taking a breath and trying to be patient.

"You told me it's the most beautiful ride in the country. I have to go to San Francisco, for this audition. I *want* to take the train. It was a birthday present."

"You said that already." She glares at me. "It's *my* train."

Last night, she seemed so good. That last moment before she went upstairs, sharing a secret with me, it almost felt like she was normal again. Clearly, we're back to reality now.

The stairs creak and Gram appears in the front hall. "Are you ready, Rose? Your dad's just looking for his keys." I look from Gram to Mom and back to Gram, trying to clue her in on the impending outburst.

"*It's not. Your. Train,*" Mom says, excruciatingly slowly, her volume rising.

"El," Gram starts, coming into the room, "Rose is taking one of the trains on your map. You *want* her to take this train, remember?" Gram has patience with Mom that I can't even comprehend. Or if she doesn't, you'd never know from the tone she musters.

Dad comes downstairs with his coat and hat, all ready to go, not yet recognizing the familiar, building tension in the room. "Tally ho, ladies. Rose, your chariot awaits."

Mom's reddening face and increasingly jerking head and extremities mean she's getting worked up. Then it all explodes.

"It's not your train! It's my train! My train! You're always trying to sssteal my fucking things!"

Gram chuckles, as if Mom's just kidding. "Well, technically it's not your train either, is it, El? Unless you're the bloody CEO of Amtrak." She's trying to lighten the mood, but I can tell Mom's already too far gone to be brought back with humor.

"El, come on." Dad puts what he intends as a calming hand on each of Mom's shoulders. Sometimes it works, but not this time. She shakes him off violently.

"Just ssstop treating me like a child!" she growls. "You"— she points at me—"you have no right to make *my* life . . . your life."

I don't even know what to say anymore. If only she still understood irony, she'd hear the ridiculousness of what just came out of her mouth. As if, under any circumstances, I would want to make her life my own. If there were anything I could possibly do to avoid that, believe me, I'd be doing it. Unfortunately, that's a choice I don't have.

"Mom, I'm going," I tell her, not giving an inch to the rage boiling in my gut. "Bye. Love you, Gram, I'll call you from the road. Or track, or whatever." I plant a quick kiss on my grandmother's cheek, grab my suitcase, and make for the car. By the time I get buckled in and see Dad heading out after me, closing the front door behind him, I've already wiped the tears from my cheeks and taken a deep breath. Done. Ready to go.

Twenty

THE LONG-DISTANCE AMTRAK WAITING ROOM IS IN THE basement of Chicago's Union Station, an unfortunate, low-ceilinged room hiding under what is a quite majestic train station upstairs. The floor is lined with threadbare blue carpet, and big luggage lockers line one whole wall. There are a lot of bored-looking people waiting for their trains with their feet propped up on coolers and suitcases.

Lena, Caleb, and Dad booked me what Amtrak calls a Superliner Roomette, which is the smallest of the sleeping compartments. When they call "All aboard" for the Zephyr—and they actually do call "All aboard"—a woman in a navy vest and hat directs me to the first car on my left, and a man in the same uniform takes my ticket at the door and points me up a staircase barely wide enough for Mom's suitcase, to room number three on the upper level.

The California Zephyr isn't exactly the old-fashioned Orient Express—complete with a steam engine and red velvet seats—that I was picturing for my epic train ride. "Room three," it turns out, is basically two single seats facing each other with barely a foot of floor space between them, and a silver door with a glass panel that slides closed just to the right of the seats. In other words, a closet with two seats stuffed in. But there's a big window, and a table that folds out from the wall, and since there's only one of me I can prop my suitcase on the backward-facing seat and sit facing forward. There's a tiny bottle of water resting by each seat, and I noticed coming in that there's also a selection of juice and a coffee pot right by the bathroom at the top of the stairs. Not too shabby, this Amtrak thing.

By the time I get settled in my compartment, I've almost cleared my head of the exchange with my mother. Almost. Dad and I drove pretty much in silence to the airport. As we pulled off the exit ramp for Logan's Terminal B, he said out of nowhere, "It's the disease. It's not her."

"I know. Obviously. I get it."

"I'm sorry, Ro. That's not how I wanted you to start this adventure."

"It's not your fault," I told him. "It's the disease, remember."

He pulled over by the American Airlines entrance. "You're a good kid. I love you."

"You're a cheeseball. Love you too."

Sometimes, when I'm feeling especially irritated about the particular genetic mishap that may or may not have happened to me before my birth, I remember that Dad didn't even inherit this crappy luck. He married it. And you can't divorce the woman with Huntington's disease, even if you want to, because that makes you a massive jackass. Not that I think he wants to leave her—but maybe sometimes, I guess. It has to be enticing, to think that you could just put it all behind you and start over.

I click a few pictures of my temporary home with my phone. Just on the other side of the narrow corridor, an older woman with a slight hunchback is getting situated.

"Hiya," says the woman, calling over to me. Midwestern. "This your first time on the Zephyr?" I nod. "Mine too. I'm going to Sacramento. Where you headed?"

"All the way to the end. San Francisco."

"Oh, wonderful," says the woman, dreamily. "Are you all by your lonesome over there?"

Actually, now that I'm getting settled in the roomette, it does feel a little strange to be alone. Which is unexpected. I figured it'd be like last summer, when I went to a two-month summer program at New York City Ballet. I was away from home by myself for a lot longer than three days. But that time, my parents delivered me right to the dorm, helped me get my bags upstairs, and put sheets on the bed. Not that I can't put sheets on my own bed. I can. But still, it's nice to have your parents do it for you, sometimes.

"By my lonesome," I say with a smile.

"Me too," she says, returning the smile, but she looks almost concerned.

"My grandparents are picking me up on the other end." I don't know why I tell the lie. Just to make this stranger feel better I guess, like my life is all good. It's normal.

The same Amtrak-uniformed man who directed me to my compartment appears in the corridor. He introduces himself as Jay.

"Rose," I say, shaking his hand, which swallows mine. He's handsome, in spite of the unflattering polyester he's forced to wear, dark-haired, with the most incredibly well-coiffed beard I've ever seen—every strand looks like it's been individually combed and placed exactly where it is on his chin. He doesn't speak with an accent, but his English is textbook-precise in a way that makes me think he learned it in school, not at home. He explains where the lounge car is, and that the dining car attendant will be around just after departure to take our preferred dinner reservations (really, reservations), and that he'll be around to fold down our beds any time after dinner until eleven o'clock.

"That's when I turn in for the night. I'm right here in room one if you need anything in the meantime."

At two o'clock on the dot, the train pulls slowly out of the station, and I watch the tracks coast by out my window. I text Dad first, to let him know I'm off, and then send Lena and Caleb the first few pictures I've taken. Within fifteen minutes, the high rises and shabby, boarded-up brick buildings of train-track-adjacent Chicago give way to flat, dry cornfields, and we're on our way.

They make big states in the middle of the country. Sounds obvious, I know, but I'm used to being able to drive across Massachusetts in three hours or less. In the middle of the country, we spend hours passing through shifting landscapes without crossing state lines. The flat land goes on for ages. It's beautiful in its own way, dead brown cornstalks for miles—it isn't really corn season yet, I guess—and dotted with tiny towns along the train tracks, ranch houses, above-ground pools, churches and schools with American flags flapping out front, scrap yards and recycling centers. And flatness.

Once we're moving, I explore the train from end to end: My sleeping car is the last on the train, followed by three other sleepers, the dining car, the observation car, with windows stretching to the ceiling, and three coach cars. The coach cars in particular are full of uncertain smells, each one slightly different from the last—one like someone's McDonald's hamburger, the next like disinfectant, the next like the toilet's not quite working. A few passengers are trying to sleep, even in the middle of the day, with T-shirts or masks draped over their eyes, which strikes me as a little defeatist, considering that the ride has only just started and there's plenty of interesting stuff to check out. At the end of one of the coach cars, a group of scruffy twenty-somethings are sitting on the floor, wearing pajama bottoms and drinking Sierra Mist. One of them strums an acoustic guitar quietly, which strangely doesn't seem to be bothering anyone sitting nearby.

Somewhere still in Illinois but hours from Chicago, the Zephyr stops long enough that passengers who are continuing on are allowed to get off the train and stretch our legs—a smoke stop, they call it. I step outside and jog up and down the platform a few times. I guess I can't really blame Lena and Caleb for not considering that fifty-two hours in a tin can wouldn't do wonders for my pre-audition body, because honestly I didn't think about it either. I'd pictured a sleeping compartment big enough to stretch on the floor, but the reality allows no such thing. So on the platform, I mark out a short combination we learned last week in class, trying to ignore the stares from Jay and my fellow passengers.

"You're a dancer, then?" Jay asks, shading his eyes from the harsh glare of the near-dusk sunlight against the cement platform.

I blush a little at the question. "Sort of, yeah."

He smiles. "It looks like more than 'sort of' to me—was that a *pirouette*?"

"A *chaîné*. But you were close." He isn't really, but it doesn't matter.

"You're practicing for something?"

"I have an audition in San Francisco."

Just speaking the words out loud makes my stomach feel like an ocean in the hours right before a hurricane hits. Churning.

Jay looks intrigued. "What's the audition for?"

"Oh, it's just a—it's nothing. Not a big deal."

"All right," he says, eyeing me like he can tell I'm not telling the truth. "Break a leg, then—do they say that in dance, or just the theater?"

"You can say it in dance, too." I roll my ankles around one at a time. "I probably won't get in, though."

"That's a bit pessimistic, isn't it? You've got the same chance as anybody else. Better, because you've got the luck of the Zephyr behind you!"

"Is that a thing?"

"Of course it's a thing! Everyone knows the Silver Lady is a good luck charm. Ask Mary in the dining car. She's a big believer." Jay gestures toward the train door. "All right, get yourself back on board. We are moving out."

I grasp the handle on the train door and step back up. I can't say I'm a big believer in the "luck of the Zephyr" myself, but I guess I'm not currently in a position to turn it down.

For my first Zephyr dinner, I'm seated across from a young French couple—one tall and dark-haired, the other smaller and blond—who are touring the States from New York to Chicago to San Francisco to Los Angeles, with one big train ride in the middle. Next to me, there's an older man with leathery skin, a worn red flannel shirt, and a cowboy hat. He used to be an insurance agent, he tells us, but now he's a volunteer park ranger.

"Americans eat so much corn?" asks the blond Frenchman, who speaks better English than his boyfriend. He nods at the cornfields—probably the fifth straight hour of them—flying by out the window.

"Mostly we eat corn syrup," I tell the French guys. They look at me quizzically. "Sugar," I say. "It makes sugar."

"Ah! Ah! Of course! *High fructose*," says the English speaker, nodding enthusiastically.

Our booth for four is decorated with a white tablecloth (heavy paper masquerading as cloth) and a pink carnation in a plastic vase. Two waitresses, Mary and Dyllis, call loudly to each other across the car and crack jokes with the passengers. Mary is instantly my favorite. She calls everyone "young man" or "young lady," or occasionally "gorgeous" or "handsome," thoroughly amusing the many senior citizens on board. I consider asking her about the luck of the Zephyr, but decide against it—the dining car is crowded and she's hustling, expertly balancing trays of meals without spilling them as the train heaves from side to side.

The insurance agent / park ranger / cowboy recommends the steak (he orders his rare), and the French guys follow his lead. I peer over their shoulders toward the kitchenette, trying to imagine the remote possibility that they might be able to effectively grill a steak back there, and order the roast chicken instead. But when Mary brings our meals out, my dinner companions' steaks are nicely pink on the inside, and topped with a dark wine sauce that looks pretty good.

"So tomorrow, you'll want to get to the observation car early," the cowboy tells us. "Fills up real fast, comin' out of Denver."

"The views—they are nice?" asks the blond.

Cowboy nods, his mouth full of steak.

"Have you done this route before?" I ask, when he's finished chewing.

"I've done every route," he says, wiping his mouth. "The long ones, anyway. I'm working on the shorter ones. The Zephyr beats them all."

So the cowboy is a real train buff. I wonder what Mom would want me to ask. Would she want to know about the stretches with the best scenery? Or about the conversations he's had like this one, over meals with strangers?

Our drinks shudder in their plastic cups, like we're in the middle of an earthquake.

"Why do you ride so many trains?" I ask finally.

"Why not?" He considers for a moment while he works a toothpick around in his mouth. Then he looks at me. "Nobody talks on airplanes."

The last time I was on an airplane, I was eleven. My parents sent me to visit Gram in London over April vacation, and I was mad because I had to miss four dance classes. "Don't talk to anyone who doesn't work for British Airways," Dad told me when he handed me over to a flight attendant with a smile straight out of a Crest Whitestrips ad. On the plane, I put my headphones on, turned on a movie, and didn't speak to anyone until we landed at Heathrow.

But the cowboy is right—here, it feels somehow natural for the four of us to be chatting, like the train has cracked something open between us. I wouldn't normally predict that an old-school-American-rail-buff cowboy and a hipster gay couple from Paris would find themselves making cheery dinner conversation, but here we are, upending all my expectations. Mom would love this.

"Knock, knock," Jay says, peering his head into the open door frame of my roomette around ten o'clock. "Ready for me to make up your bunk?"

"Oh, you don't have to," I say, hopping off the seat and standing awkwardly in the tiny space. It feels weird to be served like this. How hard can it be to make the bed?

As if he can see what I'm thinking, Jay smiles and shakes his head. "It's trickier than you think. Trust me. Let me do it. I have nothing to do otherwise."

"Somehow I don't believe that," I say, but I let him do it anyway. We trade places—there isn't enough room for both of us to stand in the compartment while he's pulling the cushions aside and popping the two seats down into a flat position. I watch him pull the thin mattress, already made up with sheets and a blanket, from its storage spot on the top bunk. Jay lays the mattress down across the flattened seat cushions and steps aside.

"All set!" he says, revealing a perfectly cozy single bed. He steps back out into the corridor. "Have a very good night, Rose."

Tucked into my tight bunk, with pitch-black flatlands whizzing by out the window, I send Caleb a text. "Crossed the Mississippi, ate dinner with strangers, saw a crapload of cornfields. This is a big-ass country."

I open my laptop and start *Strangers on a Train*, the Hitchcock classic. I downloaded all the train-themed movies I could think of before I left.

Caleb writes back as the opening credits are starting. "Duh. Big-ass country. Meet any crazy people yet?"

"A few," I reply. "Apparently cross-country train rides are the thing to do for singles over sixty. Remind me of that if I miraculously turn out to be a healthy old person."

"Healthy, yeah," he writes back. "Single? Doubtful." Plus a winking smiley face.

I put the phone down on the edge of the mattress and tug the thin blanket closer around my chin. It's like tucking in under a paper towel, but I feel pretty warm anyway.

Twenty-one

THE OBSERVATION CAR "DOES WHAT IT SAYS ON THE TIN," as my grandmother would say. The windows are huge, rising up to the ceiling on both sides of the car and arching over our heads to meet almost in the middle. There are swiveling blue seats, singles and doubles, facing the windows. The whole car is full of the light that pours in from every direction.

Outside Denver, a little before nine a.m., we chug along through the foothills of the Rockies, slow-rolling brown hills dotted with trees. The mountains come into view in the distance, tall and snow-peaked. As we ascend farther, the observation car jams with passengers, all straining to take pictures out the right-hand side of the train, which faces out toward the mountain range. Not knowing any better, I'd grabbed a seat on the left, which now hugs the mountain, so mostly all I can see is jagged rock faces practically pressing against the window, blocking the sky. It's not the best view, but it's still awesome, in the literal sense of the word. Full of awe.

The landscape that rolls by out the window over the next few hours tells a thousand stories. In contrast to the Rockies and the canyons that follow them—so beautiful they look almost fake—there are also stretches that look unreal to me in other ways. Or maybe too real. One town we pass through has no cars or people in sight, just a whole stretch of boarded-up storefronts. In another, I spot a shop with a sign out front that reads simply "GUNS" in neon pink spray paint.

I've never been to one of those wildlife parks where you stay in a jeep and travel along a track while giraffes and zebras wander by, even though you're in New Jersey or wherever. I always thought that seemed like a strange thing. But suddenly I feel a little bit like that's what I'm doing—passing through a world that's completely unfamiliar, viewing it from the outside in. It shouldn't be surprising, I know. I mean, it's not like I expected everywhere in the country to look like Boston. But the contrast is more striking than I expected it to be: All this land, so much open space between houses, towns that aren't bursting at the seams. And no water, anywhere. I can't fathom growing up without the ocean.

By late afternoon, the landscape looks pretty different than it did this morning—flatter and sandier, the mountains farther in the distance. Maybe we've crossed the line into Utah now— state lines don't mean anything from the Zephyr, which has no way of marking them. I think of Caleb, telling me not to hop off and set up shop in Salt Lake City. He was kidding, but it's beautiful here. I can see the appeal.

As we speed through a junction, I hear the Zephyr's whistle blow. Two little boys with one bicycle between them are playing in the street by the railroad crossing. One rides the bike in circles, yelling something over his shoulder at his brother, or friend—they look alike, white kids with buzz cuts. The one relegated to traveling by foot climbs on top of the railroad crossing and straddles it, one leg on either side.

For a split second, it looks like he wants to hop the barrier and run toward us. I take in a sharp breath and am almost out of my seat—not that I could do anything to stop him, of course—but then he doesn't. He just straddles the barrier, swinging his skinny legs and bare feet, and waves at us.

I check my phone for texts, but the service is in and out and I can't get anything. Watching the little boys, I feel suddenly, urgently alone. Even with all these people to talk to, it's strange without Lena or Caleb, or my family, to share the bizarre world-within-a-world experience of the Zephyr. It makes me feel like none of it is real. Maybe that's why I keep telling little lies—my grandparents are picking me up in San Francisco; the audition is no big deal. If I wanted, I could be someone else entirely on the Zephyr. It's like living in my mother's mind, where nothing is as you thought it was.

At seven, I dine with an older man with a salt-and-pepper beard, wearing a blue-and-white checked button-down and a big knit cap covering his hair. He doesn't say much, but when he does speak, he introduces himself as Carl, and I pick up a slight Caribbean accent. Our other companion is Kathy, a woman in her sixties with a decidedly upstate New York accent, who talks compulsively about the various medical events her family members have suffered through in recent years. Her husband self-diagnosed a kidney stone on a drive from Toledo to Albany, she tells us, causing them to pull off the road into a hospital in Cleveland where (after waiting twelve hours to see a doctor) he was diagnosed with not only a kidney stone, but also a massive pancreatic tumor. Her sister has recently had a corneal transplant. Kathy herself has suffered from vertigo and various kinds of panic attacks, which are partly to blame for why she now rides the train: she developed an acute fear of flying after her husband was bumped, unbeknownst to her, from a flight that ended up crashing. She was at home with the kids, watching them run through the sprinkler, when she heard the news: the flight she thought her husband was on had gone down in a field in the middle of New York State. There were no survivors.

Kathy's been talking for about fifteen minutes nonstop. "I still can't comprehend life without him," she says, now referring to her father, who's recently died. "He served in World War Two. He was just a wonderful man . . ." She pauses and wrestles with a Paul Newman blue cheese salad dressing packet.

"You know, he had triple-bypass surgery when he was seventy-nine years old and even that didn't stop him." Kathy shakes her head. "When he was eighty-five, he told his doctor that his only complaint about his meds was that he was having trouble getting in and out of the canoe by himself. Can you imagine? The canoe!"

"The meds affected his movement?" I interrupt.

"No, no, not the meds!" She smiles at me, like I'm a kid who doesn't know a thing about these so-called "meds" of which she speaks. Of this "illness" thing.

"No, the disease. He had Parkinson's. It was the disease that affected his movement, and the meds were supposed to help. But he still struggled with the canoe—which was a joke, of course, I mean, most Parkinson's patients his age shouldn't have been walking, let alone camping."

I know about Parkinson's. It's not so far from Huntington's—a brain disorder that affects motor skills. It's degenerative, ugly. Not as ugly, but ugly.

Kathy is still stabbing at her salad dressing packet, unable to wrench the dressing from the plastic. Without saying anything, Carl takes the packet gently from her hands and tears it open himself. He passes it back to her in silence.

She goes on (and on, and on). Her father's tremors kept getting worse, eventually giving way to dementia that turned him into someone unknown to her. Parkinson's doesn't always end in dementia, she tells me (though I already knew that); her father was just particularly unlucky.

She's making very little headway on her steak—so little, in fact, that I wonder if I'm ever going to be released from this meal. Carl gives me an apologetic smile, finally, then drops a few dollars' tip on the table and excuses himself.

"Don't let me keep you here," says Kathy, who is sitting on the aisle side of our booth, trapping me. But even though she's offered me an out, I can't quite bring myself to take it.

Nearly an hour later, Kathy finally finishes her steak and her story. I make my way back to the roomette and find Jay to make my bed up, even though it's barely nine o'clock. Under the thin blanket, I pull my phone out again and turn it on and off, hoping for a signal. Finally I get one—weak, but there—and dial home. Dad answers, confused.

"Yeah?"

"Dad?"

"Rose?"

"What time is it there?" I don't even know what time zone we're in.

I hear Dad rustling on the other end, hunting for his cell phone to check the time. "Quarter to eleven."

So we're still in mountain time. "You're already sleeping?" I picture them in the dark, in bed. Nothing wakes Mom; she probably didn't even hear the phone.

"We're old, remember. What's happening? Are you okay?"

I want to tell Dad that I'm fine, great, that I'm having so much fun. But that seems too straightforward to be the truth. "Can I talk to Mom?"

"She's sleeping, Ro."

"I know, but—I need to talk to her."

Dad sighs, and then I hear him whispering in the dark. "Ellen. Ellen. Rosie's on the phone."

"Rose?" Mom's groggy voice is even more slurred than her awake voice. "Wwwhere are you?"

"I'm on the Zephyr, Mom. The train. I'm in my sleeper compartment on the train."

"The train," she says, almost dreamily. "Hhhhow is it?"

"It's—it's just like you said it would be."

"Mmmm. Wwwhat did I sssay?"

We're passing through pure blackness, except for the stars. I lie back on the flat pillow so I can see as much sky as possible. "You said it would be different than anything I've ever done, or seen. You said planes give you a bird's-eye view, but trains give you a people's-eye view. That's exactly what it's like."

For a moment, like the tiny pinprick of Derek-the-man-nurse's needle, it stings that Mom isn't here to see this journey she read about and dreamed about for all those years. I said it's just like she described it, but the truth is that it's even more than that.

She doesn't respond. "Mom?" I say after a moment of silence. There's more rustling.

"Sorry, Ro. I think she fell asleep," Dad says. "What were you saying?"

"Nothing. It's okay. I'll call you guys from San Francisco."

"Okay. Love you. Be safe. Don't talk to strangers."

I laugh. "Dad, strangers are all I've got right now."

"Oh, right. I guess that's true. Well, you know what I mean. Be smart."

By the time I put the phone down next to my head, I'm almost asleep.

Twenty-two

I WAKE UP ANTSY, BOTH READY TO GET TO SAN FRANCISCO and get the audition over with and also anxious about leaving the Zephyr. Like somehow I've been cocooned here and now I'm not sure I can function in the real world anymore—Stockholm syndrome with a train instead of a kidnapper.

By early afternoon, we're somewhere outside the "biggest little city in the world" (that would be Reno, Nevada) when Jay comes through the observation car and pauses by my seat to say hello.

"This is the route of the original Transcontinental Railroad, you know," he says, nodding out the window. "We'll follow this into California."

When I was little, Mom told me the history of the railroads, about all those men—Chinese immigrants, most of them—who laid the tracks with their bare hands, piece by piece. A few miles could take years. They died under the weight of falling rocks, in snowstorms and landslides. Some of them probably died right around here.

"That's good train trivia," I say.

Jay strokes his hand over his smooth beard. "Indeed. It's rather extraordinary, isn't it?"

I watch while he gathers an empty water bottle, a Pepsi can, and a plastic cup with melting ice from one of the side tables.

"Do you ever get bored of riding this same route?" I ask. "Or do they switch you around, so you work on different trains?"

"We switch periodically. But I'd never get bored of riding the Zephyr. Not everyone gets paid to look at views like this all day long."

"Looking at those views while picking up other people's trash, though."

Jay holds up his handful of junk. "Some people do seem to have a hard time moving their trash from table to bin. It's a difficult concept, right?"

"Very. It's really too much to expect of the average person."

Jay chuckles as he crosses the observation car and tosses out the trash. "The mountain views remind me of home, so I'm willing to put up with some mild annoyances."

"Where's home?" I take it he doesn't mean Chicago.

"Home-home is Shimla. You know it?"

I shake my head.

"It's a city in northern India, up in the mountains." He points out the window. "These aren't exactly the Himalayas, but they'll suffice."

"Why'd you move here, then? Not to work for Amtrak, I'm guessing."

He laughs suddenly, one big, loud boom, and reminds me of Caleb for an instant. "Not exactly, no. I fell for an American girl. Just my luck, right? But what are you going to do."

"Try to fall in love closer to home?" I suggest, smiling so he'll know I'm kidding.

"You sound like my sister." Jay shakes his head, bemused, I think. "Yes, that's definitely considered a rule to live by in my family, and it probably would've been easier. But you know what they say about rules," he says, shrugging. "Anyway, instead I ended up here, riding Amtrak back and forth and seeing my wife every eight days or so, and it's a decent life. I wouldn't call it exactly a *normal* life, maybe normal-ish. But that's not too bad, all things considered."

"No, I guess that's not too bad." All things considered. "Do you have kids?"

His eyes shift to the window for a moment, flicking from left to right as they follow the passing scenery. "No kids." The way he says it, it sounds like a sad secret, an admission, not a choice. "My wife thinks this train-riding lifestyle is not conducive to fatherhood."

Lots of things aren't perfectly conducive to parenthood, and people do it anyway. But I don't say that.

"Maybe one day," Jay says, turning briskly back to me. "Well. I'll let you get on with the window-gazing." He passes back through to the dining car.

Normal-ish. Maybe he's right, and that's the best any of us can hope for.

An hour or so later, the observation car fills up again as we climb the Sierra Nevadas to Donner Lake. A guide from the California Historical Society hopped on board when we hit Truckee, and he's been giving a spirited history of the American rail ever since. Apparently some of this route is still impassable by car. Donner Lake itself looks like a huge, round oil spill in the middle of heavy woods, so still and shiny you can see the pine trees reflected in its surface. And just beyond that is the stretch known as the Donner Pass, where those people ended up eating each other in the 1840s. I snap a picture on my cell phone and text it to Lena and Caleb as soon as I have a few bars of cell service.

"The Donners were here. Should I be worried that my seat-mate looks hungry?"

Lena writes back right away: "Nah. You're too bony to make a good snack."

A few minutes later, Caleb responds too: "Yes. Watch your back. Meet any more crazies?"

Two days ago that's exactly how I thought of these people. Because who rides a train across the country unless you're a little nuts? Look at Mom and me, after all. "Nuts" barely cracks the surface. But they don't feel that way to me anymore. I can't put my finger on what's changed.

"I actually don't think they're that crazy," I write back. "They're just people with their own stuff."

Maybe that's what it is. They just have their own stuff, and it's not any more or less crazy than mine, and we're all doing what we can. Without waiting for a reply, I write to him again. "There's a lot of stuff in the world."

Caleb doesn't respond for a while. Then finally, my phone buzzes. "So there is, HD. So there is."

I slouch down and rest my head against the back of the seat. We're winding our way up the mountain through a twisted stretch of track. The Zephyr feels like it could almost careen over the edge. A woman and her young daughter—seven, maybe—slide into the seats next to me and lean toward the window. I haven't seen them on the train before. The woman takes her cell phone out.

"Excuse me, do you mind taking a picture of us?" She smiles at me. "Sorry to interrupt you."

"Oh, you're not. I mean, I'm just sitting here." The little girl presses her cheek into her mother's side. I snap a few shots in a row.

"Those are perfect," the woman says, taking a look. "I appreciate it. Want me to take one of you?"

I hadn't thought to put myself in any of the many pictures I've taken so far, but I guess it would be good to have some evidence that I was actually present on this journey. For posterity.

"Might as well. Thanks."

She takes my phone and steps back into the aisle so she can get some of the scenery behind me. "Lovely," she says. "Send that one to your mom. We like to see things like that."

I wave to the little girl as the two of them head off in the other direction, toward coach. Then I open my photo album and look at the picture. The woman's right, actually. Mom will like this one for her collection. You get a nice glimpse of the observation car itself, and the mountains are in view through the window behind me. And I look different—tired from two nights of train-sleeping, maybe. Or maybe it's that I just feel different, like the Zephyr has changed me.

Twenty-three

THE DRESSING ROOM I'VE BEEN ASSIGNED TO AT THE
Pacific Coast College of the Arts is strewn from top to bottom
with dance bags, leg warmers, spare shoes, makeup kits, sweatshirts, bobby pins, hairbrushes, and water bottles, not to mention the occasional pack of cigarettes and protein bar (a complete
meal for many of these girls, I suspect). The room is packed
with dancers, all elbowing for enough room in the mirror to fix
their makeup and tuck stray hairs into their buns. They all look
familiar: they're ballet dancers. Tall (all taller than I am), thin,
flat-chested, and generally pointy, physically and in demeanor.
There's not a lot of camaraderie in the dressing room, let's put
it that way. I guess it's no surprise—we all know that there are
about twenty girls auditioning today for each place in the scholarship program.

We're all dressed identically, which is a tried-and-true trick
of the ballet world: individualism, any kind of standing out,
isn't exactly prized. Every girl here is wearing a sleeveless black
leotard, pale pink tights, and a number pinned to her chest. Our
shoes are invariably busted—deliberately so, of course; balleri-
nas are known for taking brand-new shoes and beating the hell
out of them before we even put them on.

Mom taught me how to break mine in when I first went en pointe at twelve. "Give it a few good whacks, Rose," she'd said. "Go ahead." The shoes were so perfect, so beautiful in their pink satin—I'd been waiting for them for years. I couldn't imagine deliberately breaking these exquisite, expensive things. But Mom said all dancers do it, and I knew she was right—I'd seen the older girls break theirs in at the studio often enough.

"Go on, whack 'em."

After I'd hit each shoe several times against a cinder block in the backyard, Mom showed me how to use pliers to remove the little nail in the heel—the tack—so that the board along the sole of the shoe would bend more easily. We trimmed the board itself, too, to fit my foot better. Then there was glue to add to the inside of the toe block, and pink ribbons to be sewn on.

"Dental floss," Mom said. "It's stronger than thread."

Now I do it without thinking, with every new pair of pointe shoes. But back then it was like being initiated into a secret world of knowledge.

The girls surrounding me in the dressing room all speak the same language, follow the same rituals, but I feel uneasy around them anyway. This morning, too early to be awake, I did most of my makeup in the shared bathroom of the PCCA dorm where the admissions committee put us up last night, and I'd averted my eyes from several girls who wandered around buck naked, all ribs and collarbones and flat chests. It was almost alarming. I've never thought much about having a "ballet body"—although I guess I have one, minus the height. But these girls looked skinnier than any of my classmates at NEYB, and something about all those bones on display made me queasy.

Now, in the dressing room, I try not to focus on their bodies or their height or anything but my own reflection in the mirror. By some minor miracle, I manage to find myself a corner of the room where I can hole up for a moment and take a few deep breaths while I sew myself into my shoes. I want to be entirely focused on the task ahead of me, but I can't quite clear my head of a jumble of thoughts that are careening around in there. I'm still on the Zephyr in my mind, and I need to get back to reality.

Exhaling deeply, I redirect my focus back to the room. Across the room, I spot a redhead who smiled at me earlier, almost clandestinely, like she knew it wasn't really normal to make friends at these things. Most likely it was because she recognized me as another slight underdog—her red hair, my inadequate height, even those tiny things make us stand out from the crowd, put us at that much of a disadvantage.

An ageless woman with a tight, gray ponytail and plastic glasses pushed up on top of her head swings the door open and announces that it's time for us to head to the studios. Grabbing my water bottle and checking myself one last time in the mirror, I follow the crowd out and down the chilly hallway.

A long table is set up at the front of the room, strewn with papers and discarded numbers and coffee cups. A handful of ballet-ish–looking adults—a few women who have the slightly leathery, sunken-chested look of former dancers, and a short, ponytailed man in jeans too tight for his age—are gathered around the table, chatting in low voices and jotting notes in pencil on their clipboards.

The ageless woman directs us to the barres around the room. We start the audition with a standard class, led by one of the former prima ballerina types. Then she demonstrates a quick combination—complex, but not overly long—and splits us into three groups. I'm relieved not to be called in the first one. While the unlucky eight make their way to the center and jostle for the best places, the rest of us shuffle to the sides of the room, grabbing sips of water while we can. It's clear right away who's with it and who isn't: there's the one who trips up the double *pirouette* and curses under her breath, and another who adds an extra flourish at the end, which is met with a disapproving glance from the instructor. There are a handful of girls who stand out. They're Georgias: not a hair out of place from their buns, nothing distracting them, flawless technique.

There's something else about those girls, too, and about a lot of the girls in this room. It's obvious on every inch of their bodies how badly they want this. They breathe ballet. They're built for this world. I miss Lena, all of a sudden.

I mark out the combination with the second group as they go. I think I have it, but there's a section in the middle that's quick and I wish we'd had one more opportunity to practice it with the instructor before being left on our own. My group is called last. I find a spot toward the front, but not right front and center, which is fine by me. The pianist starts in, and I spot my reflection opposite and focus solely on that, trying to ignore the other girls around me and particularly the judges sitting at the table between us and the mirror.

The combination goes relatively smoothly, I think, although I have to think a little harder than I'd like to in the middle section. When we're done, they take a few minutes to chat silently and then call out the numbers of the girls who, as they put it, "have done enough for today." Done enough to get themselves cut, in other words.

But my number's not among them, and with the group thinned out to about half of our original, we're taught a much longer and more complicated combination, with series of inward and outward *pirouettes*, and a trio of *fouettés* with an *attitude* turn thrown in the middle. Scoping out the room, I notice that the redhead is gone.

The prima ballerina leading the audition gives us a two-minute break before the first group goes, and I take a long swig of water and wipe my forehead with the back of my hand. Our scheduled time slot should be finished in twenty minutes—the next pack of girls, more of us in the same black leotards—are probably already warming up in the hallway. Twenty more minutes and this will be done. At least then I'll know one way or the other if San Francisco is even an option for next year. Once I know my test results, too, I figure the answer to my life will magically dawn on me, like the result of some fancy algorithm of possible outcomes.

I roll my neck around to the front a few times, and then to the back, trying to forcibly push all thoughts out of my head to get through this last twenty minutes and those complicated turns.

There's nowhere to hide, this time: each group is small enough that there is no front or back row. I choose a spot toward the center. I can feel the judges' eyes on me, so I close mine. In the darkness behind my lids, I'm alone in the room, just me and the music and the floor under me. I might as well be in Studio D at home, not dancing for anyone other than myself—not the audience, not the judges, not even Caleb. I count in my head as the music starts, and then I give in to it, and nothing else matters. And then I'm soaring.

When we finish and I deliver myself back into the real world, I know I've killed it. The judges whisper to each other, glancing from one of us to the next, and jot some notes. I see the prima eyeing me, nodding, but I don't need anyone to tell me that it's gone well. I know it has. This is how I expected my last show at NEYB to feel—like everything I've been working toward for all those years has finally come together. It feels complete.

They don't make another cut that afternoon, just let us go after the second combo, with a promise to "be in touch soon." In the dressing room, I turn my back to the room and slip my bra and T-shirt on as quickly as I can. While I throw my stuff in my dance bag, I eavesdrop on the girls next to me, both willowy brunettes, five or six inches taller than me apiece.

"I heard Galina is retiring this year. Or they're pushing her out, who knows," one of the girls says, clipped and low. Galina Kadirova is one of the BPC's star principal dancers.

"Well, she's been injured, like, three times this year," the other replies.

The tone is familiar—the almost hopeful speculation of someone else's downfall. It's like Georgia, sometimes, looking down her nose as another girl rolls an ankle in rehearsal or puts on a few pounds. It makes my stomach turn.

I slip out of the dressing room without making eye contact with anyone, and retrace my steps back toward the lobby. The PCCA rehearsal center is all floor-to-ceiling windows and long corridors with shiny marble floors that even my flats click loudly against. Huge black-and-white prints of BPC dancers punctuate the walls, pressed between panes of thick glass. Students float by, invariably dressed in rehearsal clothes—beat-up leotards, warm-up shorts over their tights, leg warmers. They all have the ballet walk, even the guys: feet turned out, posture like they have wires running through their spines.

I should want to be one of them. I should feel like these are my people. That's what I expected to feel. But I don't. Instead, the black box at Cunningham College comes rushing back to me, full of that feeling of shared love for dance that somehow managed to be coupled with . . . fun, abandon. There was an energy there, a sense of boundless passion, that I can't grasp here.

Outside in the cool, bright sun, I dig my phone out of my bag and find a text from Caleb, full of question marks. I can only tell him what my gut says about the audition: nailed it.

What I don't tell him is the other piece of my gut reaction. That nailing it, the rush of flying above the crowd and dancing my best when it really mattered, might be enough. The rest of this might not be for me. Not anymore.

Twenty-four

JUST A FEW HOURS AFTER THE AUDITION FINISHES, I'M ON my way home, by air this time, on a red-eye. From the window of the 767, I watch the jagged topography of the West stretch out beneath us as we pass through the setting sun. I have the sense that now, having crossed from east to west on the ground like a pioneer—minus the covered wagon—it's all my land. I feel like I know it well, this big old country. That children's song "This Land Is Your Land" floats through my brain and gets lodged there.

Somewhere down there, probably in the midst of some cornfields, the Zephyr is tracing its way back toward Chicago. I feel a pang of something, almost homesickness, for the long, narrow corridors with their shiny silver doors on both sides. I thought I'd get to PCCA and feel like I'd found a new home. I certainly did not expect to feel like that about a *train*. But now I miss dinners with strangers. I miss my roomette. I don't know how you can be homesick for a place where you lived for two days—but that's what it is.

Already, my memories of the hilly streets of San Francisco, the echoey halls of PCCA, and even the audition itself are fading. It's like when you wake up from a dream and at first it's vivid in your mind but then by the afternoon, it's gone. But the Zephyr is real. If I close my eyes, I can practically feel the movement of the train. I wish I could keep riding, back and forth through the flatlands and the mountains, and let everything else fade.

We're halfway home, the plane still and dark except for the occasional reading light marking the other sleepless passengers, when I remember that "This Land Is Your Land" isn't actually a children's song—it's a folk song. By Woody Guthrie, the world's most famous Huntington's patient.

Dad seems exhausted when he picks me up at the airport early in the morning. I pile my stuff into the trunk and settle myself in the car next to him. There are dark circles under his eyes and I swear he's even balder than he was four days ago. He leans across the gearshift to give me a kiss on the top of my head.

"So, child, tell me everything. We missed you around here."

"Okay, Dad," I say. "I was only really gone four days, you know."

"Sure, sure. That's what they all say when they grow up and leave their pitiful fathers behind." He's acting normal, cueing up his usual mix of self-deprecating Dad jokes, but there's something about him that seems off. Like he's trying too hard.

"So you had a good time?" Dad says after a few minutes of silent driving.

I think about the Zephyr, the whole country passing by us outside, and all those people with their lives and their stuff, and the audition that might be the final moment of my dance career. "Good time" hardly seems to cover it.

"Yeah. It was good. The audition was . . . It went well."

"Of course it did. And if they don't let you in, you know what I say to that." I do know what he's going to say, but I let him say it anyway because it's his favorite line. "Fuck 'em if they can't take a joke."

Hearing Dad drop an F-bomb makes me well up with affection for him. I actually get a little bit teary for a minute.

"What's up with Mom?" I ask.

It's started raining, almost-ice crystals forming in the raw, April morning air and racing along the windshield. Dad clears his throat. He hesitates. "What? Did something happen?" I say.

He shakes his head, like maybe he's pushing back some tears. "Nothing in particular. Just, you know. It never really sinks in that it's not as bad yet as it's going to be."

I focus on a single ice crystal and watch it trace its way across my window until it disappears where the glass meets the door. It's an old habit, watching the raindrops rush along the car window. I used to pretend they were racing each other, each with some place really important to be. Now I see they're just following a path they can't deviate from. The winners and the losers are predetermined by the angle of the window and the rain and the wind; nothing those raindrops can do will change their fate.

My bedroom is cleaner than I left it—Gram must've vacuumed and picked up. It smells like fresh sheets, and there's a pile of laundry, folded and sitting on my armchair. I have a strange feeling, like I'm somehow different than I was the last time I stood in this room. I climb into bed without even bothering to close the blinds against the morning light.

Who knows how long later, my phone buzzes with a text, waking me. It's almost one already.

Caleb: Home yet?

I write him back quickly: Affirmative. Just woke up.

Caleb: Can I swing by?
Me: Yes please.

Twenty minutes later, I hear a knock at the front door, then Dad's voice. "Caleb! You didn't waste much time, did you?"

Caleb laughs. "Hey, four days without Rose is a long time."

"I'll give you that," Dad says. "Good to see you, come on in. The child is upstairs, of course. I think she might be sleeping."

The stairs creak and then Caleb's in my room, and then my arms. I almost forgot how solid his chest feels against my face when I press my cheek up against it, breathing him in. His shirt smells like Tide, the ocean-fresh kind. Usually when we kiss, he starts and I follow. This time, I lean up toward his face and find his mouth with mine.

"Young people!" Dad yells upstairs, fifteen, maybe twenty minutes later. I really have no idea how much time has passed. Caleb does that to me. "Chinese okay for lunch? We've got a ton of leftovers."

"Great," I whisper. "Because it went so well the last time we all had Chinese leftovers together."

Caleb kisses the tip of my nose. "I think it went well. I got you to kiss me, didn't I? Pretty sure your mom and I were in cahoots about that."

"In cahoots, huh? Okay."

I kiss him back, this time on his eyebrow, which has one crazy strand twisting away from the rest. "Sounds good, Dad!" I call toward the door.

I give them the full play-by-play of the trip over lunch. Mom doesn't seem completely focused on my retelling of where I was, but every time someone nudges her, she acts excited all over again. At least we're not repeating the conversation we had before I left for San Francisco—if you can call it a conversation. Maybe one-sided irrational disease-induced rampage is a more accurate descriptor.

When I get to the audition itself, I struggle to find the right words to describe what happened. "I don't know," I say. "I can't explain it."

"Is that a good thing, or a bad thing?" Caleb asks.

"Good. It felt really good."

"All right!" Dad says. "That's my girl. I'm sure they were all blown away."

"Everyone was really good, Dad. It's a different league than NEYB. Don't get your hopes up."

But I saw the way the judges looked at me, and every fiber of me felt how well it went. Even though the competition is stiff, I know I'll be right in the mix. So maybe I'm really warning Dad about something else.

$$\text{* * *}$$

After lunch, I force Caleb into an intense Scrabble match on my bedroom floor. We kneel opposite each other on the floor with the board between us. I'm crushing him. He's a visual person, as he always reminds me whenever he's losing at Scrabble.

"Prepare to be impressed," I say, adding an *I* and an *S* to the *Q* in "quietly."

"God. You are freakishly good at this." He leans over to survey the board. "Wait. 'Qis' is not a word. No way."

"I swear it is."

"You swear wrong."

"Are you really going to make me go to the dictionary for this?" I ask, sitting up on my knees.

"We're so going to the dictionary."

I'm dead certain that "qis" is Scrabble-eligible—only because I've spent some time perusing all the legit Q-words in the online Scrabble Word Finder—but I let him pull his phone out and check anyway. "You're going to be embarrassed . . ." I say.

"I am rubber and you are glue," he says, waiting for the Internet to give him an answer. "Your words bounce off me and stick to you."

"What are you, ten now?" I toss a tile at him.

"Evil twins' influence," he mutters. "Qis . . ."

His face falls and he puts his phone back in his pocket. "So, never mind, then. What were we saying?"

"Oh come on!" I say. "What'd you find, my friend? Do tell."

"Fine," he grumbles, pulling his phone back out. "But this is truly ridiculous. It says: 'No definition of "Qis" found—it's still

269

good as a Scrabble word, though!'" He looks up at my grinning face. "What does that even mean?"

"It means I'm right and you're wrong," I tease. "Obviously."

"Who knew you could use words that don't even have *definitions* in Scrabble?"

"Um, well, I did." I lean across the tiles and put my face so close to his that our noses practically touch. "So there."

Caleb leans a few centimeters closer. "Well," he says, barely audible, "you are a nerd who studies obscure, definition-less vocabulary for the express purpose of winning Scrabble." His lips brush against mine with every word.

When we pull apart, just by an inch, he holds my face gently in his hands. "Hey," he says.

"Hey."

And suddenly, I can tell where this is going. It's like the Zephyr pulling out of the station, slow and steady but unstoppable.

"I love you, HD."

There it is. Those three words stop everything. They stop the white noise from the street outside and the sound of our hearts beating. Maybe if I don't breathe, if I don't move, I won't have to respond. I want to say it back. I want to be a person who can love back the person who loves me, especially when he is so good.

I can't. This is why I have a rule about this in the first place. It's one thing—one extraordinary thing, apparently, judging from the way it makes my chest want to explode—to be loved by someone else. But to let yourself love them back, to *tell* them that, that's like . . . setting yourself up for loss, right? What if I let myself love him and then he lets me down? What if he changes his mind? I don't think I can love another person who's going to disappear. It's too much.

Instead, I kiss him again. He kisses me back, but even without words I can feel his disappointment.

"I should go," he says, getting up and zipping up his sweatshirt.

I walk him downstairs and stand in the foyer in my socks, the welcome mat prickly under my feet, wanting to get rid of this terrible awkwardness that seems to have materialized out of nowhere.

"Sickle Cell . . ." I say, tugging at his sleeve. "See you tomorrow?"

"I have some stuff to do for my dad, but maybe. Give me a call." He kisses me one more time, just lightly on the cheek. Then he goes, leaving me with the moments before tying themselves in knots in my stomach.

Trying to shrug it off, I import all 386 new photos from my phone to my laptop and find Mom. She's more than happy to sit at the dining room table and watch as I scroll through them, giving the best explanation I can of each one (all the various rock formations start to blur together—I wish I'd taken notes).

Midway through the pictures of what I think is Utah and the salt flats, she closes her eyes, breathing in sharply through her nose.

"You all right?"

She holds up one hand to stop me from saying anything more. Then after a moment, she opens her eyes again. "Wish I could see it . . . myself." She reaches out and tries to smooth my hair with an unsteady hand. "Okay. More."

"There's like three hundred and forty more to go. We can skip to the highlights if you want."

"No."

So we paw through picture after picture, even the ones that mostly look the same. I try to make up interesting details to help the narration. "When I took this one, I was talking to the French couple," or "This is when I was eating lunch—the veggie burger was shockingly good!"

It feels good, hanging out with Mom—sometimes, she still seems like the parent in the equation, and it's like a balm on everything else going through my brain right now. Once we've finished going through the pictures, I turn on the TV and find us some *House Hunters International.* In the current episode, a young, hip American woman has moved to Paris to be with her French boyfriend, and now they're looking for an apartment in the eleventh *arrondissement,* which apparently used to be run-down and precisely for that reason is now the place where all the young, hip people want to move.

It seems like Mom's body is more committed to a project of constant motion than it was less than a week ago. Or maybe a few days away just makes it that much more obvious to me. The skin on the pads of her thumb and forefinger is raw from the way she constantly rubs them over each other. Her limbs, her head, everything looks like it's on vibrate all the time, with the mild vibrations punctuated by more violent movements. I know this is the chorea advancing—Dr. Howard has been honest with us about how this would happen—but it doesn't look anything like a dance. That part was a lie.

Grunting at the television, Mom shakes her head with great effort (the irony being, of course, that her head shakes on its own with no effort at all when she doesn't want it to). "It's always the ssssame," she says. "Some girl gives up her life . . . for a man."

It's a fair point, really. By now we've seen countless episodes of this show that involve American women moving overseas to be with their foreign boyfriends/husbands. And somehow the boyfriends/husbands always seem to get what they want in a house, while the women are inevitably like, "Oh, I'd really like to be near the city because this is my first time living abroad, but okay, Francois/Alejandro/Baz, you're probably right that we'll get more for our money in this run-down suburb where you can easily commute to work in your Smart car/motorbike/Segway and I'll be stuck forty minutes by public transport from the city center." You can sort of see the unraveling of their relationships before it even happens.

Sure enough, the second house the realtor shows this particular young woman and her particular French boyfriend is a bigger, cheaper place in the suburbs, and I don't have to watch the next twenty minutes to know how it's going to end.

"Rose. Listen," Mom says over a commercial. "Don't ever give up your life for a man."

"Okay, Mom." If only she knew what just happened with Caleb. Throwing myself too far, too fast into a relationship probably needn't be at the top of her list of worries for me.

"Or for me," she goes on. "I don't want you to put your life on hold, for me."

I put my hands over hers on the couch. They stop moving, fluttering gently to a halt like a butterfly you've cupped in your hands. "I won't, Mom. Really."

She doesn't say anything else, and we turn back to the show.

"Ma," I say when the episode ends (spoiler alert: they take the place in the 'burbs), "you know we'll take care of you at home, right? No matter what?" Dr. Howard has warned us that this is almost impossible, but I'm sure Dad has said it to her a thousand times anyway. I don't know if I ever have.

"Babe," she says, her head quivering continuously, "one day ssssoon, I won't even . . . be myself."

My face gets hot and a lump forms in the back of my throat, solid and painful. I don't say anything. I can't.

Mom shakes her head determinedly, forcing it to move the way she wants it to for once, instead of its own way. "I want you to live better."

With that, she takes my hand and pushes herself up off the couch with a grunt. I help her into her chair, and she buzzes off toward the kitchen, leaving me alone in the living room with her cryptic message and an ensuing marathon of *Love It or List It*.

Twenty-five

On Monday morning, when I'd like to be catching up on my sleep—school's out for some kind of professional development day—Dad bangs loudly on my door. "Rose, I need a favor!" he says, busting straight in, per usual.

"What the—Dad, what?" I come to, trying to orient myself to the day and time. I've been home from San Francisco for two days, and my body is basically clueless as to the time zone. When I find my cell phone, I see that it's barely eight o'clock.

"Sorry to wake you. I'm late for work. Gram has a headache and wants to stay in bed and your mother has an appointment for physio at ten. I need you to take her. Sorry, babe."

I groan and force my eyes all the way open. "Okay. Fine."

"You're the best, love you, ten o'clock, don't forget, bye!" He closes the door behind him.

An hour and ten minutes later, I've got Mom situated in the car, her wheelchair folded up in the back, and we're headed to Mass General, to her physical therapist's office.

"Thanks for taking me. It's your day off." I can tell it pains her to need me like this—to have to rely on her only child when I should still be able to rely on her.

"It's okay. I don't have any plans today." That's not totally true—I was hoping to see Caleb, but we haven't talked since the other night. I'm not sure he wants to see me.

"Good. I don't want to be a bother."

"Okay, Mom. You're not." I don't know why it exasperates me when she says stuff like that. I know she's being genuine, but for some reason it irks me. I don't like the idea of her being some saintly sick person. It doesn't feel like Mom, the saintly or the sick.

"What do you do in physio, anyway?" I ask her, to head off any more maudlin comments.

"Bullshit. Pick things up. Put them down."

I laugh and she joins me. Even though her speech is slurred now, her laugh hasn't changed that much.

"Hey!" She jabs my right arm. "Let's play hooky."

"From physio? No way. Dad'll kill me."

"Come on! Don't be a spoilsport."

I know that Dad *will* kill me. But I also know that it won't kill Mom to miss a physio appointment. One might ask what is the point of them, period. They're not actually making her better. I suppose they make Dad feel like we're doing something other than watching her deteriorate.

"Where would we go instead?"

Mom doesn't say anything for a minute. She looks like she's concentrating really hard.

"The theater?" she says finally. "The ballet?"

I shake my head. "It's Monday. No shows. Anyway no matinees, for sure."

"Oh right." She pauses again. I'm mulling it over too. Where could Mom and I go, where we could have fun? Fun like we used to have. Not shopping—I can't remember ever enjoying shopping with Mom. Something special and unusual that only she and I would want to do together. Then I remember the signs they've got plastered all over the subway stations.

"Hey, Mom—we could take the train to Maine."

That's what the signs say—"Take the Train to Maine." They're ads for the Downeaster, Amtrak's service from Boston to Brunswick. There's a picture of a train skimming a coastline, a couple seagulls, a lighthouse in the distance.

Mom grins at me, and in that moment, smiling at me across the car, her eyes asking for trouble, she doesn't even look sick.

Which is how we find ourselves at North Station twenty minutes later, stashing the car in an overpriced, all-day parking lot and buying two round-trip tickets on the next train to Portland, which departs at eleven thirty-five.

The Amtrak agent situates us at one end of the car, where there's extra space to accommodate Mom's chair. But she doesn't actually want to sit in the wheelchair—"looking like a damn invalid"—so after the agent secures the chair to the wall and disappears with a sympathetic, uncomfortable smile, she gets out and crosses to the empty blue seat beside me.

"Should we tell Dad now, or later?" I ask as the train pulls slowly out of the station. No turning back now—we're on our way.

Mom laughs. "Later. Definitely. Later."

* * *

The Downeaster travels north out of Boston, through the ugly backsides of industrial Massachusetts mill towns. The non-pine trees—the deciduous ones, I think, the word coming back to me from eighth grade—are bare still except for a few early buds. Thirty minutes or so go by with not much to see. I was expecting the train to run along the coast all the way, but we're going through the woods most of the time. Every now and then there's a break in the trees as we pass through a little trailer park.

I glance over at Mom. Her eyes are closed, but I can tell she's not sleeping. She has a little smile on her face, uneven because her muscle control is better on the right than the left.

"What are you smiling about?" I ask. She opens her eyes.

"Foamers."

"Huh?"

"Foamers. I remembered. That's what they call them."

"Who calls who? What are you talking about?" I wonder for a moment if she's confused, thinking of something else, or if maybe I actually did wake her from a dream and she's not sure where she is.

"Rail folk. Foamers. Train fans who fffoam." She gestures to her mouth.

"Like foam at the mouth?"

Mom nods.

"That's what they're called? That's gross."

She smiles and puts a hand over mine, gripping it as forcefully as I think she's capable of.

"Well, I don't get where the water is. I thought this was supposed to be a coastal ride. Scenic," I say.

Mom points awkwardly out the window, toward a rusty smokestack. "That's scenic."

"Yeah. Lovely, Mom."

"*Child.*" She always used to call me "child," just like she used to call Dad "husband." She hasn't done either in a while. "Trains are about ssseeing things ddddifferently. It's not all pretty."

"I know, I know. It's about the journey." I roll my eyes—she's like a broken record, figuratively and kind of literally now, too, so focused on the same things. But then I think of those empty crossroads in the middle of Colorado, with their worn-out motels with half-lit cable TV signs and dust rolling by in the shadow of the mountains, and all the people between here and there and the other side. And I know she's right.

Mom smiles. "See? You learned ssssomething from your old mother."

We sit in silence for a while, watching the North Shore become southern New Hampshire. More pines, more unpleasant scenery. This isn't the Zephyr, that's for sure. But it is a train, and Mom's on it, and I feel like we've done well.

Outside Durham, I lean into Mom's shoulder, like I used to when I was little. I can't distinguish between the movement of the train and the movement of Huntington's rippling through her.

"Hey, Mom? Can I tell you something?"

"You can tell me anything," she says.

"I did something without telling you and Dad." It's like Russian roulette, telling my mother this. If she's angry, she'll tell

Dad. If she isn't, she won't. Who knows which way the day will go.

"Mmm-hmm," she says.

"I took the test for the Huntington's gene."

She twists her body as much as she can to look at me. "Why didn't you tell me?"

"Dad and I had a fight about it, a while ago. I didn't want to repeat that, with him or you. So I just did it. I wanted to know my status before I make any decisions about next year. About school, and dance. And just in general, for my life. I wanted to know."

"You could have told me. You think I'm not sssstill your mother?"

She's still my mother, but not in the talk-through-your-problems, make-you-feel-better kind of way. Not in the protect-you-from-the-ills-of-the-world kind of way. I think I've learned pretty well that no one, not even my mother, has that power.

"I'm telling you now. Will you not tell Dad? Please? I just want to tell him myself."

She stares at me, kind of sad, searching. She must take this personally—how can she not? I'm basically saying, I want to know if I'm going to end up like you before I decide how to live my life. In not so many words.

But then she doesn't say anything else, and after a few minutes I hear a halting snore come from her, and I see that she's fallen asleep. I stare out the window at the depressing views, waiting for the water to show up. Finally, when we're practically to Portland—Old Orchard Beach, Maine, where we used to come in the summers to play miniature golf—I catch a glimpse of the ocean through the pastel motels, not yet open for the season.

"Mom, look," I say, nudging her gently. "Finally, some ocean!"

I can see the kitschy boardwalk, too, where I used to beg my parents to let me play arcade games and eat cotton candy. Mom and I would do skeeball tournaments until I'd have enough of those little tickets to turn in for some stuffed animal that crinkled when you hugged it, like it was filled with newspaper. And there was the Ferris wheel, which rose up so high that all you could see around you was water and sky.

"Mom, you're missing the view." I nudge her again. Then I feel her jerk awake, next to me.

"What the hhhell?" she grunts, way too loud.

"Shhh," I say calmly, trying to bring her back down. I shouldn't have let her fall asleep. Sometimes she gets disoriented when she wakes up.

"Where the hell are we?" she shouts. She slurs less when she's shouting.

The passengers nearby are looking at us with those sort of combined sorry-for-us-but-also-annoyed-but-also-fascinated kind of looks. They're pretending to be concerned, when really they're just enjoying the show of the crazy woman and her poor sucker of a daughter.

"Mom, we're on a train," I say in a low voice. "You love trains. You and I are on the train to Maine. For fun!" I force a smile. "See? Look." I point out the window. As if on cue, a gull comes by, flying low, close to the tracks.

"Why the hell would we do that? Leave me alone! What the fffuck is wrong with you?" She pulls her arm away from mine and pushes herself abruptly out of the seat. Just then, the train shudders to the left, and she stumbles across the aisle, whacking her head or her face—I can't really tell—on the arm rest of the seat across from us. And then she's lying there, in a quivering, jerking pile.

"Dammit," I say, jumping up. "Mom, are you okay? Look at me, Mom." I turn her gently toward me. She has a pretty nasty gash on the side of her face, but she's conscious.

"I'm ffffine. Leave me alone." But she's quieter now, subdued. A man from two rows behind us has jumped up and is hovering over us.

"Is she all right?" I glance up and see that everyone else is peering into the aisle and over the seats in front of them now, watching the excitement.

"You can ask her," I say. The man looks horrified. He turns bright red and trips over his words.

"Sorry, of course—I mean—ma'am, are you okay?"

"Fine, I'm fffine," Mom mutters.

An Amtrak agent comes hustling down the aisle. He has a first aid kit and a walkie-talkie in hand, and he fusses over Mom like all he can think about is the looming lawsuit that happened on his watch.

The train slows to a halt, and I hear passengers murmuring to each other, no doubt griping that they're going to be late getting to the outlets at Freeport or wherever they're going. I can feel their eyes on us, wondering why I'm alone with this obviously sick, insane person. Wondering why we chose their train to get on, their trip to ruin.

The Amtrak agent buzzes around us nervously. Mom's sitting up now, a deep bruise already rising from the corner of her eye all the way down her cheekbone. She'll look like a victim of domestic abuse tomorrow, for sure. I help her back up into her seat and hold a piece of gauze to the gash on her face. The blood seeps through it pretty quickly, much to the Amtrak agent's obvious horror. He has a look on his face like he's never seen blood before. Or maybe it's everything else about Mom that horrifies him, it's hard to tell.

What the fuck is wrong with you? I repeat in my head. The disease's words, not Mom's. But still, what *is* wrong with me, thinking we could take this trip like we were normal?

We're waiting on the tracks for what feels like an hour. They've called an ambulance to come meet us, and the whole car feels like it's getting more and more restless, agitated. My foot's falling asleep under me, and when I stand up to stretch, I see three or four passengers look away quickly.

"Mom, I'm going to get you some water, okay?" She doesn't respond—she's pretty out of it still—but the Amtrak guy gives me a nod, so I make my way down the car.

As I pull a paper cone cup from the dispenser, a woman brushes past, then stops and stares at me. Even though I keep my eyes focused on the water, she doesn't move. Then she leans in close to me, like she knows something I don't.

"That woman shouldn't be out in public like this," she says. "She should be in a home." She shakes her head. "She's a danger to herself and others."

My ears and cheeks prickle with heat. "That woman is my mother. Mind your own damn business." She looks shocked, like how dare I question her on this matter about which she knows nothing at all. She starts to open her mouth to say something else, but I walk away.

Mom has three stitches in the side of her face by the time Dad comes charging through the double doors of the emergency room at Maine Medical Center in Portland. He gives her a quick kiss on the forehead and inspects her face, the bandage, the swelling.

"You okay, babe?"

She nods. "Fine. Just ssstupid."

"You're not stupid. It was an accident. It could happen to anyone on a train." Then he looks from her to me. "What the hell were you thinking, Rose?"

"I don't know—I just . . ." The words get caught around each other in my mouth and nothing real comes out. Tears stream down my cheeks.

"Goddammit, Rose! You didn't think to tell me where you were off to on your little holiday jaunt? What about your mother's physio? She needs her physio."

I wipe the tears from my cheeks. "Oh yeah, she really needs it, Dad. It's clearly having a marked impact on her quality of life."

I storm past my father and out the doors into the parking lot. The air smells like salt. It reminds me that we're in Maine—formerly the site of so many happy moments for our family, until that summer I was twelve, with the stupid ticking stripe. Now Maine seems to be a harbinger of doom. I should remember not to come back here.

I stomp back and forth for a few minutes, trying to regain my balance. Finally, Dad comes outside, pushing Mom in her chair. Without saying anything, he takes me in his arms and kisses the top of my head.

Inexplicably, I burst into tears all over again, out of relief this time.

"Hey, hey," Dad says. "It's all right. I just got freaked out on the drive up here. So your little mother-daughter adventure went awry. Everyone's okay." I sniffle into Dad's coat.

"You should sssee the other guy," Mom adds. Dad and I both turn to her, dumbfounded. I don't think either of us has heard her make a joke in ages.

"All right, then," Dad says. Then he leans over and kisses her on the lips. I can't remember the last time I saw him do that. "Do you ladies mind if we take an automobile home rather than a locomotive?"

Mom sleeps, knocked out with painkillers and stretched across the backseat, all the way back to Boston, and I stare out the window at 95 South as it rushes by.

"Sorry, Dad," I say, after we've listened to a whole segment of talk radio in silence.

"You wanted to do something nice with your mother. I get it."

"It was stupid, though. We could've just gone to the movies or something."

"She could've tripped in a movie theater."

"She took a nap," I explain. "And when she woke up she didn't know where she was. That's why she freaked out and tried to run down the aisle."

Dad doesn't say anything for a minute. Then he nods, slowly. "Yup. Well, that's where she's at now. It is what it is."

And it's only going to get worse.

When we're almost back in Cambridge, Dad calls Dr. Howard and asks if he can see Mom quickly this afternoon. Mom grumbles in protest, but I can tell Dad wants Dr. Howard's reassurance that she's okay. When he drops me off at home on their way to the doctor, Gram comes rushing out of the house, looking frantic.

"She's fine, she's fine," I say.

"And you? All right?" Gram says, grabbing my hand. I shake my head. Am I fine? I don't even know. She pulls me in close. Her breath smells like old tea, but it's somehow comforting.

"Go have a rest, then," Gram says. "I'll go with them to see Dr. H."

Inside, the house is breezy with the first few warm drafts of spring, and it has the fresh smell of the weather warming up. I text Caleb, giving him only the briefest of explanations of the day, leave the front door unlocked behind me, and go upstairs to my bed. It's still light out but I could sleep for days.

Fifteen minutes later, maybe twenty—I've already dozed off—I hear the door.

"HD?" Caleb calls.

"Upstairs!"

Without saying anything, he slips into the bed next to me. I crawl into the nook between his arm and his chest, and he holds me tight in there, no questions asked. Then I roll over onto his chest, and kiss him.

I was half-asleep a minute ago but now I'm fully awake, a rush of adrenaline beating rapid-fire through my whole body. I know immediately that we're going somewhere we haven't been before—and I don't stop to think about it anymore. I tug my shirt over my head quickly and he does the same, then pulls me into his warm, smooth chest and kisses the back of my neck, pushing my hair out of the way. He unhooks my bra.

I don't want to think about loving him or not loving him in this moment. All I want is to disappear into him, to fall into his eyes and mouth and forget the day behind me. We can't possibly get any physically closer than we are right now, but I want more. I wrap my arms and legs around his, until we're as close as we can to becoming one being with eight limbs and two brains, and two hearts beating really, really fast on top of each other. The feeling I've been afraid of all this time, of losing myself in someone else—right now it's all I want.

We've never been completely naked in front of each other, and as we peel off clothing, our eyes and hands roam over each other, figuring things out. I find another scar, a Harry Potter–like lightning bolt, smack in the middle of Caleb's chest. "Stepped on with a soccer cleat, fifth grade," he says when I run my finger over it.

"Are you sure about this?" he asks, pulling my hair out of my face and twisting it around his fingers. "What I said the other day . . . I didn't say it so you'd have sex with me."

I take his glasses off carefully and shake my head. I already know that. And I'm not doing this to make up for not saying it back. Or maybe I am, just a little. I don't care. In this moment, I'm sure.

"Are *you* sure?" I ask.

He nods, then kisses me again.

The actual sex part isn't as easy as I expect it to be. He has a condom, but it turns out that they're easier to unfurl over bananas in "growth ed" class than they are in real life, and we both fumble with it. The sexiness of the moments before disappears into awkwardness. But then we lock eyes again and I don't care if it's awkward. Right here in my bed, with the April sun peeking in like it's keeping our secret, we're safe.

Twenty-six

IT FEELS LIKE TOO MUCH HAPPENED IN THE LAST TWENTY-four hours to be held in one day—the train to Maine with Mom, the accident that landed us in the Portland hospital, Dad freaking out, Caleb coming over. Caleb coming over.

I text him from the bus on my way to school. "Hey. How's you?" But he doesn't respond.

By the end of the day, I'm starting to get genuinely worried. I text him again, then a third time, and I hear nothing. He always has a chance to text me at lunch or during a study hall. My overanxious brain goes into hyperdrive. Car accident on the way home last night? Maybe he was distracted. Or maybe he's regretting the whole thing and wishing it never happened— wishing *we* had never happened, and he's trying to figure out how to tell me.

It's the first really warm spring day of the year, so I tell Lena to meet me on the playing field after school. We lie on the grass in the late afternoon sun.

"Okay, so what's this update?" She pushes her hugely over-size, tortoise-shell sunglasses higher on her nose and rests her head on her bag. "Did you hear from PCCA already?"

When I tell her, she goes from lying down to sitting up straight so fast I barely register her moving.

"I cannot *believe* you didn't call me immediately. This is a big, big deal."

I wish she'd make a little less of a big deal of it, actually. I expected this response from her, of course, but I've been busy trying to downplay the whole thing in my head all day.

"But now he's not texting me back. What do you think that's about?"

Her smile sets into a hard line. "He needs to text you back. He's probably just . . . I don't know. Being a dude about it."

"I guess so," I say. The thing is, Caleb isn't usually inclined to "be a dude" about stuff. At least not since his *Nutcracker* fail. My gut is telling me there's something else going on.

"Well, Caleb's obsessed with you, so you'll hear from him."

"He's not 'obsessed' with me."

"You know what I mean. Anyway, details please. Was it fun?"

I'm just considering what pieces to give Lena, and how, when my phone buzzes with a text.

It's Caleb. "Sorry didn't text sooner. Ella's at Children's, pretty bad."

Of course. I kick myself, once again, for assuming his silence had anything to do with something as small as our relationship. This is the second time Ella's been hospitalized in the six months we've known each other. That seems like a lot for a kid with sickle cell.

"I—um—I have to go."

Lena stares at me blankly. "What do you mean?"

I show her the text. "I should go. To the hospital."

"You don't have to go. He's with his family." Lena shakes her head at me like I've lost my mind. "Do you even know if he wants you there?"

I know what she means, but it still stings. I hop up and dust the grass off my jeans. "I'm going. Sorry to ditch you."

Lena shrugs. "Whatever. It's not like you've never chosen Caleb over me before."

"Come on, Lena." I wait for her to wipe the petulant look off her face. It's not like she's never ditched me for a guy before. And this is for an actual decent reason.

"All right," she says. "Go. I hope she's okay."

"I'll call you later, friend."

"Yeah, yeah."

"Love you, friend."

"Yeah, yeah," she repeats, lying back on the grass again and crossing her arms over her chest.

I grab my bag and hustle across the field toward the street, completely certain that I'm doing the right thing. If I can't tell Caleb how I feel, I can show him.

I wait until I'm already on the Red Line before I text him back. "On my way."

It's my second hospital visit in as many days, and the two places couldn't be more different, as far as hospitals go. The lobby of Children's is almost convincingly disguised as someplace fun. The walls are splashed with bright colors and jungle animals, and there's a huge kinetic sculpture that looks like it belongs in a science museum. I duck into the gift shop, thinking I'll buy something for the girls, and quickly realize that I might as well be shopping at FAO Schwarz. I hunt around the section near the checkout counter, where there are tall plastic bins of small items—Super Balls, figurines, magic wands. There are a lot of kids in this place who could use those wands. But Ella and Nina seem too old for magic—or at least too world-weary for it—so I pick glow-in-the-dark Silly Putty instead, in purple and green.

The hallways are as colorful as the lobby, with bright symbols painted along the walls and on the overhanging signs—a purple moon, a green boat, a blue fish—to help guests navigate the abyss of the hospital complex. Caleb told me to follow the fish, so I do, finding my way up to hematology.

I loop around the floor, trying not to stare too hard into the patient rooms. The place is at once buzzing with a kind of sugarcoated cheerfulness, the nurses bubbly in their purple scrubs and roller-skate sneakers, and also oppressive. It's hard to believe there are enough sick children in the whole world to fill this space, and this is just one wing of one floor.

I can hear Caleb's family before I see them—Ella's room has to be the one with raucous laughter coming from it. Sure enough, when I poke my head around the door, I see the whole slew of them—Valerie and Charles, Ella propped up in the bed and Nina lying next to her on top of the covers, Caleb, and a purple-clad nurse, all cracking up over something. Even here, the Franklins manage to make it look like they're having fun.

Valerie spots me first. "Hello, gorgeous," she says, waving me into the room. "You're so good to come by."

"Hey, ladies." I give the girls each a high five. "How you feeling?" I ask Ella. She shrugs. Ella's completely dwarfed by the hospital bed—you'd think they'd have littler beds here—but otherwise she looks more or less the same as usual.

Caleb tugs me away and gives me a quick kiss, sending his sisters into a fit of giggles.

"All right, all right. Nothing to see here," he says, slipping his hand into mine and pulling me into the hallway. Away from the prying eyes of his family, he gives me a longer, better kiss. It feels different than our old kisses, somehow. "Thanks for coming."

"Obviously," I say. "No thanks required." I dig in my pocket for the Silly Putty. "I come bearing gifts."

"Silly Putty, my favorite! You shouldn't have." He snatches the green plastic egg from my hands and tosses it once in the air.

"Oh, was I supposed to get you one of your own? I didn't realize," I say, grabbing it back. "How's Ella doing?"

Caleb bites his lip. "She's all right. They're strong kids."

"I guess they must be kind of used to this, huh?"

His demeanor shifts, subtly but unmistakably. "Does your mom get used to losing her motor control?"

"Um, *no*."

"Okay. Well, my sisters don't get used to being in chronic pain either. It's not really the kind of thing you get used to, you know." He turns away from me and chuckles to himself, like he can't believe my idiocy.

"I wasn't downplaying it, Caleb. I just meant . . ."

"Forget it. Sorry. I didn't get enough sleep last night." He shakes his hands and face like he's trying to release the tension of the day, but I can tell he's still annoyed. "Anyway. Are you as good at Monopoly as you are at Scrabble?"

"Um, there's not really skill involved in Monopoly, per se. It's a very different ballgame."

"*There's not really skill involved?* Oh man. Clearly, you have never played with the Franklins before."

The six of us play Monopoly for over an hour with the board spread out at the foot of Ella's enormous bed, and Caleb's right—apparently there is skill involved, and it has nothing to do with the skills involved in Scrabble. When I've been wiped clean of cash by a mean hotel-packed stretch owned entirely by Nina, I offer to go down to the cafeteria and retrieve some snacks. As I leave the room, I glance back over my shoulder at them, gathered there around the bed. They're the perfect family, never mind what their genes say.

I return twenty minutes later, carrying as many Sun Chips, chocolate chip cookies, green apples, and bottles of water as I can hold, to a very different scene.

Ella is on her back, writhing on the flattened bed and crying in pain while a nurse fills one of her intravenous lines with something that I can only assume is killer pain medicine. On one side of the bed, Valerie grips Ella's shoulder with one hand and strokes her hair with the other, whispering something in her ear that I can't hear. Charles holds her legs against the bed, massaging them. Across the room, Caleb is holding Nina, who has buried her head in his shoulder. Monopoly pieces are scattered across the floor. I step on a purple fifty-dollar bill as another nurse pushes past me into the room.

I meet Caleb's eyes and then retreat out the door and into the hallway. He follows me, still carrying Nina.

"Hey," he says to both of us. "What do you say we check out the playroom down the hall? Sound good?"

Nina nods, wiping her snot on Caleb's sweater. "Um, thanks for that," he adds.

"What happened?" I ask in a low voice, once we're settled in the otherwise empty playroom and Nina is investigating the collection of DVDs.

He shakes his head. "Pain flare-up. They needed to adjust her meds."

"So what'd they give her?"

"What don't they give her?" he says. "They have to get this under control before they send her home, obviously." His eyes follow Nina, on the other side of the playroom. She looks like she's missing something without her twin next to her. "Ella's worse than Nina. They're looking at a stem cell transplant for her."

"A stem cell transplant? Seriously?" I had no idea that was a possible treatment for sickle cell.

"Yes, Rose. Sickle cell isn't a freakin' day at the beach, you know." Like before, his tone turns suddenly harsh.

"I didn't say it was. I just didn't know, Caleb. I didn't know you could do that for sickle cell."

"Well, yeah. There's a lot you don't know about sickle cell." He's right, but it still cuts. I know Caleb's stressed, and tired—I get it—but I don't like that he's taking it out on me, especially today, after everything.

"So tell me. Who would donate?"

His face relaxes a bit. "Siblings are ideal donors, but of course Nina's affected too, so that's out. I might, if they decide to go that route, or it's possible they'll be able to use her own stem cells."

"I'm sorry. I didn't know." I had no idea.

He takes my hand in his and squeezes it. Then he squeezes harder and harder until I let out a yelp.

"Ow! Excuse me. What was that for?"

"It was a love squeeze."

A love squeeze. I wonder if it's deliberate, his use of the word—a reminder for me that I still owe him something. I squeeze his hand back, but I don't say anything, and I see the disappointment flicker across his face.

Nina trots over to us with a DVD of the *Annie* remake.

"You have that at home," Caleb says.

"But we're here right now and I don't have it with me."

Caleb turns to me. "I don't know why I bother arguing with her."

"Neither do I," I agree.

"Neither do *I*," Nina says. "Put the DVD in, please."

Nina and I get comfortable on the undoubtedly germ-infested sofa while Caleb turns the television on and gets the movie set up. When he sits down next to me, Nina crawls over me to squeeze between the two of us. Caleb sneaks his arm behind her and finds my hand on the couch. His fingers intertwined through mine feel normal and solid. But something has shifted between us, and I'm not sure when or how I'll get it back.

Twenty-seven

"IF I DON'T GET IN TO NYU, I'M GOING TO TAKE A YEAR off and try again," Lena says, flipping through a *National Geographic* on my bed without paying attention to the words on any of the pages. She and Caleb came over to "do homework," but it turns out that it's true: seniors in high school don't feel much like doing homework by the time spring rolls around.

"You are so not going to do that," I say. "What would you do all year?"

She looks up from the magazine and wrinkles her forehead. "Get an internship at some design agency. Work night shifts at the Town Diner? I don't know—something like that. I'm desperate. Seriously."

Lena fell into a deep and irrepressible love affair with NYU when she went to visit last year. She said it spoke to her "major metropolitan soul." It's true that Cambridge, even all of Boston, has always seemed too small to hold Lena.

"What about you?" Lena asks, chucking a balled-up pair of socks from my pile of freshly folded laundry at Caleb's head. "Any word from RISD yet?" Most of the admissions announcements are due in two days, but there were rumors at school that some of them were coming out early.

Caleb catches the socks. "Nothing yet. My parents are about to burst an aneurism."

I shoot him a look. He knows I hate expressions like that. They're just begging the universe to screw with you.

My phone buzzes against the desk. Unknown. I let it go to voice mail.

"Well, PCCA won't tell me until the end of the month," I say. "So you can all go off partying together while I'm still at home obsessing."

Caleb mutters something to himself.

"What?" I say.

He throws the balled socks up toward the ceiling and catches them, twice. "Nothing, Rose. Nada." Then he tosses the socks back into the laundry basket and goes back to the tattered copy of *Moby-Dick* he's been working his way through at the rate of approximately one-half page per hour.

"What?" I repeat. I don't even know why I'm pushing. Lena's face tells me to stop, and I want to, but I cannot do it. It's been a week since Ella came home from the hospital. Caleb and I have hung out like we normally would, but nothing has been quite normal since.

"Yes, you're going to be at home obsessing," he says. "Your favorite pastime."

"Excuse me. I only obsess over things that are worth obsessing over."

He laughs. "Rose, if you were a country, obsessing would be the national sport. Overthinking is to Rose as baseball is to America."

"You don't get it," I say.

Lena shifts her weight on my bed and pulls her cell phone out of her pocket. She focuses closely on what I strongly suspect is a fake text message.

"*I* don't get it?" Caleb asks. "I think you're the one who doesn't get it."

"That's not fair." I stare at him, hard, challenging him to push me further, but he doesn't.

"I gotta go," he says finally. "Lena, you need a ride?"

She shakes her head. "Thanks, though."

Caleb gives me a perfunctory kiss on the cheek, but I don't turn my face to him to offer him anything more. "Later," he says.

When we hear the front door squeak closed, Lena tosses her phone aside. "Well, *that* wasn't at all awkward for me. What's got his shorts in a knot?"

I'm afraid if I speak the heat in my cheeks and the back of my throat will turn into a total meltdown. It wasn't a fight, not really. But I know what Caleb's really upset about, and it certainly isn't whether or not I'm going to go to PCCA.

"He's just . . . I don't know," I say, swallowing back the lump in my throat. "He doesn't like that I'm not as sure about everything in my life as he is about everything in his. He thinks I'm exhausting."

Lena considers this for a moment, twisting a strand of hair around her finger. "You're not exhausting, friend. But . . ."

"But, what?" I ask, when she doesn't finish her sentence.

"Well. You know, it's just that . . . you're not the only person who has hard choices to make. Maybe Caleb feels like you don't really acknowledge that enough."

We sit in silence for a minute. Finally, Lena reaches out and touches my arm. "I'm not saying that to be a bitch. You know I love you. I'm just being honest."

"I know." I don't know what else to say to her. Sometimes, she's the only person who can get away with speaking the truth to me. I hate her and love her for it.

"Can we talk about something else?" I say, climbing up onto the bed next to Lena, our backs leaning against my pillows.

"Please. Let's. How about, how's the s-e-x part going?" she asks.

Caleb and I have had sex exactly three more times. No one has bothered to tell me to leave the door open when he's here, or any of the other conventional things adults say to children to keep them from having sex. I'm not sure if that's because the adults in my family are smart enough to realize that saying those conventional things doesn't make any difference, or if they're just too distracted to notice, or if they notice but figure they have bigger problems to deal with than my burgeoning promiscuity.

I indulge Lena's curiosity. "Can we talk about condoms and how they're more complicated than advertised?"

"We *could* talk about that," Lena says, "but it would be the most boring conversation on the topic of sex that we could possibly have."

"At least it would be an honest one. More complicated than advertised, you heard it here first."

"Thank you for that public service announcement," she says, smirking at me. "So have you guys said the L-word yet?"

"As in, lesbian? Literal? Lugubrious?"

"I don't even know what that means. You know the L-word to which I am referring."

Obviously. Her powers of intuition are eerily good sometimes.

"Not yet," I say, wanting to avoid the conversation in which I tell Lena that Caleb said it and I haven't said it back, and that that's what he's really upset about. It has to be possible to let yourself care about a person, and want to be with that person, and still not feel ready to tell that person that you love them. Right? Because love is, like, a big deal. Love is like—you're my person, and I'm your person—and that means you need to be ready to be anyone's person other than your own. And you have to trust that, you know, neither of you is going to regret it. That it's not going to blow up in your face.

After Lena goes home, I stretch on the floor of my bedroom and stare at my phone, willing Caleb to call. Or text. Or something. He doesn't. Finally I give in and dial his number.

"Hi, you," he answers.

"Hey."

"What's up?"

"I'm sorry about before," I blurt out. I'm not even sure what exactly I'm apologizing for.

"Don't be sorry." Calmness settles back over my body. "Look, I'm just nervous about RISD." He sighs.

"You're getting into RISD."

"Your vote of confidence is appreciated, but considering that you can't tell a Rothko from one of my sisters' finger paintings, I'm not sure you're the most reliable judge."

"Point taken."

"Anyway, we'll see. I guess I just keep thinking, if I can't even get into art school, I have no business hoping for an actual *career* as an artist. Who am I kidding? But I can't imagine myself doing anything else. I mean, would you want me as your doctor? Or your dentist?"

"You do have steady hands," I offer.

"Chuckle, chuckle," he says, wryly. "But you know what I mean, right? I have to paint. There's nothing else. You get that."

"Yeah." I used to. I'm not so sure anymore. But I keep that thought to myself, because I know Caleb doesn't want to hear it, and let the silence hang between us for a minute. "All right," I say finally. "I should go. I didn't get any homework done this afternoon."

I hang up and look back at my missed-call log. There it is, staring me in the face, just like it has been all afternoon. Unknown. I click on the voice mail and bring the phone to my ear.

"Hi Rose, this is Roxanna. Give me a call when you get a chance and we can set up a time to have coffee." Then she repeats her number, twice.

At first, I struggle to wrap my head around why Roxanna would think I would want to have coffee with her—isn't that a violation of some professional code of conduct? But then I remember that she warned me that she'd leave an "ambiguous" message if she reached my voice mail. It's protocol, apparently, not to identify the genetic counseling clinic in a voice mail so that the patients' privacy is protected. I told her it was my cell number, that no one would listen to it but me, but she said it was *protocol*. I can tell Roxanna is the kind of person who takes protocols very seriously. Maybe that's a prerequisite for her job.

I start to hit Roxanna's number to call her back, but then I stop myself. I'll do it later.

There's a soft knock on my door maybe an hour later, when I've finally forced myself to turn my attention to the introduction for my English paper. As usual, Dad pokes his head in without waiting for a response. He doesn't ever seem to worry that I might be buck naked, or making out with my boyfriend, or doing any number of other things he definitely doesn't want to see his daughter doing.

"Dinner's ready, Ro," he says. He seems a little off—worried, or tired or something. Like he has been a lot lately, I guess. Only more so.

"I'll be right down. Everything okay?"

"Fine, fine. Just come on down." He disappears and pulls the door shut behind him. I save my English essay and close my laptop, shooting a quick IM to Lena first: "Dinner. Dad's acting weird."

"Weird like Chico Lederkranz?" she replies, referring to a card she gave me years ago for my birthday with a ridiculous poem about some weird guy named Chico Lederkranz. It had a cartoon picture of a skinny old man making a stupid face, and it became one of those jokes between us—"you're weird like

Chico Lederkranz"—mostly because it meant nothing at all. No one else thinks it's funny, but it cracks us up every time.

Downstairs, my parents and Gram are already sitting around the table, passing slices of pizza around. As usual, "dinner's ready" really means "dinner has been removed from its takeout vessels."

I slip into my seat and Dad passes me a slice of mushroom and peppers without asking or even making eye contact. He looks watery, like he's been teary-eyed recently, and I glance from him to Mom to Gram to see if I can gauge what's actually going on here. Everybody just looks strange. Uncomfortable or something. Worried.

I take two bites of pizza, chew, swallow, drink some water, and look around again. No one says anything.

"Okay. What's up? Why are you being weird?" Chico Lederkranz flashes through my mind again, but now I know whatever this is, it isn't going to be funny.

Dad looks hard at Mom, who is shakily sipping water through a straw. "El, I think you should tell her."

"Tell me what?" My heart's pounding now, making that kind of fuzzy white noise in my ears. "What is going on?"

"Sssweetheart. I've made a decision. I'm going to make arrangements. For long-term care."

My mind goes blank for a split second, like a TV at the moment the picture disappears. I've been turned off.

"Wait—what does that even mean?" I look from her to Dad. Mom gestures awkwardly at him, telling him to explain further in words that form more easily than hers do.

"It just means she's chosen a facility that she likes. And we're going to make the arrangements. Now. No one's moving anywhere just yet," Dad says. "Just yet," he says—but what I hear is that Dad's promise to keep Mom at home, the one we've both now made to her, was a lie.

"Okay, but when? When will you move?"

"We'll just wait and see how things progress—" Dad says, but Mom cuts him off.

"When I sssay so."

I stare at her. She's coherent. She doesn't need a feeding tube. She doesn't need round-the-clock care. Sure, she's been getting worse—she needs her wheelchair now more often than not, she can't bathe herself safely, and the chorea is more pronounced than it was a year ago. And yeah, I suppose those outbursts, the moments when she loses control, lashes out at one of us, are more frequent than they used to be. But she's not a danger to herself. She's not a danger to us. It made me angry when the woman on the Downeaster spouted that bullshit. It makes me furious that my own parents are now, apparently, doing the same thing.

"It's absurd," I say. "You can't. You're not dying."

"Rose, this is your mom's decision," Dad says. He hasn't touched his pizza. I can see the cheese congealing on his plate, getting that cold, dull look.

"No it isn't. This is a family! That's a family decision. She doesn't just get to decide to leave us!"

Gram reaches across the table to touch my arm, but I pull away. "She's not leaving us, Ro. Even when she does move, you'll still see her whenever you want."

"That's BS, Gram, and you know it."

Mom raises one arm awkwardly in the air and slams her hand down on the table, shutting us all up. My glass rattles.

"Hey!" Mom says. "Hey."

I meet her eyes with mine and force myself to hold them there.

"I want to do this, fffor you. I want you to go to college and not worry about me."

Mom tugs her napkin from her shirt collar, where it's tucked like a bib on a two-year-old, and turns her wheelchair away from the table. In the threshold between the dining room and the living room, she turns her chair back around to face us again.

"I'm ssstill your *mother. I* get to decide what's best fffor you, one last time." Then she buzzes out of the dining room. I hear her shift herself into the stair lift. Gram, Dad, and I sit in silence until we hear the bedroom door click quietly closed upstairs.

"Don't be selfish about this, Rose. She really does think this is the best thing for you," Dad says after a moment.

"*I'm* being selfish? You're the one who just let her spring this on me."

"Babe, this is for the future. She's not going anywhere yet. It could be months, hell, it could be years before she actually makes the move."

"That's not what it sounds like to me. It sounds like she's decided on a place, and that's it. How am I supposed to react to this?"

"You're supposed to say, 'I love you and support whatever decision you make for how you wish to live the remainder of your life.' She wants to be in control of this. You and I might not understand that or like it but we have to respect it."

Like Mom, I push my chair back from the table and leave them sitting there. Maybe I am being selfish, if that's what you call this, this not wanting my mother to give up on her life before it's really over—this. If that's selfish, then I guess I am.

Twenty-eight

PETRILLI GIVES US A UNIT TEST ON THE WEDNESDAY morning that I'm supposed to hear back from PCCA. Coupled with Mom's announcement, this is a less than ideal combination of events in terms of my ability to focus on calculus (or anything, really). As we wait for our classmates to get settled, Lena glances at my knee, which is bouncing rather conspicuously up and down under my desk.

"What is your problem, dude?"

"It's the thirtieth, *dude*."

Lena looks at me, clueless. She got her acceptance to NYU last week, like I knew she would. Caleb got into RISD. And I got into Cunningham, with a nice financial aid package, too, which felt like more of a relief than I expected it to. Still, PCCA is PCCA. It's everything I should want.

"PCCA decisions are out today," I whisper loudly.

"Oh shit!" Lena practically yells.

Petrilli looks up. "Come on, Lena. Seriously?" That's the kind of teacher Mr. P. is. No detention for swearing, not even a "that kind of language isn't tolerated in my classroom"—just a deadpanned "Seriously?" That's why we love the guy.

"Sorry, Mr. P." She turns back to me, whispering again. "Shit, I forgot. You're so getting in."

"Ah—right," Petrilli says, clearing his throat. "Got a quiz today, no open book, no open notes." He passes a stack of scribbled papers—Petrilli always handwrites his tests—to the kid in the front row with unfortunate white-boy dreadlocks whose name I always forget. "Good luck and thanks for playin'."

Finally, after slogging through Petrilli's test and the rest of the day, the blaring fire alarm masquerading as our bell system announces that it's two thirty. My stomach rolls over itself a few times as I make my way to the public library. It's a slightly more anonymous locale than the computer lab or the school library, better for checking the admissions decision, no matter what the outcome is. Earlier I was feeling grateful that Lena had volleyball practice and couldn't come with me—I have a direct order to send her a text message once I find out the verdict—but now I sort of wish she were here. Or Caleb, obviously.

I check my phone. Caleb sent me a text about thirty minutes ago: "Fingers crossed. Let me know ASAP."

The thing is, I don't know what my own fingers are crossed for. I've thought this thing through and through, and I still don't know what I want the decision to be. I guess I'll just be relieved to know one way or the other.

I sign up quickly for an Internet station and log in. My fingers are barely functioning properly as I open my e-mail. Sure enough, there's a message there saying that the decisions are now available online, with a link to my personal outcomes page.

What if they mess up the links and you get a URL to someone else's decision? Like that woman whose book got nominated for some huge prize and then they realized, oops, we confused your book with some other/better book with a similar title. Too bad for you.

I click the link. The library computer is a little slow, and it takes about five seconds longer than I think I can stand to open the page.

"Rose Alexander Levenson," it reads at the top—good, they haven't mixed me up with someone else, I guess— "Congratulations! You have been admitted to The Pacific Coast College of the Arts Dual BFA/Ballet of the Pacific Coast Apprenticeship Program!"

Admitted. In. I'm in. I feel a kind of numbness all through my extremities. A split second of joy and relief washes over me and then passes, replaced with a fresh wave of nerves: what about the money? The scholarship information isn't there on the same page, but scanning the letter I find another link down at the bottom: *For more information about your scholarship and financial aid decisions, please click here.*

My phone vibrates loudly against the wooden desk. Caleb. "Don't leave a sickle cell hanging." I click the link to the scholarship page and find what looks like a generic financial aid profile with all the possible funding sources listed, alongside the amounts I've been offered—most of which are zero, because they're scholarships I didn't qualify for, like one for minority students from California and several other in-state-only things.

I see that I haven't been offered any need-based aid, which hardly seems fair, considering that Mom can't work and her medical expenses are pretty ridiculous.

For a minute I can't even remember what I'm looking for, but then I spot it there, just one line among many. *Grierson Scholarship Award: Full tuition, room and board. All expenses covered.*

And that's it. No cheering, no fireworks shooting out of the computer, just a tiny little line, "all expenses covered." I'm one of the chosen few. I can go for free. To San Francisco. To dance, to start the rest of my life—and my career—as a ballet dancer. If I want to.

I waste most of the afternoon in Harvard Square, looking at flimsy sundresses I have no interest in buying. Then I walk up Mass. Ave. to the bookstore in Porter Square, where I slump down in the back corner of the nonfiction section and skim a book about psychopathy for an hour. At least Mom's not charming on the outside and a narcissistic, pathological liar and potential serial killer on the inside. Being in the bookstore reminds me of my first "date" with Caleb, when we met here on the pretense of coffee and ended up getting ice cream instead. It feels like years of my life have passed in the interim.

Caleb and Lena both wanted to go out and celebrate, but I feel strangely deflated. Maybe I've just been thinking about this moment so much, for so long, that now that it's here, it doesn't seem real. I've been imagining this exact opportunity since I first fell in love with the BPC. Here I am, a decade later, with a chance into the company. I should be doing *tour jetés* down the street. Instead I walk all the way home from Porter Square, imagining myself in San Francisco, with my days full of ballet. I think of being in the studio for even more hours than I'm used to now, for the next however many years. I think of being surrounded by bunheads all the time, like the girls at the audition.

I push the front door open with some effort—it's warping as the weather has warmed up—and survey the sounds in the house to figure out where everyone is.

"I'm home," I call upstairs.

"Kitchen!" Dad says. He's sitting at the island, working. He glances up from his laptop as I put my bags down on the radiator, but he doesn't say anything. It's been tense like this ever since our dinner conversation about Mom. I haven't brought it up again and neither has Dad, but it's lingered in the house.

I sit across from him, not saying anything. Finally, he looks up again. "What's up?" he asks.

"I got in," I say.

"PCCA? The scholarship?" I nod. "All right!" he says, pumping a fist in the air. "That's my girl! Yeah, baby!"

"Dad, Dad. Dad! Stop."

His brow furrows, like a dark cloud has blown in, out of nowhere, over his face. "What? I thought this would be the happiest moment of your life to date. This is what you've always wanted."

The man sitting across from me is a person who, I suddenly understand, would do anything to give me the tiniest glimpse of a decent future. My situation is in no way his fault—the bad genes aren't even on his side of the family—but that doesn't matter. He'd do anything to erase the uncertainty.

I get up from my seat and give him a hug. When I pull away, he's got tears in his eyes, of course. "What's that for?" he asks.

I shrug. "I'm sorry for being a jerk the other night about Mom. Also, you're a pretty good dad."

"Pretty good? That's the best you can do, you little ingrate?"

"Quite good. Significantly above average."

"I'll take it," he says, closing his laptop. "So what's up?"

I look over at the refrigerator door, where there are pictures of me in full dance regalia from various performances over the years and a yellowing *Cambridge Chronicle* article from sixth grade, when I won a big statewide ballet competition. The most recent addition to the collection is a program from this spring's showcase. Looking at the ever-rotating items on the fridge used to give me this feeling of crazy awesomeness. I know that sounds super egocentric, but somehow remembering all my best dance moments made me irrationally happy. Now, they might as well be pictures of someone else.

Going to PCCA means living and breathing ballet for the next four years, and if I'm successful there, which I think I could be, and if I'm lucky—which who knows—then for however many years after that.

I feel Dad's eyes on me, waiting for a sign of what's going through my head. "Remember how Mom used to tell me to flip a coin when I couldn't make a decision, to check my gut reaction?"

Dad nods. She said it so many times to me over the years, it's hard to imagine he'd forget.

"So I sort of feel like, the coin flip came up the way I thought I wanted it to. But my gut doesn't feel right."

"All right," Dad says. "So what do you think that means?"

I take a breath. "I didn't feel like I belonged there. Maybe I just don't belong in the ballet world anymore. I love ballet, but it's not how I want to spend what could be the last healthy fifteen years of my life."

Dad cringes when I say "the last healthy fifteen years of my life," but he doesn't contradict me. He just waits, maybe to see if I'm finished or if I might still change my mind again. Finally, he says, "Okay. What about next year, then?"

I take a deep breath. "Cunningham. That's my choice. I can dance there—and try something other than ballet. That's what I want."

The skin around Dad's eyes crinkles a little bit. He looks almost proud. "You can try all kinds of things other than ballet there. Modern, jazz. You could choreograph. Hell, you could try biology."

"*Dad.*" I cut him off, rolling my eyes. "So how do I tell Mom?"

"You just tell her," he says.

"But I know she always wanted me to be . . . you know. A successful dancer."

"Did you not just get into one of the premier ballet programs in the country? You are a successful dancer, Ro. She wouldn't want you to go there for her. Please. You know she'd kick your butt if she thought that's what you were doing."

"I strongly suspect Mom has lost the ability to kick my butt, Dad. If she ever had it."

"I wouldn't be so sure," he says. "I bet she could still muster a decent right hook, given the right motivation. For you, I think she could."

* * *

Mom is lying on the bed with a mask over her eyes, but she pushes it up when I knock on her open door and come into the room. The mask rests awkwardly on her forehead, sending her hair in ten directions. I sit next to her and slip it off her head, smoothing her hair down.

"What's up?" she says, smiling at me.

"I have news," I say. "About next year."

"Okay." She waits for me to say more, but I can't tell if she really understands what I'm referring to, or if she even remembers about PCCA in the first place.

"So, you remember how I auditioned for the scholarship at PCCA? In San Francisco?"

"Of course I remember that. I'm not sssenial, you know." But from the way her eyes flicker when she says it, I can tell she doesn't quite believe it herself.

"I got in."

Mom's face lights up. "I knew you would. See, I told you ssso. Didn't I?"

I don't remember her telling me so anytime recently, but maybe she's right in the global sense. All my life, in one way or another, she told me so.

"Yeah. You did. But, Mom—the thing is . . ." I trail off, afraid to see her obvious pleasure turn to disappointment.

"What's the thhhhing?"

"I don't want to go."

She struggles to prop herself up on one arm, so she can get a good look at me. The left side of her face twitches as she stares me down, just like she used to when I was little and she wanted to know if I was telling the truth. "Are you still worried that my plane is going to crash?" she'd ask before leaving for a business trip, and then she'd give me that deep stare-down until I'd admit that yes, I was still worried about her plane going down in a field. Then she'd take me straight to the Internet and show me all the statistics on how many planes fly safely every year, to calm my fears.

She's still trying to be that mother now, even as her body is betraying her.

"You don't want to?"

I shake my head. "No. I want to go to Cunningham. Remember, where we saw that dance show last year?"

She closes her eyes, maybe trying to bring back the memory.

"Are you sssure? That's what you really want?"

"Yes. Really." Saying it again, to Mom, makes me feel even more certain. That I won't have a six-hour flight—or a two-day train ride—between us is a bonus.

"Okay, then. Did your fffather order dinner?"

On Saturday, Dad makes me invite Lena and Caleb over for what he calls a "celebratory dinner for talented people." I humor him. In exchange, he actually grills, like he used to all the time.

"I'd like to raise a glass to all of you completely amazing youths. Here's to big things!" He raises his pint glass with one hand and reaches over to squeeze Mom's shoulder with the other, as he blinks back predictably sentimental tears.

"Hear, hear!" Gram adds, hoisting her beer. Gram rarely drinks alcohol, but tonight she said it was an occasion worthy of a "fine ale."

"So you're making a shift toward vegetarianism, I see," Lena says, surveying the spread of chicken, steak tips, and sausages.

"You only live once, Lena," Dad says. "Might as well enjoy your meals."

I wonder if Dad's new gospel of living in the moment has anything to do with Mom's decision to reserve herself a place in a care home, and the newfound glimpse it offers into the life she's headed for—sitting in a wheelchair in a room that smells like urine faintly disguised by disinfectant, smearing soft food across her face, playing "games" with aides in pink smocks and other people in varying, withering states of incapacity. (Or at least that's how I'm imagining it. Dr. Howard says it's not really like that.)

"YOLO, Dave," Lena says, clinking her iced tea against his Guinness.

"What what, Lena?"

"Never mind, Dave." Under the table, where our knees brush up against each other, Caleb squeezes my leg.

When Lena leaves, Caleb and I manage to extricate ourselves from the rest of my family and slip upstairs. I close the door behind us, shove him back on the bed, and straddle his lap, pulling my shirt over my head at the same time. He looks pleasantly surprised, but also a little concerned, glancing toward the door.

"Whatever," I say, kissing his neck. "We'll just be quiet." I open my laptop and turn up the volume on iTunes. If they hear anything, they'll hear Adele, and maybe they'll wonder, but I don't even care. He runs his hands down my torso to my waist and kisses me back.

Afterward, we lie on my bed, on top of the covers, not doing or saying much of anything. I lean against his chest, and every now and then he twists a strand of my hair around a finger.

"I'm doing the right thing, right?" I say after a few minutes. "About school?"

"You know what I think."

"You think I should do what I want."

He nods.

"But that's just you being a good human being. I want to know what you really think."

Caleb sighs. "That *is* what I really think. I can't tell you what to do. Do I know what I would do in the same situation? Yes. But that's me."

"You would take the scholarship and go to PCCA."

"Hell yeah, I would go. I can't imagine just giving up on the thing you love."

I lean against his chest and press myself up so I can see his face. "I'm not giving it up, though. I'm choosing something else. And I can still dance at Cunningham."

He nods, thinking. "I know. That's what you're telling yourself. Are you sure you're not just scared?"

"Why would I be scared?"

"I mean, you've been waffling about this from the beginning, from before you even auditioned. Don't you think that's about something else?"

"No. I think I'm making a *choice*, which you've been pushing me to do for months, and now you just don't understand that choice so you're being weird."

"You *asked* for my opinion. I'm just giving it to you. Ballet is your life. You have a chance to do it at the best place in the country, for free. So no, I don't get not going. I didn't get a scholarship to RISD and I'm going anyway, because it's the right thing for me."

"And because you can," I remind him. As soon as the words are out of my mouth, I know I shouldn't have said them. But he can't possibly think our situations are the same: his parents can afford to send him wherever he wants. His eyes harden and he pulls away from me, ever so slightly but I notice it anyway.

"Yeah. Because I can. Do you want me to apologize for that, Rose?"

"That's not what I meant."

"Because, you know, you've been asking me for a lot of apologies lately. Apologies for not having my family's illness, apologies for not having to worry about money, apologies for having what you seem to think is an easy, uncomplicated life."

I sit up on my knees, alarmed by how quickly this conversation has taken a turn. "Hey, I never said that."

I know Caleb worries about his family, that their illness weighs on him. I've never doubted that, but now it's creeping into my head that maybe I haven't said that out loud to him very often. Or ever, really.

"Come on. You've been competitive about whose life is harder right from the beginning. Let me ask you this. Have you ever heard the phrase 'twice as good'?" He folds his arms across his bare chest. "Have your parents ever had that talk with you? You don't know what I'm talking about, do you?"

I have no idea. I just stare at him.

"Yeah, because white kids don't get that talk," he goes on.

"Wait, when did this become a conversation about race?"

"We're not talking about race, Rose. We're talking about us. I'm trying to tell you something about me, and you don't want to listen."

"How are you allowed to lump me in with white kids in general and then claim we're not talking about race? I don't lump you in with black kids all the time."

Caleb laughs then—not his good laugh, the one that makes me smile, but a different one, distant and cold. "This is exactly what I'm talking about. This isn't about 'lumping in.' This is about our different experiences. And you always thinking my life is so pristine. But since when do you even ask me about my life?"

With that, I'm silenced. I swallow, hard, and feel my face heating up. Warm tears are already spilling down my cheeks but I don't wipe them away.

"I'm just saying, Rose—as *you* told me from the train, we all have our own 'stuff.' "

He puts air quotes around "stuff" in a way that bugs me, but I don't say anything, just wait for him to go on, which he does.

"And you were right. We do all have our stuff. When I was eight, my father sat me down and told me not to run in white neighborhoods, including our own. Get that? Then when I was fourteen, he explained to me how to behave around cops, which I can assure you is not the same way you can behave around cops. At work, my mother had to publish more articles and teach more hours than any of her colleagues before she got tenure. And she's done it with a chronic illness, which, although it is not Huntington's, as you've pointed out many times, is still pretty freakin' bad. Okay? You got a tough hand, sure. You didn't get a monopoly on struggle."

He finally pauses, exhaling deeply and threading his hands together behind his neck. Wiping my face, I swallow hard enough to speak, even though I barely trust myself to get a coherent sentence out. "I didn't—I don't think I have a monopoly. I get that we all have our own . . . complications. Okay? But you have to also accept that I might deal with my particular set of complicating factors differently from how you would."

Caleb nods, a vaguely skeptical look on his face, and chuckles again, mostly to himself.

"And we're all supposed to just excuse you for everything as a result of these complications, right? It's always complicated with you, Rose."

Well, yeah. It is. I'm sorry if that's new information for him. The realization that he's just been rolling his eyes at me this whole time is ice cold as it slithers through me. And the coldness pushes me to say the thing I've been holding in, the thing I've known and haven't wanted to accuse him of.

"You don't get this, okay? You don't get what it's like to *not know*. You don't know what it feels like to have this big dark thing hanging over your head."

"I get it, Rose! I have a family of sick people too, remember? Just because our sick isn't as bad as your sick on your continuum of suffering, it doesn't mean I don't understand pain."

"Watching other people be sick is not the same as living with the possibility of being sick," I say. "I don't get what it's like to be black in this country? Okay, you're right. Obviously I do not. I'm sorry about that. Maybe you shouldn't date a white girl if you want to be with someone who automatically understands how you have to act around cops. But you don't get what it's like to be at risk for this disease. So you don't get to sit around judging me."

Abruptly, Caleb pushes himself upright on my bed and disentangles himself from the pillows. "Yup, that's what I'm doing. Judging you. That's what this is. Sure. You want to know what I think?"

He's raised his voice now. If my family didn't hear us hooking up before, they're definitely hearing us fight now. Caleb looks like he's about to cry, or yell, I'm not sure which. He pulls his jeans on and moves toward the door. "You make this huge thing about how you don't know what your future holds, and it makes your life so hard." He tugs his sweatshirt over his head. "So go get your stupid test results! You've been talking about 'taking control' for months now." He does the air quotes around "taking control," like it's a joke to him. "But the information is there for you to take and you're just waiting. So go do it. Otherwise you're just floundering in the dark, all the time, and it clearly is not working for you. Or us."

It's the "us" that stings, even more than the implication that this is all just me being some silly, high-maintenance girl. This is exactly why I wasn't supposed to have a boyfriend to begin with. Because I knew a boyfriend wouldn't get it, that he'd think I was just being needy, and then someone would get hurt.

"And you know what really gets me?" he says, more quietly now, running a hand over his head and exhaling hard. "You're always pulling away, and I'm all in. If that test comes back positive, I just want to be there for you. But you won't let me."

"Is that what you want, then? For me to find out I have it, so you can be the perfect hero boyfriend?"

I can't get the words back. They land with what might as well be an audible thud on my bedroom floor.

"Okay," he says, completely evenly. "I'm done." He closes the door softly behind him as he leaves.

I want to stop him, but I don't know how, so I don't even try. I hear him on the stairs and then going out the front. He starts the car and idles in the driveway, maybe giving me a chance to come down and fix this, but I don't move, and after a minute he drives away.

I sit on my bed in the same position for what feels like a year and a half, thinking that Caleb and I just fought about so many things at once that I can't even remember what we were really fighting about. A soft knock interrupts the crazed thoughts that are hamster-wheeling around in my head. Gram pokes her head in.

"Well, that was bloody dramatic."

"You heard us?" I ask.

"It's a small house." She doesn't come in, just hovers there in the doorway. "You all right?"

I nod.

"Right then," she says, ever matter-of-fact. She looks like she's about to turn and close the door, but then she stops and gives me a hard stare for a minute, buying time.

"You know, every choice you make to share yourself, every time, it's a risk. No matter what. People get sick, they get scared, they get stroppy . . ." She trails off and laughs, like a memory has just floated through her head. "My point is, you don't know. There are no guarantees in this life, about anything. Full stop."

It means "period"—full stop. It's the British term, so much better than ours. Period makes you think of the obvious unpleasant things. And it doesn't mean anything. Full stop says exactly what it means. This is the end of a thought. Full stop.

"Okay," I say, not sure how else to respond.

"I have learned a thing or two over the years, you know. You're not the only old soul around here." She winks at me. "Goodnight, Rosie girl."

When Gram leaves, shutting the door behind her, I dig a quarter out of my backpack. "*That's* how you know how you really feel," Mom used to say. I toss the coin into the air and let it fall to the floor. It spins on the hardwood for a few seconds before toppling over. Heads. I check for my automatic, natural response, and then I go to my desk and pull Roxanna's business card from the mess of random papers in the top drawer. I know it's too late to talk to a human being, but I dial the office number anyway and leave a message.

Twenty-nine

THREE DAYS. THAT'S HOW LONG IT'S BEEN SINCE CALEB walked out of my room, and he hasn't returned my calls or my texts since. The last time he went MIA, it was because his sister was in the hospital—and I realized how silly I'd been for thinking it was about us. This time, I know it's about us. And it terrifies me to care as much as I do.

The McClaren House isn't as bad as I'd imagined it—it smells like a hospital, like too much cleaning and not terribly good food, but it doesn't look that much like one. Mom and Dad went to see a bunch of these places, but McClaren is the one she chose, so now she wants me to see it, too.

According to Dr. Howard, most Huntington's patients stay at home until their behavioral symptoms become too much for their families to cope with. He says most families—*most families*, like this is a common problem, like there are a lot of families like ours—find it easier to deal with the deteriorating physical symptoms of the disease than the emotional ones. Apparently it's easier to cope with your mom losing the ability to swallow than her ability to not lash out at the people she loves. I guess I can understand that, based on the previews I've seen— the words "ungrateful bitch" come to mind. But I still feel like even being here for a visit is a betrayal. We said we'd take care of her at home. We promised.

Celeste is the family liaison assigned to show us around Mc-Claren and answer our questions—to convince us, essentially, that McClaren is a halfway decent place for my mother to die. But even so, I like her right away. She's not overly chipper and she doesn't make it seem like this is going to be super fun for all of us. She's basically like, well, this sucks for you. Let me try to make it the least sucky it can possibly be. Which I appreciate.

On the first floor, she shows us the main recreation room, which looks like a big living room filled with old people. Dr. Howard warned us that because McClaren doesn't specialize in Huntington's, most of the patients would be much older than Mom. It's hard to imagine her sitting here with these people. These people are debilitated.

Nonetheless, the recreation room itself is pretty decent, bright and painted a cheerful yellow, instead of some awful industrial puke color. There's a fireplace (probably just for show; I'm pretty sure it's considered a best practice to keep people with advanced dementia away from open flames), and several bookcases, a few round wooden tables, and lots of comfortable-looking seating options. I note that any sharp edges have clear, padded covers over them. Subtle.

"And we have morning yoga classes," Celeste is saying, "and art and music therapists. Weekly movie nights, and of course there's a library with books and DVDs you can borrow anytime."

It all looks and sounds like a souped-up bed and breakfast for sick people, which I suppose is more or less what it is. I tune Celeste out. There are patients—"residents," as Celeste carefully refers to them—scattered around the common areas, playing games or sitting by themselves, looking out the windows or just staring off into space.

"Look, Rose, they have Sccccrabble," Mom says, pointing to an old guy and a girl a couple years older than me—I can't tell if she's an aide or his granddaughter—who are playing at a nearby table. I inch a little closer, careful not to make it obvious that I'm watching them. When I'm close enough to see their Scrabble tiles splayed out on the table, I realize that the words the old guy is spelling out aren't words at all; they're just a jumble of letters. The girl doesn't say anything, just lets him put down whatever nonsense he comes up with. I like to think I'll have that kind of patience when Mom loses it completely, but the truth is I'm not sure. I'm not sure Mom would *want* me to let her come up with nonsense words, anyway.

Celeste takes us to a model bedroom. They call it a "studio apartment," but that's a joke because it doesn't have a kitchen or a living room or a dining room. It's a room with a bed at one end and a couch and two armchairs at the other end. There's a matching wardrobe and bureau, from IKEA I think, and a flat-screen television (with cable, Celeste notes) mounted to the wall.

"Most of our residents make their apartments very homey. Lots of artwork on the walls, family pictures. You can bring a quilt from home if you'd like," Celeste says, smiling gently at Mom. "We encourage you to do whatever you want to make this place feel as much like your own as possible. We know it's only the second best thing," she adds, glancing at me, "but we hope it can be a close second."

"Nice," Mom says, surveying the room, the way she used to when we'd go to open houses on the weekends. Even though we weren't looking to move, Mom would go online, find some open houses nearby, and take me with her to check them out. ("It's like a free pass to snoop in someone else's house, Rose. Think of *Rear Window*.") As an architect, she always loved looking at other people's homes, and she passed her curiosity along to me through those visits to grand old mansard Victorians and pastel-painted Colonials all over Cambridge. Of course, the real Mom would *not* have found this place up to her standards. It's basically a white box with some furniture—none of the character Mom loves, or used to love, anyway. No crown molding, no quirky nooks or built-in shelves or anything, and the floor is clearly laminate, not real wood.

"Chhheck out the view," Mom says to me over her shoulder. I push her chair over to the window and we survey the backyard gardens.

"This is just a model unit, Mom. Your view might not be this nice." Dad shoots me a look, but I'm not saying it to be mean. It just seems like they shouldn't make the model unit have the nicest view in the whole place. It's manipulative.

"Can I request a room with a vvview?" Mom asks Celeste.

"You can. We'll do our best to accommodate your preferences. Of course it depends what's available when you . . . uh . . ." She trails off. It's the first time I've seen Celeste search for the right words. Like she hasn't rehearsed this part, or she's forgotten her lines. "Whenever you make the decision. To transition."

On a table by the window, there's a potted plant with purple flowers. I reach out and run one of the petals between my fingers. Fake.

"I'll leave you folks here for a few minutes," Celeste says. "I'll just go get some paperwork, and I'll be back in a few."

Dad nods at her. After she's gone, the three of us look around the room, numbed. Stunned, maybe, I'm not sure. We've certainly gone silent.

After a moment, I clear my throat. "I have to tell you guys something." My palms are sweaty, and a wave of nausea sends a tingling sensation through my spine and gut. "Well, I already told Mom this."

Dad looks confused. He turns to Mom, alarmed. So she kept my secret.

"I took the HD test. More than a month ago."

"You did what?" Dad's voice is low and angry, or maybe just scared.

"There's no point in fighting about this again, Dad. It's done. I've done it, and I made an appointment to get my results. And I'm hoping you'll come with me."

"Ro—come on. I know you think that this is the right thing, but . . . are you sure you want to do this?" he asks. "You could go off to Cunningham, enjoy yourself, not worry about it for a few years."

"I'm sorry, Dad. But I can't *not* do this. I need to follow through."

Of course, since I took the test, I've managed to lose the person who was actually willing to be with me through this whole thing. Or maybe "lose" is the wrong word—throw away. I've called him four times since our fight—and I've lost count of the unanswered texts. I've steeled myself to the fact that he meant what he said: he's done.

Dad shakes his head, but doesn't say anything. I forget, sometimes, that these results dictate my father's future as well. He'll watch me suffer, after he's watched her suffer. A car accident that killed all of us probably wouldn't be the worst thing that could happen.

"You told your mother about this, but not me?"

I shrug. I wish I could apologize, but I'm not sure I know how. Dad stares at the floor for a minute, and I wonder if he's going to yell, or cry, or tell me I've betrayed his trust. But then he nods, like he understands.

"*Chhhild,*" Mom says suddenly, opening her mouth wide to get the word out, like she does now. "If I had known about thhhis"—she gestures around the room—"I might not have had you."

Dad gets up, his eyes full, and goes into the hallway. It's just Mom and me, staring at each other over the fake purple plant. Mom almost never talks about her diagnosis. In fact half the time she seems less aware of her symptoms than we are. "Unawareness" is a symptom itself, Dr. Howard has told us. Mom never talks about her feelings about living with the disease, about deteriorating, about dying. But as soon as I think how strange that is, that she never talks about it, I realize that I never ask her. Maybe that's why her decision to make these plans was so surprising to me. I've stopped thinking of her as a person with feelings as complicated as my own.

It occurs to me, only now, that when Dad said that Mom wanted to take control of her life by choosing McClaren House, it was the same as me choosing to take this test. When there's so much out of our control, we deserve to make whatever choices we can hold on to.

"This disease is ugly," Mom says, her tongue protruding and then disappearing back into her mouth as she forms the words. "But it isn't everything."

Thirty

THE NEXT MORNING, AFTER SEVERAL MINUTES OF SPEED-pacing around my bedroom, I call Caleb again. This morning is the last time I will be this version of myself. By this afternoon, I'll be a person who knows my HD status. This version of me will never talk to Caleb again, unless I do it now.

His phone rings a few times, then goes to his deadpanned voice mail that I'm now getting used to hearing, the one that tells me he regrets falling in love with me: *"Greetings. You have reached the answering service of Caleb G. Franklin. Please leave a message after the beep and I will return your call as soon as humanly possible."*

I've never asked him what the G stands for in Caleb G. Franklin. Suddenly that seems like a weird thing not to know about him, and I need to know right away. I call back two more times, but he doesn't answer.

Dad pulls into the underground parking lot and finds a spot near the elevator bank. We sit in silence in the car, the engine still humming. Inside the clinic, there is a person who knows my fate.

"Ready?" Dad asks, turning to me. "This is what you want, right?"

I nod. It is what I want. I think. Of course, I won't completely know if it's what I want until I know the outcome of the test. But by then it'll be too late to change my mind, so I just have to trust that this is the right thing to do.

As we ride up to the fifth floor on the elevator, I think about the return trip. I visualize the concrete barricades between the rows of parked SUVs, the low-hanging ceiling, the parking attendant collecting tickets, validated in the hospital lobby for everyone lucky enough to leave alive. The parking lot smells of gas and hot air, I remember that. It will smell the same when I leave. Everything will be the same, but nothing will be the same.

The receptionist smiles at me, a closed-mouth sympathetic smile, as Dad and I take seats in the waiting room.

"I'll let Roxanna know you're here," she says. It's Roxanna who will deliver the news. I've known this all along, since I met Roxanna, but it's still chilling. Roxanna knows. She already knows. The paper is in front of her, and all she has to do is open her mouth and tell me.

We wait for two minutes, or maybe ten, I can't tell. There's a light buzzing in my ears, like the sound of everything around me is heightened a little bit. I sip water from a thin paper cup, but my mouth doesn't absorb any of the moisture.

And then she comes out, looking just like herself: it's business as usual in the field of telling people bad news.

"Rose, are you ready to chat?"

Chatting. That's what this is, apparently. I turn to Dad. He just stares back at me, like he's trying to look straight through my eyes and see my brain.

We follow Roxanna into her office.

"Please, sit down." She gestures toward the sofa and sits herself in an armchair opposite. If it were good news, wouldn't she just tell me?

She looks me in the eye—maybe it is good news. Would she look at me, if she were about to deliver me a death sentence? I stare at the same old sand dunes painting over her head. You know how they say your life flashes before your eyes right before you die? I think I'm having a moment like that, except it's not my whole life; it's just the piece that's happened since the last time I sat in this office and was subjected to the crappy painting on Roxanna's wall and her earnest head-cocking.

I didn't sleep at all last night, which I guess isn't a surprise. I just lay there on my bed, staring at the ceiling where the constellations once glowed. Constellations my mother wouldn't have made, for a daughter she wouldn't have had, if she'd known she was going to get sick. Going through the motions of getting dressed and eating breakfast this morning, in a house my mother will one day soon not live in, I felt like myself inside out and maybe having just gone through the spin cycle on the washing machine. If only they'd invent a washing machine for cleaning out genetic errors. Wouldn't that be a clever way to resolve this situation. Although, on second thought, I suppose that's what the eugenicists thought they were doing, and look how that turned out. So never mind.

All of this goes through my mind in an instant, staring at Roxanna's wall. I look directly at her now. She has freckles spread across the bridge of her nose and a large, hard-to-ignore mole under her left eye. I wonder if it's annoying in her peripheral vision, or if she's so used to it she can't tell it's there anymore. She cocks her head to the left. Then she squints at me, purses her lips, and cocks it to the right. It must be bad news.

"Rose, remember that whatever your results are, they won't change anything about the way you live your life right now," Roxanna says. "You aren't sick today. You won't be sick tomorrow. You can go to college. You can work. You can have a family. All of that. It doesn't change."

I can love the journey. That's what my mother would say.

"Even if you do test positive, you have years left to live normally," Roxanna adds.

She's wrong. I'll never live normally. But normal-ish, at least. I hear Jay, suddenly, echoing in the back of my mind. "You know what they say about rules." I didn't know what he meant the first time, but now that I hear it again in my head, I understand.

As Roxanna opens her mouth, I put up a hand.

"Stop." I take a breath. "Dad, I want to go."

"What?" He looks confused.

"Let's go."

"But, Ro—you were so sure—don't you want to—"

I shake my head. "No," I say. "No. I'll wait."

I'll wait.

SUMMER

Rule #4: Rules are meant to be broken.

Thirty-one

I GET AN ICED TEA AND WAIT NERVOUSLY FOR CALEB ON the rickety yellow bench in front of the bookstore in Porter Square. It's one of those perfectly bright, dry, sunny days, and it feels like every resident of Cambridge is out and about, buzzing around, wearing the wrinkled short sleeves they've unearthed from the bottoms of their drawers.

Seeing him makes me want to melt. It's been almost a month. After the first week, when I called him and got his voice mail so many times in a row, I forced myself to stop trying.

Now graduation is just a few weeks away. My mother has lashed out at me three times since I last saw Caleb. I skipped the prom last Friday, even though Lena tried to force me to go— which was fine, really, because a night in a crowded, sweat-filled hotel ballroom, in a fancy dress and high heels, isn't exactly a must-have life experience for me. But as much as I tried to ignore the thought as it lurked around in my brain, it did occur to me that Caleb would've made me go. And that he probably would've made it fun.

So I called him again, and this time he answered, and agreed to see me. Now, here he is, just like normal, in a red T-shirt and jeans. He has new glasses and his hair looks recently buzzed, but other than that, he's the same.

"I'm sorry," I blurt out, barely waiting for him to sit down. "I'm sorry I was a jackass. All you wanted to do was be there for me, and I'm just incapable of accepting a good thing. You were being great, and I was awful."

"You weren't *that* awful," he says, smirking a little. "Look, I'm sorry too. I'm sorry I left like that and didn't call you back. My mom says I was being selfish, that I was pushing you too hard, and she's right."

"Your mom said that?"

He nods. "I get that you need to make the decision that's right for you, whatever that is." I think he's rehearsed this. "And it's not easy. I'm sorry." He looks at me now like he's going to cry.

I inhale as hard as I can. I have to tell him what I've come here to tell him. "Can we have us back now? Please?" I ask.

Caleb puts a hand on my knee. "HD, I've done a lot of thinking about this, and I've come to a conclusion."

"What conclusion?"

"That I do not care."

"You don't care?" My voice comes out sounding small, and it feels like my heart has traveled to my stomach. Or my stomach's in my throat, or something. Whatever it is, something is mixed up with my insides.

"Nope. I don't care if you're sick, or healthy, or want to ride trains around the world forever, or whatever other ridiculous things you have planned. I just want to be your person, for now, and I would like you to reciprocate. So yes, HD. I would like to have us back. If you would."

His forgiveness unravels me. He cups one hand around the base of my neck, and wipes a tear off my cheek with the other. Then I have to say the other thing, without thinking too much about it. "I went to see Roxanna. For my test results."

Caleb sits upright on the bench. "You what? What happened?"

Quickly, I tell him about Roxanna, and the waiting room, and walking out without my results. When I come to the end, he looks as confused as my dad did in the moment.

"So in the end, you went with—nothing? Your decision is indecision?" A deep rut forms between his eyebrows.

"It's not indecision." I chew on my straw and try to find the rights words to explain what's in my head. Or my heart. I can't tell which is which anymore. "This *is* my decision. I can't know yet. I need to try to be normal for a little while. Or at least normal-ish."

"Normal-*ish*?"

"What?" I say. "It's a thing."

"Normal-ish," he repeats, nodding slowly. "Okay. We can live with that."

We.

"And here's the thing," I say.

I've broken all my rules already. There's no point in trying not to, not anymore.

"I love you. I know it took me a while and I know I'm a pain in the ass but . . . that's the thing. I love you. Okay? Happy now?"

Caleb gives me a wry half smile, the look he always has when he already knows something and I'm reporting the realization as if it's breaking news.

"What?" I ask. "Aren't you going to say anything?"

He shakes his head. "You are truly one in seven billion, HD."

"So, is that . . . okay? That thing I just said?"

"It is okay."

After I let the relief flush through me, I lean up toward him and kiss him, hard. I've never done that before in public. "Can I ask you something?" I say, when I pull my face away and he looks at me, bemused.

"Yes."

"What does the G stand for? In your name?"

"Giles. For my grandfather."

Of course. Caleb Giles Franklin, named for his grandfather the artist, who gave him a sketchbook and the gene for art.

"One more question," I say. "Will you still watch paint dry with me?"

He laughs, big and raucous, his shoulders bouncing up and down, like I haven't seen in too long. I've missed that laugh.

"I will still watch paint dry with you, HD." He wraps an arm around my shoulder and pulls me in close. "Maybe we could make it the quick-dry kind, though." —

I punch him in the arm and then burrow myself in his chest, where I think I'll stay for a while. Or at least for now.

Acknowledgments

FIRST, A DISCLAIMER: THIS BOOK IS JUST ONE IMAGINED story—it isn't intended to be a comprehensive account of Huntington's disease or the experiences of families coping with it. To explore these topics in greater depth, the Huntington's Disease Society of America (www.hdsa.org) and the Huntington's Disease Youth Organization (www.hdyo.org) are great places to start.

That said, in writing Rose's story, I relied heavily on those who know much more about Huntington's than I do. Nancy Downing, PhD/RN, generously answered my questions and shared excellent resources. Masha Gessen's brilliant book *Blood Matters*, as well as the research and writings of Alice Wexler, Nancy Wexler, Amy Harmon, Gina Kolata, and Kevin Baker, all provided invaluable guidance.

I've had the great fortune of working on this book with some extraordinary women. Joy Peskin is a magical editor. Mollie Glick is a badass agent. Both gave their whole hearts and great minds to this book and it is immeasurably better as a result.

Thanks too to Zoey Peresman, who dove in with incredible enthusiasm and thoughtfulness (and reminded me that a prom matters); and to the teams at FSG and Foundry Literary+Media, for everything they've done to bring this book into the world.

Several dear friends were vital sounding boards. Ellen Shanman and Brooke Lyons Osswald gave time and love to early drafts. The women of the TCFBWC—Anna McCallie, Heather Peske, Meagan Comb, Maria Fenwick, and Ellie Eckerson—competed for the best plot ideas and urged me forward. Leslie Kwok Potter and Alexis Carra Girbés are my Lenas, and I'm grateful to them for everything that means.

The good people of GrubStreet make Boston a better place to be a writer. Thanks to the community I met there, in particular to Emily Terry, Jennifer Barnes, Jennifer Johnson, and Beth Jones, for their insights along the way. Most importantly, of course, to Elaine Dimopoulos, who taught me much about the craft and business of writing for young adults, and to Laura Chandra, the plot whisperer; this book wouldn't be itself without them.

I won the family lottery, and I try not to forget it. To all the McGoverns and Lewises, genetic and otherwise, much love and gratitude. A special shout-out, too, to my excellent niece and nephews, Addison, Connor, William, and Nicolas.

The only bittersweetness of this experience is that my grandmother, Alice Lewis, isn't here to share it. But if she were, she'd probably say, "What? MacDougal wrote a book? Well, of course she did." Gram was sharp-witted, fiercely independent, and bookloving; her influence remains singular and salient, and I thank her for that daily.

Finally, my parents, Kathryn Lewis and Jim McGovern: They raised me in a house full of books and made me believe I could write them. Their love carries me through this world.